What happens when the girl of your dreams turns out to be the very one to destroy them?

With the sting from not being drafted still fresh, Dalton Boyd gets sent to the strictest coach with the most rules in summer league ball.

Was it mentioned the coach also serves as his host family? No? Well, everyone knows the player staying at the coach's house has the most brutal regime.

But here's the thing.

Dalton wouldn't be in this situation had he not followed his heart and ended up ghosted. As much as he'd like to change the past, he can't.

So, he sets a goal to stay out of trouble long enough to get through this summer and impress the coach and scouts.

It's an obtainable goal. Or so Dalton thought until walking into his coach's home and seeing the reason for rule number one—don't touch the coach's daughter—is none other than Cassie Greenburg, his rule follower ghost.

Summer just got a whole lot challenging.

CAUGHT LOOKING

Cessna U Wildcats Book Four

KIMBERLY READNOUR

Rae-Allen Publishing

Cover Design by Daqri Bernado of Covers by Combs

Editing by Missy Borucki

Proofreading by Kaitie Reister

❀ Created with Vellum

NOVELLA OFFER

Pick up your FREE novellas today for joining my newsletter, and be among the first to learn about my new releases and giveaways. Find out more after you read *Caught Looking*.

AUTHOR NOTE

Thank you for your interest in *Caught Looking.* I wanted to make sure you were aware of the prequel *On Deck.* In keeping with the timeline for the *Cessna U Wildcats* series, the prequel takes place prior to Dalton's freshman year.

On Deck gives the backstory to Dalton and Cassie's beginning. Coming in at a little over 24K words, their backstory would make too long of a flashback, and I felt the backstory was too important to cut. My solution was to turn it into a prequel, which can be read at anytime during the series.

CHAPTER ONE

DALTON

THIS IS SUCH BULLSHIT.

And I don't mean arriving at the San Francisco International airport. Nope, I mean my destination—Baytown, California. But I can't let my frustration show through. I'm about to meet my summer league coach, and you can bet your sweet ass I'll be sporting the widest grin possible. I'll own that first impression like a novice gymnast sticking a perfect landing. The coach won't know what hit him.

At least, that's the plan.

Stepping up to the baggage carousel, I silently curse the baseball-powers-that-be for sending me here in the first place. I ended the regular season with a .352 batting average, twelve home runs, eighty-two hits, and fifty-five runs batted in. And what accolades do I receive for these accomplishments—none, other than punishment.

I'm not amused.

Obviously, the fallout from not getting drafted still stings. Couple that with Dad's echoing words that my dream will never materialize, and annoyance doesn't come close to describing how I feel.

I'm fucking pissed.

My phone buzzes in my pocket right as the conveyor belt kicks to life. With plenty of time left before my luggage arrives, I pull it out and smile at the name, Noah Geren, sprawled across the screen. Noah is one of three former teammates-slash-roommates. I couldn't have asked for a better group of guys to share these last two years with—the fact they won't be at school when I return sucks. Especially since I haven't exactly made friends with any other teammates.

Noah: *Whatever you do, don't fuck up. You're welcome.*

A self-deprecating laugh escapes, but I take note of his sound advice. Messing up isn't an option. Not now. Not when it's the summer before my last year of college. They redshirted me my freshman year, so technically, I could tack on another academic year, but funding would be an issue. Unlike my former roommates, my funds aren't unlimited, and the baseball scholarship only covers so much. I've accrued a shit ton of student debt, and it won't disappear on its own. I *need* this upcoming year to work out for me.

Me: *Stellar words of wisdom.*

I spin Gramp's ring on my finger as I wait for a reply.

Noah: *Seriously, good luck. The guy may be a hardass, but he's a good coach. Whatever you do, don't get on his bad side.*

Don't get on his bad side, I repeat the words to myself. That may be an impossible task, considering *The Guy* is also my host. Yep, my life-long dream to live with the head coach has now been fulfilled.

Whoever coined the phrase "when life gives you lemons, make lemonade?" is a fucking dick.

I grind my teeth, watching the baggage carousel spit out every piece of luggage but mine. Am I being cynical? Maybe. But my entire life has been nothing but rotten lemons. Unless some vodka spills into that shit, I'll have a tough time enjoying it.

Northern California isn't where I want to be. My ass should be training with either a single- or double-A baseball team—not stuck in some Podunk town getting an attitude adjustment.

2

That's the *real* reason I'm here.

Not to improve my game. To improve my attitude.

And I only have myself to blame.

Because here's the kicker—Cessna University wasn't my first choice. I turned down my dream college with a full ride to become a Wildcat. And *why* would I do such a thing?

That's easy to answer.

I didn't want to live my life in constant *what-ifs*. No regrets, no remorse has been my motto my entire life. This time, it may have gotten me in trouble. Or maybe it was my dick. Blame him for turning down my top-choice school to chase a ghost. Or better yet, blame temporary insanity. Either way, it was a matter of being stupid.

But honestly, I thought the ghost I followed was *the one*. The girl I would spend my happily ever after with, or whatever bullshit thought went through my head at the time.

How fucking stupid was I?

Now, my "what-if moment" is wondering if I would've been drafted by now had I attended the other school. I know for sure I wouldn't be attending the worst summer collegiate league in the program. And I certainly wouldn't be sentenced to the preacher's house as if I'm under house arrest.

Oh, did I mention the coach moonlights as a preacher? No?

Well, like I said, "Fuck the person who makes lemonade."

"Whoa, looks like you're in need of some company while you're in town." The low, seductive voice draws my attention from the baggage carousel to a tall brunette. Her gaze rakes along my body, lingering on the tattoos sleeving my arms. Appreciation fills her eyes.

I bite back a sigh and transform the scowl shaping my mouth with my sexiest smirk that has worked in my favor since . . . well, since puberty. But if I'm honest, this whole seduction scene gets tiring. All I want to do is settle into my new home for the next three months and focus on my game. It's been a long week staying at my former teammate's house, followed by a turbulent airplane ride. After the fourth or fifth bump and dip, the lady next to me had to make quick use of the paper bag tucked in the seat pocket.

Yeah, that was awesome to watch.

And smell.

The brunette raises a perfectly manicured eyebrow, clearly waiting for an answer. What was her question? Oh yeah, if I needed company. Far be it for me to be rude. In my confident—often misconstrued as being cocky—voice, I ask, "Are you volunteering?"

Lashes too long and thick to be real sweep up to meet my gaze, followed by her own confident smirk. "I can be."

And that's my cue to take whatever this chick is offering. Her body is like a wet dream with long tanned legs sporting miles of flawless skin and tits that are more than a handful, considering her tiny waist. I'm out of my mind not to go for it, but I don't know. Even with a body most women would kill for, I'm just not interested.

I'm more fucked up in the head than I realized.

At my hesitation, she sweetens the deal by brushing that generous rack against my chest as she reaches across for her luggage. I remain stoic. If she knew how many girls make this type of move, she'd realize it's not that unique.

Before I can abort this whole seduction scene she has going on, my suitcase comes into view. I waste no time grabbing and sitting it on the ground. She positions those tanned legs right in my eyesight. I hold back a chuckle. *She's a persistent thing. I give her that.*

As I click the handle up and stand taller, I have no choice but to drag my gaze along that tight body. Miles of flawless skin lead me to a face angled by model-like precision. Her hazel eyes are dusted with too much eyeshadow for my liking, but her calculated look holds heat. The little temptress is gorgeous, no doubt.

Ah, screw it. I may as well partake while I'm in purgatory hell. Maybe this sentencing won't be so bad after all?

As the idea resonates in my mind, uneasiness settles in my stomach. Having sex is the last thing I should focus on right now.

But like the fuckup I am, I ignore the warning and ask, "What's your name?"

"Jenni with an *I*."

"Well, Jenni with an *I*, I'll be playing for the Baytown Crushers. You should check out a game."

"I think I will." The corners of her lips curve upwards. "A baseball player, huh?"

"Yep."

"Hasn't the season already started?"

We exit the baggage claim, and my phone buzzes again. This time it's Garret Cartel. I stayed at his parents' house before coming here. "It has. I had to finish the College World Series first. The Crushers were on the road when we won, so I had a week's downtime."

"Oh, you must be good."

"One could say that." *But apparently, I'm not good enough.* Garret, Noah, and Braxton, the third teammate-slash-roommate, were lucky enough to get drafted. There may be some jealousy involved, but I certainly can't be mad. They're damn good players and deserve to have a shot. And it was a good thing too. Unlike me, who had just completed my junior year, they were all seniors. It was either that or the unthinkable plan B.

I have no plan B.

I shake off feeling sorry for myself and read Garret's message.

Garret: *Just talked to Mom. She said you should be arriving there any minute. Wanted to warn you to keep your head in the game. The Preacher isn't as bad as they say.*

Yeah, right.

I heard he doesn't allow us to go out at night. But they also say the curfew is at nine o'clock, which contradicts the previous statement. One thing everyone seems to agree upon is how he runs the team. They say he acts like a drill sergeant, constantly barking orders as if we're recruits at boot camp. Sorry, but I've already lived that life. Except the barracks was my house, and the sergeant was my asshole father. The last thing I want is a repeat of that scenario. Cue in why I stayed at Garret's parents' house for the time between the College World Series and arriving here. I haven't been home since freshman year.

Before I respond to Garret's text, a message from Braxton's sister, Shannon Smith, dings through.

Shannon: *Good luck. Let me know what your surroundings are like. You're close to my hometown. I may be able to swing by for a visit when I come back.*

The corners of my mouth lift despite my mood. A visit from a recognizable face would be great.

"Uh-oh. Girlfriend?" Jenni with an *I* guesses.

"Not mine." I don't delve into my friendship with Shannon. This woman couldn't care less that Shannon's completely enamored with Noah Geren. But Shannon and I formed a bond, and I consider her a close friend. She's a year younger than me, and we'll be the only ones left from our group when we return next semester.

Without my former roommates, the next school year is going to suck.

"Good because I have plans for you," Jenni says. The look she gives holds heat. I should be turned on or, at the very least, interested, but again, I feel . . . nothing.

This is new.

Maybe I'm more keyed up about my situation than I want to admit. Or perhaps I'm feeling sorry for myself thinking about Cassie the Ghost and the lack of detective skills I possess for hunting her down. Had I not tried to find her, I wouldn't be in this situation.

"The only thing you have plans for is to find your ride."

Jenni and I snap our attention to the stern, demanding voice. The man stands about two inches shorter than my six-foot two-inch frame. Flecks of white streak his otherwise blond hair that *surprise, surprise* is cut into a buzz. It wouldn't shock me to learn if he was ex-military. The man stands with his arms crossed at his chest and a scowl settled across his features. His razor-sharp eyes zero in on me.

Fuck.

This is not how I wanted to meet my new coach and host for the summer.

So much for making a positive first impression.

Jenni hesitates and flashes a wary smile. "I'll, uh, catch you later." She gives a small but forced smile to the preacher, er, coach, and skitters away.

"We need to lay down ground rules," he says unamused.

I bite back a sigh. This is going to be a long forty-five-minute drive.

That vodka-laced lemonade sure sounds good about right now.

CHAPTER TWO

CASSIE

"I BETTER CHANGE BEFORE DAD GETS HERE. WEARING A BIKINI while meeting the new houseguest will drive my dad over the edge." The suggestion comes from me, but I make zero effort to move. Floating on a raft in a heated pool with my cousin, Nicole, outweighs the risk of getting caught. I skim my fingertips along the water surface and let the warmth from the sun imprison me. It feels too good to move, as proof by the contented sigh leaving my mouth. Nothing could top this day.

"Puh-leeze. If Uncle Nolan had his way, you'd be wearing a one-piece straight out of the thirties," Nicole says.

"Even that would show too much skin." Sarcasm drips from my every word. To say Dad was strict would be an understatement. He's the epitome of authoritarian.

"I still can't believe Uncle Nolan didn't send you away this year," Nicole says.

The protest that I'm twenty-one years old and have every right to stay in my house dies on my tongue. Because face it, she's right. When summer league baseball rolls around, Dad always sends me packing. Lord forbid, one of his players gets a glimpse of his daughter. And to make matters worse, besides coaching, Dad manages the team and serves as a host, opening our home to a

9

ballplayer. But only one. We have a spare room in our ranch-style home, and I refuse to let a stranger sleep in my bedroom. The office gets converted to an extra bedroom for three months out of the year.

"I wonder if he'll be cute?"

Warmth coats my cheeks. "What does that matter?"

"It'll give you something good to look at. If you're going to have to share living space with a stranger, he may as well be hot as fu—"

"Okay, I get it." I laugh, cutting her off. I'm not as uptight about foul language as I used to be, but we are at my parents' house. Well, my dad's house. A twinge of pain squeezes my chest, but I push away the memory that causes it. I don't want to think about the last three years. Not today. Not when I'm finally enjoying myself.

"What? You know I'm right." Nicole won't let it drop. I shouldn't be surprised. She's what my dad calls "boy crazy."

"That may be so, but I don't want to think about sharing a bathroom with a hot guy. The only guys that stay here are the ones needing discipline. Bad boys are hardly my type."

"You sure about that?"

My eyes narrow. Nicole never brings up my bout with said bad boy. That bad boy was Dalton Boyd, whom I met three summers ago when Nicole and I stayed at Aunt Jan's house in Bellow Bay, North Carolina. Any discussion about Dalton is considered taboo. It's not like I want to forget him—as if that's even a possibility— but it hurts too much whenever he enters my mind. And yes, I still think about him—a lot. "Positive. And even if I did, fate had other plans."

"Enough about fate. The missed chance with him is all on you, not from the lack of invisible love gods playing cupid. There are things called cell phones. We had his number. You made me delete and block it."

Yeah, not my wisest decision.

Nicole was his only contact, considering I wasn't allowed to have a cell phone at that time. Thank goodness Dad changed his stance once I got to college.

"I really thought we'd find a way." And I did. After leaving Bellow Bay, I wholeheartedly believed fate would bring us together. Call it naivety or plain stupidity, but I once thought that when two people loved each other, they were destined to be together.

I could not have been more wrong.

"I don't see how." Nicole's quipped response reveals how much she believes in fate—zero, zilch, nada. All of which she told me three years ago.

"You know my dad would never approve of anyone like him."

"Okay. So what you're saying is, CC's the better choice?" CC being my boyfriend, Bobby. He earned the name Carbon Copy—shortened to CC—after visiting my dorm one night while Nicole was tipsy. Appalled she partook in that "ungodly act of drinking"—his words—he lectured her about being underage and the consequences of getting caught. After he left, Nicole rolled her eyes and said he was too rule orientated like me. Then she gasped as if discovering an earth-shattering innovation. A smirk played on her lips as she said, "He's basically your carbon copy except with a dick." Thus, CC was born.

"Quit calling him that. You know he hates it. And yes, *Bobby* is better." I frown, not liking what that statement implies. Bobby may be the better choice to garner Dad's approval, but that doesn't make him a better person. Dalton may have his share of faults, but he never showed them around me.

"Yeah, whatever, but from your lackluster expression, I'd have to disagree. I don't understand how you put up with *Bobby* all these years."

"We've only dated two of them, and he was . . ."

"Safe?" She fills in when my voice trails off.

"Yes, I mean"—I shake my head in frustration—"no. It doesn't matter. I'm breaking up with him when he comes home."

"Think you'll go through with it this time?"

I let out a groan. Before Bobby left on his mission trip, I tried to break up, but I did a poor job conveying it. I had dropped subtle hints that he either ignored or didn't get. Frustrated, I gave up trying since he was leaving for four months and decided to save the argument for later. Later has come. "Yes, but it will still be hard. He's done nothing wrong. For the most part, he's a dutiful boyfriend." *He's just controlling.*

"Which is why his name is CC." She slaps the pool water, causing a spray of droplets to rain down on me. I jerk away, tipping the raft, and almost fall off.

"Don't make me tip over," I say, laughing. "I don't want my hair messed up. I don't have time to fix it."

Nicole's eyes narrow as she gauges me. "Wanting to look good for the new roomie?"

"No!" I shake my head again but then shrug. Because, really, who am I fooling? "Well, okay, somewhat good. In my defense, I wouldn't want anyone seeing my wet hair." With my blond curls piled into a messy bun on top of my head, it's not as if I'm at my best, but my hair gets funky when wet. A wild, frizz monster isn't the impression I'm aiming for.

"Fair enough." Nicole settles back onto her raft, staring up at the blue sky.

Bellow, my miniature pinscher, starts yelping. He wags his tail and goes over to the screen door.

"Oh crap. I think Dad's here already." *This is not good.* I paddle my hands along the side of the raft, but Nicole blocks my way. I need my towel to cover myself up before Dad sees me in this bikini. He'll throw a fit. "Hurry up."

"I'm trying, but—"

The slide of the screen interrupts what she says. I close my eyes momentarily and prepare for Dad's wrath. Dad's strictness never used to bother me. I got used to being the daughter of a preacher, but these past three years have been suffocating. He's gotten worse after Mom's passing.

Nicole's shocking gasp pulls me out of my thoughts. My eyes

fly open, but I can't see anything but her stiffening back. *Oh no.* Dad must sport that mean look he gets when angered.

"Nicole, move. I need to get out of here." I try to shift to see around her, even though staying out of sight would be smarter. But I need my towel. Covering up is the only thing I can think about.

"What are you doing?" Dad's voice booms across the backyard.

Breaking free from the logjam Nicole created, I go to respond, but my answer dies a quick death the moment I spot the black leather jacket.

It can't be.

My gaze darts to the face the jacket belongs to. Dark brown eyes meet mine and widen in shock. Then everything happens at once. Nicole grabs my raft to shove it behind her at the same time I rear back from the surprise. The sudden shift jerks my body to the right as the raft pulls to the left. I try to steady myself, but I'm off-balance. My feet tip upwards. I grab hold of the side, but I can't hang on to the slippery vinyl. I slide off and slip beneath the water's surface.

All noises cease to exist, but I welcome the silence and let gravity pull me under. I don't know what's more shocking to my system: the fact I'm sinking to the bottom of the pool or Dalton Boyd—the boy I waited for fate to bring me—is here as our new houseguest. Part of me wants to remain submerged forever because what's waiting for me on top of the surface is nothing but trouble.

CHAPTER THREE

DALTON

MY FEET STAY FROZEN ON THE CONCRETE PATIO. THE AIR, suddenly too thick and heavy, heats a few degrees. I struggle to catch my breath as I fixate on the expanding ringlets circling the splash.

Holy shit. This is not possible.

The thrumming in my ears drowns out Coach's voice. I stand shell-shocked and wait for the blonde to reemerge. She sputters as water sheets off her face, but the moment those wide, blue eyes turn to meet mine, the entire world stops spinning. Life hits pause as my brain catches up to my eyes and confirms the girl in the pool is Cassie—my ghost—and Coach's very unattainable, untouchable, and I-will-end-your-career-before-it-starts daughter.

Fucking rotten lemons.

This can't be happening. She can't be the same Cassie. Cassie's last name is Green not . . . *Greenburg.*

I blink and then blink again, staring numbingly at eyes mirroring the same shock as I feel. She's still as beautiful as I remember. Even with wet, messy hair, the girl steals my breath. No matter how much time has elapsed, no matter how hard it hurt that she left without so much as a goodbye, the woman still wields power over me. And I know at that moment why every other female hasn't measured up.

"Dalton, head back inside the house."

Coach's low, menacing tone pulls me out of this endless time warp capsizing my body. I pull my gaze away and try to focus on my new coach—the same man who'll have my head if I so much as glance at his daughter. Coach's face is red and blotchy. Dread seeps into my bones. I've already blown my first impression. I'm sure standing here ogling his daughter doesn't score any bonus points. I somehow muster a nod and retreat into the house without a backward glance.

The breath I was holding sputters from my lips the moment my feet hit the hardwood floor. Safe inside, I think clearer. I shrug out of the jacket I put on to stop Coach's prying eyes from staring at my tattoos and stumble to the oversized island separating the kitchen and living room. I grab hold of the cold granite slab. I've been physically knocked on my ass by my father's upper hand, but this feels ten times worse.

I actually found her.

Three years after searching Cessna University's large campus, countless nights scouring the internet, and repeatedly dialing her cousin's number that had clearly blocked mine, I finally found my ghost without even trying. Relief clashes with anger. Cassie lied to me. If she lied about her name, what else has she lied about? *Us? Was I just a means for her to lose her virginity? Or some act of defiance against her overly strict father?*

I close my eyes to keep the room from spinning. I'm suddenly five years old again and sitting on the concrete steps in front of the elementary school, waiting for a mom that never came. I don't want to be the one that gets left behind all the time—that weak, helpless boy crying over a loved one who failed to love him back.

Fuck that.

Anger stabs my heart, but it's aimed more at myself than at her. The blame is on me. I fell for this girl who never wanted to be found. That's the essence of her wish, right? The fact she didn't want me to find her. They say actions speak louder than words. Well, her lack of communication speaks volumes.

Had I listened, I wouldn't have wasted a year chasing after her, and I wouldn't be here playing for a wannabe boot camp team. I'd be drafted. That, I guarantee.

Coach's loud voice filters in through the sliding glass doors. Words such as indecent and ungodly are tossed around. He's clearly upset at their choice of swimwear. Given what I know about him, I'm not surprised, but he's beyond ridiculous.

But then, Cassie speaks. Her melodic voice sets me back from my hard stance and wraps around my chest, thawing my cold heart. I try to resist the sound, but I can't stop picturing her embarrassed expression whenever I called her Choir Girl.

Shit. How is living under the same roof as her going to work? My friends back home know I push the limits and don't care about rules. I've been low-key these past few years, focusing on baseball. And that good deed left me smack dab in boot camp hell. But having the girl I spent all of freshman year searching for is temptation overload. It's like dangling a mouse in front of a tomcat and expecting him not to play with it. That situation never works out.

Coach cannot find out that the boy who chased his daughter that summer in Bellow Bay now stands in his kitchen. That would drive the final nail into my coffin. The man lives for his rules. That was evident when we got alone in his truck, and he laid down the law.

No showing up late to practice.

No talking back.

No questioning the play calls.

Show respect to coaches and teammates.

The list went on and on before segueing into the social aspect.

No alcohol.

No dancing.

No staying past curfew—especially during away games.

No cursing.

No girls.

Church is a requirement, not a choice.

And last but certainly not least, absolutely no fraternizing with his daughter. I quote, "If I catch you with as much as one lustful gleam, you're kicked off the team, sent back home, and will no longer be NCAA eligible."

I seriously doubt the man wields enough power to ruin my NCAA eligibility, but I can't risk being sent home.

The need to flee overwhelms me. I'm itching to go for a run or take a hot shower—anything to be alone. I need time to think and formulate a plan. My gaze pushes past the large sectional, landing on my luggage by the front door. I'd snatch it up and hide in my bedroom if I knew where it was. After we arrived, Coach led me straight to the backyard. Their miniature pinscher was barking its happy greeting outside the sliding glass door. But the ranch-style house isn't overly large. I'm sure the bedroom is down the only hallway to the left of the kitchen and living room.

The backdoor slides open, and the sound of feet tramping across the hardwood floor fills the silence. *She's here.* Nicole leads the trio and gives me a side-eye glance as she passes. I barely register her as my gaze slides to Cassie. I soak every inch of her up until those vibrant, blue eyes meet mine. I stand a little straighter, powerless to stop the rush of memories flooding my mind. I picture the way her face glowed in the moonlight three years ago, all innocent and bright. *Angelic.* And her taste. God, the way her sweet taste filled my mouth as waves lapped the shoreline.

And then our last night together.

I shut that thought off and will my breathing to slow down before the ache in my pants makes it apparent how much I remember. One thing is for sure—three years isn't enough time to get over this girl.

Coach clears his throat as the girls disappear down the hallway. "Sorry about that. As I said, this is the first year Cassie's home during baseball season. She won't be parading around half-naked anymore."

Shame.

But is he for real? Her bikini was modest at best. The US beach volleyball team sports less material than Cassie's two-piece.

I clear my throat. "That's okay, sir. I'm here to play ball."

He eyes me for a long moment before breaking away. He steps to the counter behind me, grabs a packet, and tosses it to me. "That is your schedule. Read through it. I expect you to know every detail. We have practice tomorrow, so be ready. You'll ride with me. I spend a lot of time at the church, so on those days Cassie will run you to practice, or you can find a ride with someone from the team. The ones who brought cars are listed on the blue paper. You'll find the calendar highlighted when I can't give you a ride. You're only to find rides on the days I'm not available. Otherwise, it'll be me taking you. Got it?"

"Yes, sir." It takes great strength to stop myself from rolling my eyes. I can't believe this man. He seems like a control freak. Maybe this is part of his punishment regime—forced proximity with the coach.

Lucky me.

"This is the kitchen. You'll find the refrigerator stocked with the essentials." He points to a white door. "The pantry is through there. There's a shelf containing high-protein snacks. That is yours. It's your responsibility to keep it stocked. I expect you to accompany us to church as I already told you. We observe the sabbath, so be sure to stock up before Sunday as there are no purchases to be made on that day."

I nod, trying not to clench my teeth. Church and I don't get along. Even if there is a God, he abandoned me long ago.

Christ, this is going to be a long fucking summer.

"Grab your jacket and suitcase and follow me." He waits until I grab my belongings and then stalks down the hall. The corridor is long and skinny. It consists of three doors—one directly at the end and two on each side. Pointing at the closed door on the left, he says, "This is the bathroom. You'll find the towels and everything you need in there. Since my daughter insisted on staying home, you'll have to share it with her. Her room is here." He points to the other closed door at the end before turning to the door on the right. "This is your room."

Great. Right next to Cassie's. That won't be awkward or anything.

"Thanks." I place my luggage on the hardwood floor. The miniature pinscher trots over and gives a tiny yip. Then he wags his undocked tail and stares up at me. It's a cute little thing. The short black and tan coat shimmers like polished black obsidian.

"This little guy is Bellow."

My gaze snaps to Coach for a beat and then back to the dog. Surely, the guy isn't named after my hometown, Bellow Bay. It must be a coincidence. I crouch down, extending my hand to pet his head. I belt out a laugh as he burrows into my palm, clearly basking in the attention.

"Huh, he must like you. Normally he yaps his head off at strangers. He bit the kid staying here two years ago. But Bellow's almost three now. He has outgrown the puppy stage."

"You got him three years ago?" I ask before I can stop myself.

"More like two and a half, but yeah. We haven't had him for too long."

"Huh." Perhaps staying in my hometown did mean something to her.

When I don't say anything else, Coach leaves me to my room with Bellow on his tail.

Traitor.

Although, I suppose Bellow switching allegiances to Team Dalton would be deemed a traitorous act. Coach is his master, after all.

I push my way inside the bedroom. With one glance, it's easy to tell this room serves mainly as an office. The old-fashioned metal tanker desk houses an outdated computer. *Computer?* I step closer to examine the relic. No, I take it back. That's an old word processor. I didn't think those were still in existence. I knew he wouldn't allow Cassie to have a phone, but surely, they have internet. I pull out my phone and search for a connection. Sure enough. No internet. Did I step back in time? I spin the ring on my finger and glance around the room, landing on an oversized painting. "Jesus Christ," I belt out.

"Yeah, that's him," a baritone voice says from behind, startling me.

Can I catch a damn break? Curbing my language is going to be more challenging than I thought. I glance back at the portrait of Jesus praying on some rock. *I have to sleep with this guy peering over me.*

"It sure is. I wasn't quite expecting something so . . . prominent," I say, trying to play off my brashness.

"Yeah, well, it wouldn't hurt to start praying to him. You'll need his guidance."

You got that right.

I bite back my sharp rebuttal and agree. "Yes, sir."

"I wanted to inform you that supper will be ready at six o'clock sharp."

"Thanks, sir."

He gives a quick nod and stalks away. I place the suitcase on my bed with a shake of my head, searching for soap and shampoo. I need that shower. Although, I think it will take more than hot water to get used to these living conditions.

I snatch the containers and sneak another glance at the religious figure. Yep, Coach is right. I'm going to need a lot of help. I tip the shampoo bottle to the painting and nod. "What do you say, Big Guy? Can I count on you?"

When silence greets me, I shake my head and mumble, "That's what I thought."

Heading to the bathroom, I pass Cassie's room, and my traitorous eyes stray to her door. I want to barge in there and demand answers, but another part of me wants to ignore her existence. I need to cling to the latter as if my life depended on it because it kind of does. I can't think of anything more off-limits or damaging to my career than associating with her.

But this is Cassie.

The girl I spent an entire year trying to find.

The girl I thought I loved.

The pang in my chest returns. I ignore it and push my way into the bathroom. The door ricochets shut with more force than intended. Thrusting my hands through my hair, I lean my back against the door and gaze upward. "Lord, if you exist, give me strength because Cassie just became my worst sinful combination —a forbidden temptation."

CHAPTER FOUR

CASSIE

THE SLAM OF THE BATHROOM DOOR REVERBERATES OFF MY WALLS and snaps me to attention. I turn to face my cousin. She looks as perplexed as I feel. We're sitting on the edge of my bed in a trance. A state we've been in since walking past Dalton and heading in here.

"What are you going to do?" Nicole's voice cracks at the end. That hint of despair does little to calm my frayed nerves.

"I-I don't know. How is this even possible?" The question is rhetorical, but I can't formulate an intelligent response right now. *He's really here.* Dalton Boyd, the boy I wished fate would bring us together, is right outside my door for the next eleven or so weeks.

"Do you think he's here because he found out who your dad is?"

"Um . . ." I ponder her question for a moment but quickly dismiss that notion. The look on his face was pure shock. "No. He looked blindsided."

"Yeah, he did seem rather surprised," Nicole admits. "But, seriously, what are you going to do?"

It takes a moment to formulate an answer because I have no clue how to proceed. Never in a million years did I predict this situation. I may have dreamed about Dalton finding me, but that hope fizzled when I had Nicole block his number. Since I wasn't allowed to have a cell phone and Nicole was his only contact, we never heard from him after that. I forced myself not to look him up on the internet. It was tempting—oh, so tempting—but I knew any information about him would only break my heart more. What if he popped up on the screen with another girl? It would've crushed me even though I had no right to be. It's not as if we had a normal relationship with an actual ending. I just disappeared on him.

And now he's here.

In my house.

Playing ball for my dad.

This can only mean one thing—Dalton needs a stricter regimen to work on his attitude. He certainly doesn't need me as a distraction.

"I have no idea. I don't understand how this is possible. Players from the University of South Carolina don't play in this conference." He had told me he was attending U of SC.

"Maybe he went to a different school?"

"Maybe." But where? The air conditioner kicks on, the forced air causing me to shiver. I wrap my towel around me tighter and bring my hand to my forehead. I gasp as wetness coats my palms. "Oh no. My hair."

"Believe me, he wasn't looking at your hair."

"But I look awful. He hasn't seen me in three years, and I look like *this*." Plopping on my back, I let out a wince.

"It's fine. Speaking of fine, did you see how he's filled out?" She stands up and walks over to my desk, where her clothes lay in a heap.

"The whole ten seconds I saw him, I couldn't get past those deep brown eyes."

"Just wait, honey. Your libido is about to kick into overdrive. Wearing that black leather jacket over a white T-shirt and those ripped jeans, he looks like an eighties heartthrob ripped straight from the cover of *Tiger Beat*."

I press my lips together to keep from smiling. Okay, I did notice that. But I can't think about Dalton that way. It's too risky.

She slides into her flip-flops. "Okay, I'm out of here. I need to get ready for my date."

"Are you sure you don't want to cancel, so I don't have to face him alone?" I sit up and give her my best pleading eyes, but that only draws up a laugh.

"Chicken."

"I won't deny that." I force myself to stand. Wallowing in self-pity won't help my cause. I'm damp, cold, and could use a good shower.

"You know, you wouldn't be in this situation had you talked to him."

"Yeah, yeah, yeah. I don't need a voice of reason right now." What I need is to harness good acting skills.

She wraps her fingers around the door handle and glances back at me. "It is ironic that he's here. Don't you think?"

"A total kismet moment," I whisper. How ironic indeed. If it weren't for my overbearing loves-to-put-the-fear-of-God-into-you father, Dalton wouldn't be here.

"I never believed in all of that, but I have to admit this is pretty weird." She glances at her phone. "Ugh, I do need to go."

"Go on. Tell Chaz I said hi." I know she needs to leave, but part of me wishes she wouldn't. I have no idea what I'm going to say to Dalton. How am I supposed to act normal when I feel anything but?

"I'll talk to you later. Good luck," Nicole singsongs as she opens the bedroom door and waves her fingers at me as Bellow trots down the hallway.

"Thanks." I sweep Bellow into my arms and shut my bedroom door. Leaning with my back against it, I let out a long exhale. I look into his dark brown eyes and ask, "What am I going to do?"

His answer comes in the form of a lick to the face.

"That's not helpful." I laugh, but it turns into a low groan.

I didn't get much of a chance to see Dalton when I slipped off the raft. I was too shocked, but when he stood in my kitchen, and his intense gaze traced my every movement, that same feeling I had three years ago slammed into me. It's as if no time had passed, and he has waited for me this entire time.

As if fate finally brought him to me.

Bellow squirms and jumps out of my arms. Pushing off the door, I catch sight of my reflection in the dresser mirror. *Jeez, I look worse than I thought.* Not only is my hair a wet pile of frizz, but the smeared eyeliner makes me look like I've been on a bender. No wonder Dad was angry. He hates me wearing makeup.

I tighten the beach towel around my waist, determined to rectify my hair's hot mess with a long, hot shower. As I swing the bedroom door open, Bellow darts between my legs, tripping me forward right as Dalton steps from the bathroom.

A small yelp escapes, followed by solid, muscular arms steadying me. I suppress the second whimper as my gaze takes in that rock-hard body. Mother of all things holy, he's hot. My focus shifts from his tattooed arms to the towel draped low around that glorious waist that I remember so vividly in my dreams. My eyes continue to climb up his body. Dalton's still fit, but more defined than I remember, maturity agreeing with him. I'm familiar with the ink sleeving his arms, but the wildcat tattoo covering his right chest is new. It takes great effort to restrain from tracing the animal's outline with my tongue. Goodness, I want to eat him up.

"You okay?"

His deep voice pulls me to those dark, brown eyes. A water droplet falls from the wet ringlets framing his forehead and lands between us on the floor. The sound I make may resemble a yes, but I really don't know. I'm so mesmerized by his presence my mind keeps reverting to when his body hovered over mine. I itch to reach out and touch him. To let my fingers wander over his defined muscles.

Dalton steps forward, backing me against the door. His clean scent encapsulates me and smells like temptations and memories. He presses a hand into the wood panel above me, leaning in farther. I'm not quite caged in—there's enough distance between our bodies for me to slip away—but my restraint weakens as heat licks my core and shivers race down my spine.

"Cassie." My name is a whispered plea on his tongue. The back of his fingers brush against my cheek ever so lightly, and holy moly, that touch conjures every intimate moment we shared as memories slam into me. Like how my heart raced when his lips touched mine for the first time. Or the wetness between my legs when he walked into his bedroom wearing nothing but a towel—like what's happening now. Or the slight pinch of pain followed by a fullness when our bodies joined in a way meant for two people. Summer lust or summer love? The answer doesn't matter because the feelings were very real.

There's so much I want to say, but his intense stare has me so tongue-tied I can't think straight. Desire may spark in his eyes, but it's at war with the anger radiating off his body. No doubt, the unspoken question as to why I ghosted him weighs heavily between us.

If only I could explain that my only goal was to avoid this exact scenario—him and me together in front of my dad. If Dad witnesses even the slightest fraction of attraction between Dalton and me, he will end Dalton's baseball career. Whatever we felt toward each other had to be put on pause. Dad will never approve of him. He may stand at the pulpit and preach about being nonjudgmental, but Dalton's the exact type of guy he judges. Tattoos and bad attitudes feed my father's prejudices. It wouldn't matter the cause behind said attitude. My dad is the most judgmental person I know. Once I learned Dalton's desire to play college baseball, I knew I wouldn't be good for him. I knew the harm Dad could bring. And I knew one summer was all we could have.

"I found you." Dalton's breathy voice pulls me back to the present—back to him. But something's off. His gentle touch doesn't match his defensive stance.

"You don't look happy," I say.

A pained look flashes in his eyes as he battles the demons haunting him. This is all my fault. If only he knew why. His gaze dips to my lips as if he wants to kiss me, but his body is stiff. It's as if he's preparing for war—a battle he feels the need to fight. I struggle for the right words to defuse the bomb. But what I really want him to do is close the small gap separating us and claim my mouth. I've missed the feel of his lips on mine. I've missed the dominating way about him that made me feel special.

I've missed *him*.

A small bark followed by nails scraping against wood alerts us to Bellow racing back down the hallway. Dalton heeds the warning and backs away a moment before Dad comes into view.

My back stiffens at the way Dad's narrowed eyes take in Dalton's proximity.

"Am I going to have to send you packing?" Dad asks.

"No, sir. I was just heading to my room."

Dad's lips tighten to a thin line as he peers at Dalton. It feels as if an eternity passes before he speaks. And when he does, his tone holds more warning than the actual words. "Don't parade around in a towel." Then his gaze snaps to me. "Either one of you."

I want to die from mortification. My cheeks flame. I can't remember a time I've ever been this humiliated.

"Sorry, sir. I'm not used to a lady being present. It won't happen again." Dalton nods and steps to his door. He doesn't look back as the door shuts behind his tall frame.

Dad stares straight at me. "Don't make me regret my decision."

"I won't. Bellow had knocked me off balance. Nothing more."

Dad's nostrils flare. "If you need to switch rooms with me—"

"Dad, it's fine. You wouldn't be comfortable in my bed. Your back would scream at you after the first night."

His jaw clenches, but he concedes and stalks down the hallway without another word.

Who would have thought I'd be so grateful for not having an orthopedic mattress? But here I am feeling exactly that. I glance at Dalton's door.

How on earth is this going to work?

CHAPTER FIVE

DALTON

PEERING OUT THE WINDSHIELD, I TAKE IN THE FRESHLY chalked turf. For a small town, the ballpark is rather impressive. Green paint coats the exterior, and I can admire the nostalgia from this vantage point. Everything from the wooden structure to the uncomfortable as hell bleachers places the timestamp at the early nineteen hundreds. But it's too well preserved for that. Maybe it's a replica? Regardless, I'm impressed.

"Surprised?" Coach asks as he places the truck in park.

"I didn't expect the stadium to look so authentic." This is my third summer playing collegiate ball. I expected the same rundown, half-assed grounds keeping as the rest of the stadiums where I've played. "It's really nice."

His eyes fill with pride from my statement. "We've worked hard to keep this site relevant."

"I look forward to playing in it."

He eyes me for a beat, his face revealing a hint of surprise as if the thought of me admiring something other than myself was unheard of. I bite back a sigh. He's hard to read, but it's obvious this man formed an opinion of me. And it's anything but flattering.

"When practice is done, I expect a detailed report for two of the five teammates."

"Excuse me?" *What is he talking about?*

Coach looks directly at me. "Didn't you read the packet I gave you?"

"Some of it." *Like a teeny tiny fraction.* The packet was thirty or so pages. I figured I had all week to catch up.

His jaw clenches, and I certainly read him now. He's pissed. At me.

"Had you followed my orders, as I had asked, you would've known about the special assignments."

Special assignments?

What kind of shit-fuckery is this? Who plays collegiate summer ball and has special assignments?

"Are these assignments for everyone?" I ask.

"No. They're for the one staying at my house."

I clamp my mouth shut as anger pulsates through my veins. Cursing would land me in more hot water, but this is such bullshit. We're here to practice and win games. This isn't summer school, for fuck's sake.

Coach continues when I don't respond, "You need to bond with five members of the team and report back with what you found. It doesn't matter who you cover as long as Jason Fowler is in tonight's report."

"But—"

"You should've done what I told you to do."

Christ. This is worse than boot camp. This is Professor Fellure's biochemistry final exam level bad. The last thing I want to do is make nice with these people and then write about it. Obtaining this level of information requires me to hold conversations with them and dig deep into their history. That's something I don't care to do, nor do I want them digging into mine. But contrary to popular belief, I have enough sense not to argue with the coach.

"Yes, sir. I'll get right on that." My voice comes out sharper than I intended, but I'm beyond annoyed. I jar the truck door open when his loud voice halts me.

"You may disagree with my coaching tactics, but one thing you will learn is respect. And the last thing I'll put up with is attitude."

I take a deep breath, still looking across the parking lot. "Understood, sir."

This guy made his assumptions about me before I arrived. He may peg me for an unruly punk, but he couldn't be further from the truth. Sure, I don't toe-the-line outside baseball or warm up to my teammates, but I never cause trouble for the team. I do the job asked of me even if it doesn't check this guy's perfectly squared boxes. Punishing me for not being a social butterfly is pure crap.

Crap?

Well, would you look at that? I can improve my language.

I'm still reeling over Coach's assumptions as he catches up to me and walks by my side. Before reaching the locker room, my phone buzzes with a text. I debate whether to read it, but it's from Marty, a friend from Bellow Bay. He's the only one who sends updates on my dad.

Marty: *I know you can't come home, but your dad's worse.*

I sigh, which earns me a side-glance from Coach. I don't acknowledge the text and shove the phone in my pocket. I don't have time to deal with my dad's bullshit today. I'll have to address this later.

Coach comes to a halt when we reach the locker room. "When the team hits the showers, I expect you to give me fifty laps. A lap is one complete turn around the stadium."

"On top of getting to know this Jason guy and another teammate?"

"Yes. Next time, listen to what I say." With those parting words, Coach pivots and stalks down the hall.

I don't mind running as much, but how am I going to squeeze time to talk to anyone? I'm still pissed when I push into the locker room. A few heads turn my way. I scan the unknown faces. Most of their glances hold curiosity more than anything, but I don't miss the few scowls tossed my way. Unsure what I did to any of these guys, I head straight to an unoccupied locker.

These are the assholes he wants me to warm up to?

I've dropped engines in vehicles easier than that.

Right as I lose hope of knowing anyone, my gaze lands on a familiar set of eyes staring back at me—Carter Drews. The corners of his mouth push to a grin the moment I spot him.

"Dalton Boyd." The only friendly face in the room comes up and shakes my hand. "Glad you made it. It was rumored that Coach ate you for dinner last night."

"He tried." I don't even try to hide my smirk. "Glad to see a familiar face."

Carter glances around the room, seemingly noticing the hostility tossed my way. "Yeah, I imagine. Anyway, are you ready to win some games?"

"You know it."

Carter is an incoming sophomore and catcher for the Wildcats junior varsity team. He didn't accompany us to the College World Series, but his stats are impressive enough to fill Noah's position. I imagine we'll get plenty of playtime together next season.

"Come on. There's a locker next to mine you can have."

No one else bothers to introduce themselves. It's as if I have the plague. Their distance would be comical if it weren't so pathetic.

"Seems like a friendly crowd."

Carter shrugs. "Your skills will win them over."

"Didn't realize that needed to happen," I say dryly.

"Yeah, well, everyone knows to watch out for the player staying at the coach's house." He raises an eyebrow. "Since they're juvenile delinquents with talent."

"Fuck off. There's nothing wrong with my attitude."

"You better not let Coach hear you cuss. There'll be another strike against you." The slight tease in the stranger's voice keeps me chill, and we turn to face the burly guy easing upon us. A playful grin dances on his lips as his fist meets mine. "Javier Tavarez. I'm the *lead* catcher." He smirks at Carter. "Congrats on one hell of a season. Your stats were phenomenal."

"Thanks." I fall silent, unable to add anything of value. Really, what more can be said? We both know my stats were good enough for me to get drafted. Yet, here I am, and we both know the reason why—or at least presumably so. It's probably why the team gave me such a wide berth when I arrived.

"I'm looking forward to winning some games, so I'm glad you're here. We could use your bat."

"That's no shit," Carter says.

I smirk. So far this season, the Crushers haven't crushed anyone, going four for ten.

"Who's the first baseman?" No better time to scope out my competition. I should know the roster by now, but unlike Javier, I haven't studied any teammates. If I had, I would've known who Jason Fowler is and maybe understand the look Javier and Carter just shared.

"He's going to be tough to dethrone," Carter says, resting his hand on the back of his neck.

"Why? Is he good?"

Another uncomfortable glance occurs between them. Their gazes dart around the emptied locker room.

"I wouldn't jump to that conclusion," Javier says.

"Then what's the problem?" I fail to understand where their trepidation comes from. If he's not a fantastic player, there shouldn't be any question about why I can't take over the starting position.

"He's sort of the team's darling," Carter says.

"And Coach's little bitch boy." The disdain in Javier's voice is obvious, and I get it. They don't care for him.

"I'm not worried." I wink to drive home my point. I'll do anything in my power to get noticed, but I won't be an ass kisser. My sheer talent will make sure I'm the starting player. Despite what my sorry-excuse-of-a-father wants to call me, I am talented. I just wish my stats would've impressed the major league scouts. But the guys still haven't told me his name, so I ask again. "What's his name?"

35

"Jason Fowler."

Well, fuck me.

CHAPTER SIX

CASSIE

"Have you talked to Dalton at all since he arrived?"

I wedge the phone between my shoulder and left ear and dip the angled applicator in a deep purple shade. Nicole's question plays through my mind as I apply eyeshadow. How do I answer without sounding whiny and pathetic? It's only been two days, but my dad has ensured we haven't had any downtime. We haven't had a second alone to talk between Dalton's baseball practice and my meetings for the church's upcoming rummage sale. I'm desperate to speak to him. "Not yet."

"Why not?"

"We haven't been able to connect. He's going as I'm coming. And when we are home at the same time, Dad's around." *Except for now.* The hospital called a few minutes ago. They admitted one of our elderly parishioners. The request for a preacher doesn't bode well for poor Mr. Barley. Although there isn't much my father can do other than offer support. He can pray to God all day long, but that won't help Mr. Barley's overall condition. I know firsthand how praying only gets you so far.

"I take it he doesn't know about CC?"

My chest constricts. I need to warn Dalton about Bobby, but I'm running out of time. Bobby's due here in two hours. It's just

I'm not sure how Dalton will take it. Part of me fears he won't care, and the thought of that kills me. From the tortured look on his face, I'd say he hates but still wants me. Maybe he hates that he still wants me. Lord knows I want him. Dalton will always be that guy, no matter how bad an idea or how off-limits he is. You know, the type that makes your flesh tingle and body throb in that delicious, sinful way.

He'll always be the one I want.

The one I love.

But I can't have him.

People will say he's not good enough for me, but it's the opposite. I'm not good enough for him. All I can offer is an abrupt ending to a career that he desperately needs. I've witnessed firsthand why he wants to make it and not end up back in Bellow Bay. And I can't blame him.

"Not yet, but I will as soon as we hang up. Dad got called to the hospital right before you called. This is the first time we have the house to ourselves." I cut the darker shade along the outer corner of the crease to define my eyes. The look is more daring than I usually sport. I never wore much makeup until I started rooming with Nicole. The change wasn't Daddy-approved.

"How are you going to bring it up? Oh, by the way, I have a boyfriend who everyone thinks is serious but me."

I cringe. Bobby is like the son Dad never had. He adores him. And what's not to love? At least on the surface. Bobby is working toward his theology degree—a path Dad wholeheartedly supports —and spent the last four months serving the Lord as a missionary in Peru. Yep, Bobby's a pure golden boy.

A freaking saint.

He'd be a catch for any girl, except he's not the one currently causing butterflies in my stomach.

"I wouldn't jump to serious." I place the phone down and switch it to the speaker before dipping the brush into the eyeshadow again. It's impossible to apply makeup while talking on the phone.

"Come on, Cassie. Everyone thinks you're practically engaged. The only thing missing is the ring."

"And my willingness," I say dryly. My stomach knots, naturally revolting at the idea of marriage—not marriage in general but to Bobby. I take the blending brush and work my eyes to perfection.

"I know that's not what you want, but are you going to do anything about it?" There's a challenge in Nicole's question. And I pause, toying with my answer.

Bobby and I have been friends ever since we could walk. His parents joined the congregation back when Dad took over as the preacher. Bobby could be my ticket out of here. The easier choice. We've talked . . . No, *he* has talked about serving our Lord, Jesus Christ through missionary work. Spreading Christianity is something he's passionate about. I remember sitting beside him while staring at the night sky the evening before he left for Peru.

"Cassie, think about it," Bobby said. His gaze held hope as he stared into the darkness. "Before too long, we'll be going together. With your nursing skills and my ability to preach, we'll be an unstoppable force, spreading Jesus's word." He gave me a side hug. "We'll finally be able to live our fairytale."

I forced a smile and died a little bit more inside.

Missionary work isn't my dream. It's his.

Sure, leaving this area and escaping the memories haunting me sounds appealing, but my passion for spreading the Word died ten months back when the Word failed me.

I blink a few times, forcing myself back to the present and back to Nicole's question of what I will do about it.

My gaze flicks to the sound outside my bedroom door, and those butterflies spring to life.

"I already told you I plan to break up with him." I need to figure out the timing, that's all.

She lets out a long, winded breath. "I think you want to but are waffling on the how."

I should've known she'd call me out. She's the only one who truly knows me. I reach up to my neck only to remember my cross pendant no longer resides there. It's yet another reminder that Nicole may know me, but I haven't fully confided in her either.

"Right now, I need to face Dalton and warn him about Bobby."

"Okay, fine. We'll chat later. But, Cassie, live your life for yourself—not your father." She hangs up, and I'm left stewing over the fact she's right. I've lived my entire life being told what to do and how to act. I don't even know if I can take charge.

I glance back at my reflection. My eyes are definitely defined. More seductive. I like the look. Hopefully, Dalton will too. I suck in all the courage I can and march out of my bedroom door. It's time to put this awkwardness between us to rest.

Stopping outside his bedroom, I rap my knuckles on the wooden panel. His door swings open, and my breath hitches as those rich dark eyes bore into mine. My gaze dips down to his bare chest and tattoos and heads straight to his abdominals. He's wearing nothing but brief running shorts. The black color accentuates his tanned skin, and holy moly, I want that body wrapped around me. He looks absolutely delicious. It's unfair for someone to look this darn good.

My voice comes out weak. "We need to talk."

CHAPTER SEVEN

DALTON

No matter how many times I tell myself this attraction to Cassie isn't real, nothing prepares me for the visceral reaction I have every time I see her. I want to scoop her in my arms and claim every inch of her body, which is why I've avoided her. But it's impossible to hide with her standing in front of me.

Long lashes fan across her cheeks before looking up at me. Her coated pink lips part, drawing my attention. A slight growl rumbles from my chest. I want nothing more than to devour those luscious lips and claim that mouth as mine. I should feel bad, but she knows what she's doing. She wouldn't be biting that lower lip, teasing me, otherwise. If she weren't turned on, she certainly wouldn't have wide eyes and dilated pupils. No, she wants me just as badly.

And that confuses me.

How can she still want me when she has avoided me at every turn?

But something about her has changed. Soft exotic eyeshadow replaces the neutral tones she usually wears. It's the most daring look she has worn yet, and my vain side wonders if the extra effort is for my benefit. Her hair hangs in soft curls framing a perfectly heart-shaped face. Shamelessly, I lower my gaze to her gorgeous body. I don't hide that I absorb every curve of her length. She lost the privilege of me caring about her opinion when she left me hanging for three years. My gaze lingers on the tiniest hint of cleavage. It's the raciest shirt I've seen her wear since my arrival. My dick stirs to life. Shit, I can't allow that to happen. She can't elicit this type of reaction from me. I look for the cross pendant to snap me from these thoughts, but it's still missing. I noticed she wasn't wearing it the first day I arrived but didn't think much of it. Most people remove jewelry before swimming. But she never went a day without wearing it three years ago.

I shut down my attraction. No matter how much my body physically wants her, Cassie doesn't reciprocate those feelings. No way will I let her abandon me again. I cross my arms and stare down at her. She flinches. The move isn't made to intimidate her but to keep my wits. I can't cave like I did the other day out in the hallway.

"What do you want to discuss?"

She barges through my door and stops short in front of my unmade bed. Her body stiffens as she eyes it for a moment. I step toward her but halt when she turns around and faces me.

"Why are you here?" The sharpness in her voice throws me off. She sounds irritated at me as if I was the one who chose to be here. This pisses me off more.

"Why do you think? Obviously, I didn't get called up."

"No. I mean, why are you in California?"

I still don't follow her question. Of all people, she should know her dad runs baseball boot camp. "Baseball players with attitudes get sent to your dad."

"I know that." She grits her teeth and takes a few breaths to calm down. "I thought you went to the University of South Carolina."

"Plans changed."

"So you switched schools?"

I don't know why this is any of her concern. She never cared where I was going before. She left without a single text or goodbye. Fuck this. I'm done answering questions. It's time she gives me answers.

"Where do you go to school, Cassie?" I step toward her. She straightens her stance but doesn't answer. Her eyes remain hard, not revealing any emotion. "It seems you have a shit ton of questions for me, yet you've never answered any of mine. And when you did, they were lies—including your name."

At least she has the decency to drop her head at my accusations, but she doesn't offer any explanation. I continue as silence swells between us, "Don't have anything to say to that?"

She turns away, her back to me, but not before I catch a glimpse of remorse crumbling her face. I should back off, but I'm too much of an asshole to let her off that easily.

I erase the distance and press against her backside. Leaning down, I place my mouth next to her ear. "Do you know how long I searched for Cassie Green?"

Her breath stutters, but I continue, "I spent night after night scouring every search engine. Why did you lie to me?"

Silence meets me.

"Why, Cassie?" I demand, my tone growing angrier.

"I did it to protect you."

"You did it so I wouldn't find you," I quip, voice filled with full-on rage.

She whips around to face me. "No, that's not it—"

"Bullshit. You lied. *You.* The most religious person I know lied to me. Don't tell me it was for my benefit. That's bullshit, and you know it. You never wanted me in the first place."

"That isn't true. You don't understand—"

"Oh, I understand that I wanted you a lot more than you wanted me." I don't mean to bear my soul, but her rejection stung. On the other hand, it feels a little freeing, getting three years of frustration off my chest. "I fucking followed you here, and you wanted nothing to do with me."

"What do you mean you followed me?"

I let out a frustrated breath, more pissed at myself than her.

Really, who's the bigger fool here? "I overheard you on the phone outside that store in Bellow Bay. You mentioned Cessna University on the phone. I assumed you were going there. After you left, I thought I could find you. So I transferred to Cessna University."

Her eyes widen. "But you would've been redshirted."

"Yeah, I was."

"Why would—"

"To find you!" I look toward the ceiling to calm myself down. "I thought what we had was special. I didn't know it was one-sided." I hate putting myself on the line like this, but maybe she'll open up to me if she hears the truth.

"Dalton, I . . . I don't know what to say."

"Tell me why you had Nicole block my number."

Her eyes soften and fill with tears. "You broke my rule."

"What rule?"

"I told you not to fall in love with me."

This knocks my ego back a step. Was I so stupid that I thought she'd actually tell me? She hasn't answered a damn question of mine. *Ever.*

"Why didn't you get in touch with me?"

"It was supposed to be a summer fling."

Damn, this girl is frustrating.

"Why didn't you get a hold of me?"

She remains tightlipped.

"Tell me why you let me fuck you. Explain why you handed me your virginity if we were nothing more than a summer fling."

Her hand flies up, but I catch her wrist before she connects with my face. Her chest heaves up and down. I see the hurt in her eyes, but damn it, she's the one who left, shutting me out. She's the one who lied. Staring into her eyes, I demand, "Tell me."

"You need to push aside whatever happened between us." Her voice is cold and devoid of emotion. I stagger backward. How can she be so callous?

"How do you expect me to do that? I loved you." *Or else, I thought I did.* Maybe it was more lust or infatuation. No. I shut that

44

thought process down. What we shared went beyond any of that. I fucking cared for her. I fucking gave up my dream college and trucked clear across the country to find her. I gave up a year of baseball for her. "Tell me why you tossed me aside. I deserve that much."

"If you get caught looking at me like you've been, my dad will send you packing. He has friends in high places. Ones that could end your career. You *have* to forget about us. I beg you." A tear slides down her cheek, and the pure devastation written across every facet of her face tells me everything I need to know. She still wants me. She's just fighting it.

I don't want to fuck things up any more than what I have. I desperately need to make this summer work, but this girl means everything to me. *Fuck.* I shove my hands through my hair and tug on the ends. I want to scream. I want to punch the fucking wall. My chest heaves as I blink and look away. My gaze lands straight on Jesus.

What do you say, Big Guy? Is she worth this frustration? I know the answer before I even ask the question. Of course she is. She's worth whatever consequence I face. My feet chew the distance between us until our bodies join. I keep moving forward until her back pushes against the wall. We seem to keep finding ourselves in this position—me pressing against that soft body of hers and her cheeks flushed and looking every bit like a woman who wants me. "How am I supposed to do that?" *You're everything to me.*

Her breath stutters. Had I said that last part out loud? I must've because I can see her internal struggle.

"This only ends badly for you."

"I don't care." I lean down to take her mouth. Her lips part in anticipation. Oh yeah, she wants this as much as I do. My lips brush against hers, but before I can fully take her in, Bellow's yelp echoes down the hall along with the whoosh of the front door.

"Cassie."

I immediately back away and growl out my words, "Who's that?"

"Bobby, my boyfriend."

CHAPTER EIGHT

DALTON

BOYFRIEND?

Questions flit through my mind like rapid fire. Who the fuck is Cassie's boyfriend, and why hasn't she told me about him before now?

I stagger backward. I feel as if someone sucker-punched me. Guilt flashes in her eyes, along with remorse.

"I'm coming," she says, her voice garbled. She pushes off the wall and steps toward the living room.

Unable to move, I stand there trying to process that Cassie has a boyfriend. I know we're not a thing anymore, but shouldn't she have told me? Or gave me a warning?

I hear their *I missed yous* and a wave of nausea rushes through me. I step out, ready to meet my competition, but stop short. She isn't mine. She made that clear by not wanting to be found, but I'm not ready to see her in another man's arms.

"What's wrong, baby? You look upset." The guy wears khaki dress pants with a dark blue polo shirt. He may as well pop the collar up like some douchebag from the eighties. Preppy Boy studies Cassie's face and brushes his thumb across her cheek. My body tenses. Those tears are meant for me—not him. I want to yell for him to stop, to get his hands off my girl, but something seems off about their embrace.

"Nothing's wrong. Just happy to see you." Her voice comes across as weak, and any sane individual would tell she's lying. This guy smiles as if he hit the multimillion-dollar jackpot.

"I missed you too. Four months is too long. I can't wait to tell you everything."

Four months?

It's been four months since they've seen each other, and they greet each other like distant cousins? Sorry, Preppy Boy, my girl Cassie doesn't like you the way you think she does.

I need to get out of here. Stepping toward the kitchen to fill my water bottle, I give a curt nod as they turn toward me. I ignore Preppy Boy's assessing gaze. I can tell the moment he notices my tats. Judgmental people are all the same. Without fail, their noses turn upward as if tasting something sour. Yeah, well, the only things sour around here, buddy, are your prejudices. I continue to the sink.

"I see your dad has another lost sheep."

"Bobby," Cassie chides. Then she grabs his hand and tugs him toward me. Lovely.

"This is our latest house guest, Dalton Boyd." She gestures toward me but averts my gaze.

I abandon my water bottle and extend my hand, not wanting to come across as a total dick even though I want to smash every bone in his preppy body. "Nice to meet you."

He reciprocates, placing his buttery smooth hand in mine and shaking it like a dead fish. Is this what Cassie prefers—delicate touches as opposed to calloused hands?

"I assume you won't be around much with baseball and all." His gaze roams along my ink again as disapproval coats his features. Usually, I don't care what people think, but his gestures bother me for some reason. Maybe because this is the guy Cassie has decided to date. He couldn't be more opposite from me.

Was I just a phase for Cassie? A way to satisfy those bad boy needs before committing to a life of boredom? My chest tightens. I always knew I wasn't good enough for this girl, but I did think what we shared was real. Maybe it wasn't.

My gaze slides to Cassie. "Yeah, I don't spend too much time here."

"Where do you attend school?" Preppy boy asks.

"Cessna U."

"Yeah, that's a good school. What are you studying?"

"Marketing."

"Really?" His eyebrows rise, and then he eyes my tats again. "You're not the typical businessman type."

"I'm aware," I say dryly. I had to declare a major and had no idea what to do. My counselor suggested something in business since I couldn't very well take mechanics. Trade school would suit me better, but those schools don't have Division I baseball.

"Hmm, I hope you take it seriously. The odds for becoming a professional baseball player aren't in your favor."

"Bobby," Cassie says while slapping his arm.

"What, it's true." He turns to me. "I'm sure you're aware."

"I'm quite aware." Anger rolls off me. Yeah, I'm aware, asshole. Why the fuck do you think I'm stuck in this Podunk town instead of some minor league team? But I don't say any of that. I'm too busy watching him wrap his arm possessively around Cassie's waist.

I would ask where he's been, but I don't want to make small talk.

He pulls her into an embrace, and it's all I can do to keep from prying his hands away from what should be mine. She belongs with me. Regardless of how better she is or how opposite we are, we belong together. There was more passion in her eyes as she stared at me sixty seconds ago. I don't care how long they've been together. By the time summer ends, she'll be back in my arms. And this time, she won't get away.

I replace the cap on my water bottle and sidestep around them.

Cassie calls after me, "Where are you going?"

"For a run."

And that's what I do. Cassie lives about a mile away from the beach. One of my favorite things to do is to run along the coastline. It's been a few years since I've done it. Once my feet hit the sand, I continue to run, formulating a plan on how to win her back from Preppy Boy.

CHAPTER NINE

CASSIE

I FLINCH AS DALTON SLAMS THE FRONT DOOR. THE SOUND reverberates off the walls like sharp lobster claws pinching my chest. This is so not how I envisioned Dalton finding out about Bobby. *Gah*, I can't stop picturing that look of hurt flashing in his eyes.

"You're early." My voice is sharper than intended, which isn't fair to Bobby, but I needed a few more minutes. Then maybe Dalton wouldn't have been caught off guard. I could've prepared him for Bobby's onslaught of questions.

"I couldn't wait any longer. Four months is a long time to be away." Bobby wraps his arms around me and pulls me in for a hug. I fight the urge to wiggle free.

But the arms I sought refuge in for the past couple of years feel wrong.

I'm not being fair to him. It's not as if Bobby's a bad guy. He's the total package on paper: good-looking, caring, and intelligent. And Dad approved. Having the same religious beliefs as me doesn't hurt either. Heck, he's practically a poster boy for boyfriend material. I wasn't allowed to date until I graduated high school. And even when I started college, Dad had to approve of the guy.

That limited the dating pool. For real. Who wants to bring a guy home for approval?

I wanted to protest, but I couldn't do that to Mom. I didn't want her to worry—not with everything she had going on. Then, after she had a bad spell, Bobby was there to comfort me. We've been friends forever, so it was only natural that I leaned on him. We were officially boyfriend and girlfriend after.

Mom and Dad couldn't have been more thrilled. I was numb.

"So, tell me about Peru." I back away and walk over to the couch. He glances around nervously. I bite back a sigh. "Dad's not home. He's at the hospital with Mr. Barley's family."

This information doesn't make him relax, but I don't miss the concern he shows for Mr. Barley. Losing church members is always hard. I fill him in with what info I have as we settle in the couch cushions.

"Sounds like your dad will be tied up for a while. I won't stay long."

"It's fine, Bobby. I think we're past the need for a chaperone." Frustration laces the edges of my tone, and I don't know why. It would be better if he left. But I know he's serious.

"Cassie, remember your place. You know I'm right," he chides.

My lips press into a thin line, but I nod, knowing that's what he expects. "Sorry, but Dad trusts you."

Bobby gives me a placating look, and I want to scream.

"You still know the rules."

"Yes." That's why Nicole dubbed him CC. I take a deep breath and try to switch topics. "You were going to tell me about Peru."

That prompts him to talk about his trip. When he details the sermons he delivered, I zone out. I can't help it. My mind reverts to Dalton, who has no qualms about being alone with me. And it may be apparent that he's mad at me, but I can tell he still wants me.

And I like that. A lot.

Because the longer I stare at Bobby sitting a foot away from me, the more I can't help but think about Dalton's hands on me.

That thought morphs to our first kiss. The first time he went down on me. And the way he caressed me after we had sex.

My mind doesn't think about my boyfriend and the *no premarital sex* rule he follows to a *T*. Goodness, he still thinks I'm a virgin. We haven't even reached first base. He wants us to save ourselves for marriage. I haven't told him that ship sailed a few summers ago.

Nicole thinks I'm crazy for not demanding more or not dumping him to find someone else, but not having sex hasn't been challenging. Like at all. Shouldn't it have been?

It's been drilled into my head that my body is for my husband. Taking things into your own hands is selfish and takes away from your partner. But how selfish can it be when your partner doesn't wish to satisfy you? And if being satisfied equals selfishness, then I'm one selfish woman. These past few years, I've taken control of my own satisfaction. The problem is it wasn't Bobby infiltrating my thoughts. It was always the six-foot-two demigod that recently ran out of the house.

"So that pretty much sums it up. I think you'll love it there. It's so fulfilling."

I nod in response, realizing I didn't listen to a word he said. "Um, yeah, sure."

"What's with you?" His eyebrows scrunch together as concern coats his eyes. "Is it that guy? Does he scare you?"

"Scare me?"

"His tattoos are rather intimidating. Plus, the constant scowl doesn't help. I can stay until your dad comes home if that makes you more comfortable. Your dad will understand."

"No, Dalton's harmless."

"I'm serious. If you're not comfortable staying here, I can move you in for the summer. My parents don't use their spare bedroom. I'm sure your dad may be a hard sell, but it's better than—"

"No! Goodness, no." My hand squeezes my neck. I finally got to stay home for the summer. I'll be darned if I'm giving up my privileges.

"Seriously, it wouldn't be a problem," he says, ignoring my responses.

"Bobby—"

"Let me call Mom and tell her to get the room ready." He whips his phone out to dial, but I place my hand on his arm.

"Please stop. Dalton's fine."

Bobby looks exasperated. Those light brown eyes I haven't seen in months stare back at me. Guilt settles in again. But this time, it is from my lack of feeling swoon-worthy. I wish I felt half of the excitement I felt when Dalton opened his door in nothing but those running shorts. It would make things so much easier. But the hard-core truth stares me in the face. No matter how hard I try, I'm not in love with Bobby.

But how can I let him down? I owe Bobby so much.

Maybe I feel conflicted because having Dalton back in my life is rekindling feelings that need to stay in the past. There isn't a future for me with Dalton, no matter how I wish things could be different. I won't be the one to destroy Dalton's dream. He doesn't have an alternative. He *has* to get drafted. I don't want him to end up back home in North Carolina with his dad.

Regardless, the breakup with Bobby is inevitable. It's not fair to him either.

"I don't trust him. You know the type of guys your dad gets," Bobby says, pulling me back into the conversation.

"I'm sorry if I'm coming across as ungrateful, but this is the first summer I've stayed home in years. Can't you understand why I wouldn't want to leave?"

"But if you feel uncomfortable."

"I never said I was uncomfortable. You just assumed. Look, I need to talk to you about our relationship."

"You're right. Please forgive me. I don't want to spend our reunion fighting."

"Neither do I, but I really need to talk about—"

"Shh." He places a finger over my lips, and I fight the urge to swat his hand away. He leans down to give me a chaste kiss on the cheek. "I've missed us being together."

"Me too." The words feel bitter on my tongue. They're not a complete lie. I have missed his friendship, but I need to end this. "Bobby, we've been friends for so long and you'll always hold a special place in my heart, but I can't do this anymore. I think it's time to break—"

He stands abruptly. "I should go."

"No, we need to talk about this. I'm trying to tell you that I want to break—"

"Your dad will be back soon, and I don't want to give him the wrong impression."

I can't help but roll my eyes. This is beyond ridiculous. "It's not as if Dad chaperones us at college." *Not that we ever do anything that needs chaperoning.*

That remark earns me a harsh glare. It's meant to put me in my place, the obedient girlfriend stepping in line. I sit taller, hating the guilty feelings swarming my body—years of being the good submissive clashing with how I want to be. To find the spine I know I possess.

"It's best I go. You know this. Besides, you have to work on my party."

My lips curve into a tight smile. "You want me to throw you a welcome home party?"

"Of course! That's what any good girlfriend would do."

"That's true, but I don't think we're on the same page. I don't want to be your girlfriend anymore."

"Come on. You don't mean that. And besides, you always take care of me. Just as it should be." He kisses the top of my head before pivoting toward the door. "I'll let myself out. Call if that guy gives you any problems."

"Everything's fine. You're being judgmental." And he is. The basis for Bobby's quick assessment is strictly from Dalton's appearance. That's hardly fair.

"I still don't like it. The offer to stay at my house is still open.

And wipe that gunk off your face. Your cousin is a bad influence. You're more wholesome without it, don't you agree?" He doesn't wait for my reply and turns to leave. The door shuts behind him, and I remain stationed on the couch, staring at the entrance. I can't believe I ever entertained the thought of marrying him. Had he proposed and I said yes, nothing in my life would've changed. Sure, the scenery may be different, but the same prison walls would still cage me. The only difference would be the change in guard.

My throat tightens.

On top of everything else, I get to plan a party for a boyfriend I unsuccessfully dumped. Wonderful. I'll get through this party and then find a way to break it off. Daddy won't be happy, and he may send me away, but I can't keep going on like this. Nicole is right. It's past time to start living my life for me—not anyone else.

CHAPTER TEN

DALTON

I STEP INTO THE LOCKER ROOM, WEARING THE SAME SCOWL THAT plagued my face the entire evening—not that anyone saw me last night. By the time I returned from my run, Cassie was nowhere to be found. I assumed she had left with her boyfriend, but I heard movement in her room after my shower. Doesn't matter. She's moved on from our, what, fling? Encounter? *Fuck!* This only proves I need to let her memory go.

Maybe Dad's right, and I am defective. Or at the very least unlovable.

A couple of guys nod as I shuffle past them toward my locker. I return a grunt. It's not the best way to bond with the team, but I couldn't care less. Coach is the only person I need to impress. Everything else is noise—women in general. I've loved two women in my life, and both relationships ended in disappointment. I need to focus on myself.

And that starts by getting on Coach's good side and completing the assignment he asked for. The short summary I bullshitted my way through wasn't good enough. Not a surprise since I hadn't spoken one word to Jason, but I had hoped. Coach took one glance at the paper and called me out. That earned me another fifty laps.

I shove my duffle bag into the locker and scan the room for my intended target. It's not that I've purposefully avoided Jason. I didn't know how to broach the subject. What do you say to someone you couldn't care less about? Hey, I have to get to know you, so tell me your deepest secrets. Yeah, that's not going to fly. I'll start by asking him to meet after the game and then worry about the logistics later.

My gaze lands on him, waltzing through the door with two other infielders. I compartmentalize my anger and step toward them. *Here goes nothing.*

"Are you ready for tonight's game? I heard coach was going to start you," Carter says, cutting me off.

I look past him. Jason steps up to his locker. When he pulls his cleats out of the duffle bag, I realize I don't have much time. "That's the plan."

I sidestep around Carter, but my cell goes off. Grunting, I make the mistake of pulling it out of my pocket and checking it. Dad. My entire body stiffens.

Damn it. Dad's the last person I want to talk to. I've already ignored his other calls. I should, by all rights, answer.

"Aren't you going to get that?"

My head snaps to Carter. I forgot he was standing beside me.

"Wasn't planning on it."

"Why the hell not? It's your old man."

Because it's the worst thing to do before a game. I don't voice that thought. I shrug instead.

"What if it's an emergency? Why else would he be calling before a game?"

Because he's drunk. Because he's an asshole. Because he hates me. I can list many reasons, and none of them are good. Marty warned me his drinking is worse and it's starting to affect what little business he still gets. I relent and answer. The last thing I need is Carter getting up in my personal life.

"Hello?"

"You worthless piece of shit. You too good to answer your dad or what?"

I grit my teeth, hoping that Carter didn't hear his rant. The glance Carter's way reveals widened eyes, so I guess he had.

"I answered, didn't I?"

Dad grunts. "You need to get home right now."

"You know I can't do that. I'm in the middle of summer league ball."

"Baseball." The word spews from his mouth as if it is poisonous. "Quit pussyfooting around. You're never going anywhere with that. It's a complete waste of time."

As his slurred words sink in, I stare across the locker room. To the guys filtering in. To their carefree laughter. Everyone has issues. I'm not alone but damn if I don't feel isolated.

"Is there a reason for your call?"

"Your brother's parole is coming up. You need to be home."

I feel eyes watching me. I remain stoic, trying not to let on that anything is wrong. We do this song and dance every summer. It's getting fucking old.

"That's not until the end of August," I say, irritated. I went home after summer ball my freshman year and arrived late to campus. My coach at Cessna U understood, but I swore I'd never visit the prison again. My presence didn't help Steve's case anyway. It's not like having his dad and brother waiting outside sways the parole board's mind. But I'll save that argument for when I don't have peering eyes on me.

"You ungrateful piece of shit. After everything your brother did for you, the least you can do is be there for him." Another one of Dad's tactics he likes to use is guilt. It won't work, but I need to get off this phone. I have a game to win.

"I'll see what I can do."

He mumbles, "Such a worthless fuck-up," before clicking off.

I don't move, the talk with Jason forgotten. All I can think about is focusing on how I've let my entire family down—my brother, Dad, and even Mom.

My mind flashes back to a bowl of Cocoa Puffs.

I had just poured myself a bowl and sat down to eat them when Dad busted through the back door. My five-year-old legs quaked. I could tell by his red face he found the pile of tire rims I knocked over. My brother, Steve, and I were playing capture the flag. He placed the flag on top of a pile of boxes in Dad's garage. I had to climb them with Steve chasing after me. The flag was within reach when Steve grabbed my ankle. I lost balance and skidded on the boxes. They tumbled over. Steve took off running. I tried to restack the rims, but they were too heavy. I bolted, hoping Dad wouldn't get too mad.

"You piece of shit. Do you know how much money you cost me?" The vein in Dad's neck popped and bobbed up and down like it did every time he yelled. He yelled a lot.

"I didn't do it." I tried to protest because it wasn't my fault. Not really. Steve made me do it. He always got me in trouble.

"Don't lie to me." He raised his hand for the first time, and I shrunk down in my seat. Before he followed through, Mom walked in the backdoor.

"Phil," she yelled. "What happened?"

"Your piece of shit son ruined Mrs. Cole's rims. This is your fault. You coddle him too much." His fingers wrapped around my arm and squeezed. I let out a whimper, and his grip tightened. Mom moved toward me, but she didn't tell him to stop. She never stood up for me, but he yelled less when she was around. She placed a hand on Dad's arm—the one that had a hold of mine.

"Let me get him ready for school, and I'll take care of it when I get back."

Her words seemed to work because he let go of my arm. I hurried to my bedroom.

"Run, you little prick. You cause nothing but trouble."

I shut my bedroom door, but it didn't drown out the yelling. I heard Dad call me another bad name. Mom tried to say something, but then I heard the slap. Then I heard Mom sob. When the backdoor slammed shut, I knew it was safe to come back out. I tiptoed back into the kitchen and saw Mom crying. She tried to hide it, but I saw the tears run along the red mark on her cheek before she wiped them away.

"You need to stay out of the garage." Her words were cold. *I had never heard that voice before.*

"It wasn't my fault."

"It's always your fault. Now get in the car. You've got school."

I hated my dad for a while, but right now, I hated my mom.

"Hey, you about ready?" Carter's voice pulls me out of my reverie.

"Yeah, I'll be right there. I need to say something to Jason first."

"Okay, man. Don't be too long."

I push aside the uneasiness that punches through my veins and make my way to Jason. He's about to head out the door with two other players.

"Hey, Jason. I was wondering if after the game—"

"Save it. I know the routine. The coach wants you to get to know me as part of his behavior modification, but trust me, there isn't anything to know about me."

"Come on. The sooner we get this done, the sooner we don't have to talk."

"Let me make this simple for you since you don't seem to comprehend. We have nothing to discuss."

"Man, what is your problem?"

"You. You're the problem. You came here with a freaking attitude that you own this team. That you own my position."

I just stare at him. Of course, the spot is mine. That's what every player in any sport would think. You must show confidence. What is this tool thinking? Maybe I should put how he's nothing but a tool in the report. *Would that fly, Coach?* I open my mouth, but before I can speak, Jason walks away.

"Let's see who the best man is at the end of the day."

And then he's gone. I pick up my hat and head out the door. Isn't this a shit kind of day?

And the shit day keeps getting worse. I think I played the worst game I've ever played. It's the top of the seventh. So far, I've swung out once and ran through the stop sign at second. I slid into third in time, but that didn't stop the ass chewing Coach gave when I got back to the dugout.

It's hard to concentrate with Dad's words still in my head. I knew I shouldn't have picked up the phone. Stupid Carter. I bet he has a good dad. One that gives encouragement.

Focus.

I need to focus.

There's a runner on third and first base with a two-two count. I played against the prick on first during the college playoffs. He's known for talking smack, and I'm in no mood for his bullshit.

Our pitcher winds up.

"Hey, Boyd, what happened? You're pretty worthless today."

My teeth grind together as I try ignoring his taunts, but the word worthless rings the loudest. I should be numb to it. It's been tossed at me my entire life.

The batter smacks a ground ball that heads straight to me. It should be an easy out. I bend down to field the ball but come up empty when I scoop my glove. The ball rolls between my legs. *Fuck!* That's my second error of the game. The right fielder sweeps in and picks it up but not before the runner on third scores.

"Damn it." I need to get my head out of my ass. I hope no one important is here at the game. I'd hate for them to see my debut performance. Jesus, it's like the Bad News Bears out here.

Coach makes a trip to the pitcher's mound and calls for relief. But that's not all he calls for. I inwardly groan when I see Jason jogging from the dugout. A double switch. Just fucking great.

Jason smirks as he nods at me. I can't believe Coach is taking me out. I get to the dugout and throw my glove against the wall. The Gatorade cooler sits there mocking me. Okay, it's just sitting there filled with electrolytes and hydration, but anything is the enemy as rage pours out of me. I knock it over, and the fluid splashes everyone in the vicinity.

"Dalton!" Coach yells. "Get into the locker room and get dressed."

I don't say a word and exit.
Fuck this shit.

CHAPTER ELEVEN

CASSIE

"ARE YOU GOING TO BE OKAY HERE BY YOURSELF?" DAD ASKS AS he grabs his car keys off the kitchen counter. "I have to run back to the hospital."

Masking my irritation with indifference, I shift my gaze from the book I'm pretending to read and look across the living room to Dad. I've never noticed how suffocating his overprotectiveness was until now. "Why wouldn't I be okay?"

His jaw works back and forth as if trying to control his temper. "I didn't send you to college to develop an attitude. I think you've forgotten your place."

That's right. Women are subservient. How could that fact slip my mind?

My hands grip the book tighter as I shift to sit straighter. I know it's rude not to ask about Mr. Barley, but staying home alone shouldn't be questionable. I should just comply so I can get to Dalton. I need to find out why he threw a fit in the dugout last night. Something must be eating at him. I'm hoping that reason isn't finding out about Bobby. "I'm sorry, but, Dad, I'm twenty-one. I'm capable of being alone."

Our stare down is like a test of wills with neither one wanting to cave. So much for conceding. I never talk back to Dad, *ever*, but he better loosen this imaginary lasso wrapped around me soon. I can't take much more.

Dad must sense he pushed too far and breaks away first. Small win, but I'll take whatever ones I can. But then he ruins the moment by glancing toward the hallway with narrowed eyes. "You're not exactly alone."

Cue my anger.

I clamp my mouth shut, suppressing the string of curse words itching to escape. Yes, actual curse words. That's how angry I am. Dad's blatant disapproval of Dalton couldn't be more displaced. He isn't a bad guy. I don't know what actions caused him to be placed under Dad's supervision, but this preconceived idea of him isn't fair. I don't believe in magic—not the genie-in-the-bottle kind—so I've never desired to own a magic lamp. The church teaches anything dealing with magic, horoscopes, or tarot cards is sinister and evil. Still, if genies were a reality, I'd use my one wish to open Dad's eyes to the sweet and thoughtful guy residing inside Dalton. That side of him hasn't appeared yet, especially after the fit he threw in the dugout last night, but I know that guy is in there. I witnessed his sweetness back in Bellow Bay.

"I'll be fine," I say finally. "Besides, he hardly leaves his room."

Dad grunts, but he knows it's the truth. Dalton has been a recluse since day one. If he isn't running or at practice, he's tucked inside his bedroom. Dad doesn't know my plan to talk to said hermit the moment he leaves. Dalton and I haven't been alone since Bobby interrupted us. Even if I had seen him, he certainly wasn't approachable after his display last night. But I owe Dalton more than an apology for not mentioning Bobby sooner. I owe him an explanation. It's just I'm not sure his reason for staying hidden is because he doesn't want to run into Dad or me.

"It's a good thing he stays in there. After last night, I don't trust him."

Dad makes Dalton out to be some loose cannon. Sure, he was angry, but there must've been a reason.

"Something had to be bothering him because his entire game was off. Did you even ask?"

Dad's expression remains stoic as he studies me, no doubt wondering how I picked up on those cues, but I got to him. I see the wheels churning inside his head. Dad may pride himself on preaching to his congregation, but he knows God's work is best served to people outside the church community. Isn't that the true calling? To help others when there's a need? Funny how that gets overlooked.

"Call if you need anything," he says through a grumble.

"I will."

The moment Dad leaves, I bite my bottom lip and wonder if he saw through my lies. I've never been good at hiding the truth. Maybe that's why he was so reluctant to leave? Ugh, why is this so hard? I should be able to talk to anyone I want.

But I find myself holding my breath while listening for the truck to back out of the driveway. Placing the book on the couch, I let another minute pass as I contemplate the best way to approach Dalton. I can't come out and ask what's bothering him. That line of questioning will put him on the defense. I also don't want to admit Bobby isn't my boyfriend. I need to keep the ruse going until after the welcome home party. It will be harder to stay away if I tell him now. The more time we spend together will deepen this attraction. And I can't be attracted to him. I won't be the reason his career ends.

When it's apparent Dad won't be coming back, I spring from the couch and dart down the hallway.

The thrumming in my chest does nothing to calm me as I stand in front of the white, wooden door. Holy moly, why am I so nervous to talk to him? I can do this. I've spoken to plenty of guys at college. I've worked beside them in the lab. *But I never actually liked any of them.*

I drum up encouragement and knock on the door. My breath escapes when the tall, broody man swings the door open, and those dark brown eyes stare into mine.

"Bobby isn't my boyfriend."

Cheese and crackers, I can't believe I just blurted that out. I blame the lack of oxygen from all the non-breathing I did. That must be the reason I lost all sense. My mind sputters as to what to say next. Dalton's blank reception doesn't help ease the tension. There's a delicate balance between wanting him to know the entire truth versus needing him to hate me enough to stay away. Perhaps, I'm overthinking it or a bit self-centered because I figured he'd at least crack a smile from learning I'm not taken. And from his bored expression, he acts as if I recited the phonebook —backward.

My hand flies to the base of my neck, my fingers fumbling with a nonexistent necklace. "Uh, I mean, I don't want him to be."

His gaze dips to my chest before returning his cold stare. "What do you want, Choir Girl?"

Despite the chill to his tone, the use of the nickname he gave me in Bellow Bay is the slightest indication that the sweet guy still exists inside him. Emotion lodges in my throat. "Can we talk?"

He studies me for a moment, and the intensity behind his stare down leaves me breathless. But he's so darn unreadable I wonder if I'm the only one feeling this way. Usually, he would erase the gap or find some way to touch me by now. He's done neither. That look in his eyes—the one where he acts as if he could feast on me—is also missing. I wouldn't say the sexual tension is missing, but more like it's paused.

I really messed things up between us.

"Please," I ask, feeling defeated.

He works his jaw and takes a sharp breath. When I think the answer will be no, he nods.

Now comes the fun game of balancing my attraction with friendship. Dad's threat still exists. No matter how badly I want to tip the scales in my favor.

CHAPTER TWELVE

DALTON

I STEP INTO THE HALLWAY AND FOLLOW CASSIE INTO THE kitchen. I'm not in the mood for head games, but I know she isn't one to play them. I also suspect her reason for wanting to talk has everything to do with my behavior from last night. That subject is a no-go. I can't afford to get closer to her than we already are. But as my gaze dips to those short shorts I guarantee aren't daddy approved, someone needs to inform my dick. He wholeheartedly approves of getting closer, as evident by the stirring in my pants. That curvy ass of hers looks too good not to stare.

Cassie whips around as if I voiced my thoughts aloud. My gaze meets her accusing eyes, and I feel guilty for ogling her. But a smirk pushes across my innocent roommate's face.

Yeah, she totally read my thoughts.

She grabs keys from inside a cabinet and nudges her head toward the patio doors. "Let's sit outside. It's too stuffy in here."

I nod, not missing the way her button nose crinkles toward the end, but I can't help but wonder if it's the quietness or her dad's lingering presence that causes the stuffiness. With Cassie's recent disappearing act, I stay holed up in my room like a damn hermit and venture out only when hunger pains strike. The house is like a mortuary, aside from the slight ticking of the wall clock and occasional bark from Bellow. There isn't even a television, for fuck's sake. The last thing I want to do is sit in the living room and watch her dad riffle through religious magazines. A shudder works its way down my spine at that thought. Shaking that image off, I step behind her as she resumes walking through the sliding glass doors that lead to the backyard. Bellow follows us outside, wagging his tail.

The warm breeze kicks Cassie's blond curls off her neck, revealing her silhouette. She's beautiful. She remains quiet as she leads me to the edge of the pool. I haven't spent any time out here since I arrived.

"Remove your shoes and join me." She points to my feet as she drops to the pool's concrete edge and sticks her lower legs into the water. I quickly follow suit. Bellow takes off to the small patch of grass by the outbuilding on the far right. I noticed the free-standing garage the other day when I went for a run but haven't had a chance to ask about it. As I said, communication around here is at a minimum.

The heated water laps against our shins as it circulates the pool. We sit there as the steady stream from the waterfall beats down like gentle rain and fills in the silence. I take in my surroundings. This isn't a pool. This is an oasis found in five-star hotels. How'd I miss all of this when I arrived? The shock from seeing Cassie must've blinded me to the beauty of their backyard because I had no idea the backdrop featured so many waterfalls. Strategically stacked boulders, which I assume are faux, form a massive wall. It's peaceful.

"It's beautiful out here."

"Thanks. I find it relaxing. I come out here to think. Or I used to when I was home."

I turn her way. The corners of her lips turn downward, and there's a faraway look to her stare. I'd give anything to know what's going through her mind, but something tells me she needs to work through her emotions. I wonder if she's thinking about her mom.

She hasn't mentioned anything about her, but something must have happened.

"I wanted to apologize." Cassie's melodic voice pulls me back to her.

"What do you have to be sorry about?"

"I can think of a few things, but I want to start with the reason for leaving. You need to know why I left Bellow Bay so suddenly." She takes a stuttering breath while her feet kick in a slow pattern. "That morning after . . ." Her voice trails off, and no matter how badly I want her to finish, I let her collect her thoughts. The morning after we made love for the first and only time played out a lot differently than I wanted. We were supposed to meet back up that night, but she was gone.

"My dad showed up that morning and surprised me." Pain cripples her features, and I have to stop myself from reaching out to her. This pain goes beyond the pain of losing me. This stems from something tragic. "He showed up at Aunt Jan's house to bring me home. My mom found out she had cancer, and her prognosis wasn't good."

Her hand rises to her chest. Her cross pendant is once again missing. Another mystery I'll let her tell me about in her own time, but I wonder if it has to do with her losing her mom. I remember she told me they were close. She had commented that she wouldn't know what she'd do without her mom. Pain rips through my chest, and even though I shouldn't, I scoot closer to her and wrap a protective arm around her.

"I'm so sorry you went through that. When did she pass away?"

"About ten months ago." She lays her head on my shoulder.

"I figured something bad had happened."

"I miss her so much, but there are days when I don't believe it's real. It's easier when I'm at college because I can pretend she's at home. But when I'm back, the house is too quiet."

"Losing a parent is one of the hardest things to go through." Even though my mom didn't die, it still stung when she left without so much as a goodbye. I suppose losing someone to an illness is different—less resentment. "I wish I could say it gets easier, but it doesn't. It just gets more tolerable."

The silence stretches between us as we watch the warm water circulate in the pool. Bellow joins us, plopping down beside Cassie. I entwine our fingers, noticing how my hand engulfs her tiny one.

"You should've reached out to me. I would've been there for you."

"I wanted to. You have no idea how badly I wanted to talk to you, but I couldn't. Aunt Jan found the cell phone under the bed before we left, and Dad was livid. He figured out I was talking to a boy, but Jan didn't tell him who the guy was. Dad didn't yell too much since we needed to get back home."

I nod, trying to understand where she's coming from, but her lack of communication was total hell for me during that time. I *ached* for her. There's only one other woman I ever ached for, and that's my mother. My temper flares, getting the best of me. "A message from Nicole would've been nice."

She flinches from the bite in my tone. "I know, and I'm so sorry. I thought a clean break would be best. I figured the goodbye would be easier. It killed me not being able to tell you."

"Did it? Because it sure never seemed that way from my side."

"I deserve that. But I had my reasons. I'm serious, Dalton. If my dad found out who you were and that you played baseball, he would've ended your college career."

"I'm sure he doesn't wield that kind of power."

"Trust me, he does. He knows people in high places, and you don't want to get on his bad side."

I let out a humorless laugh. "That ship sailed the moment I got off the plane."

"He's judging you right now, but your talent will win him over." She lifts her chin to look into my eyes. "Just don't do anything to make him upset."

"You mean like sit next to his daughter by the pool?"

A pinkish tinge coats her cheeks. She sits up straighter and pulls away but doesn't go too far. We're still close. Although, I'd prefer to close the gap completely.

I brush my leg against hers, causing tiny ripples. I study them as I ask, "What about your boyfriend?"

"Bobby has been my friend since I was little. He was there when Mom got sick, and I guess dating made sense."

My hands clench into fists as that statement shoots right through me, but when those eyes that hold so much sorrow turn to look at me, I let it go. This girl turns me to mush with just one look. I don't know how she does it.

"And now?" My voice is barely over a whisper. I gravitate a little closer.

"I'm ending things between us."

I feel her warm breath on my face. My gaze drops to those pouty pink lips. My tongue slips out and licks my bottom lip. "So no more boyfriend."

Her gaze hoods over as her lips part. Her breathing ticks up a beat. "No more boyfriend."

Warmth invades my body, which I'm pretty sure has nothing to do with the heated water on our legs. I move to close that gap, which seems to spook her. She rears back and stands up.

"I have something to show you, but first, let me put Bellow back inside."

Once we have our shoes back on and the dog put up, I follow her to the outbuilding. When she opens the door and clicks on the light, my mouth drops open. In the middle of the building sits a '57 Chevy.

"Oh sure, you show me this when we're getting ready to leave for an away game."

Her laughter makes me smile. It's the first time I've heard her relax, and the angelic sound warms my heart.

"The thing doesn't run."

"Yeah, trust me. I know." This was her Aunt Jan's car. She's the reason our business took a nosedive. She had Dad look under the hood. The woman hadn't had an oil change in forever. He warned her about the sludge buildup, but she wouldn't let him do anything. She would hire a professional mechanic, meaning one with a fancier building, in the next town over. Except she didn't. She continued to drive it until the engine seized. She turned around and blamed everything on Dad, not claiming any fault. People believed her, and our customer base shrank.

Her eyes cut to mine. "Feel free to tinker around with it."

"How did you guys end up with it."

"Aunt Jan died about a year and a half ago. Since she didn't have any children, her possessions went to Dad. He sold most everything but kept the car. He wants to restore it, but he's no mechanic. When Mom's condition worsened, he paused working on it."

"I didn't realize your aunt had died."

"I'm sure she wasn't your top priority when you went home for the summer."

"I haven't been back home since freshman year."

She gives me a concerned but knowing look. Having witnessed my dad's wrath, I'm sure she can figure out my reasoning.

"Do you miss home?"

"No. The only thing I miss about Bellow Bay is the skyline over the ocean. Oh, and my friend, Marty, but that's it. I should miss my brother, but I resigned myself to not talking to him. I knew that was coming." I certainly don't miss my old man or sweating at his mechanic shop. I don't miss the punches to the sides or slaps against the head.

She nods in understanding. "When does your brother get out?"

"His parole hearing is at the end of August. He may get out then. Otherwise, it'll be in another three years." My brother got seven years for attempted murder. It was a robbery gone bad. I don't believe he intended to shoot anyone, but he did bring the gun. Unfortunately, the gun had a hair trigger. Between my drunk father and thieving brother, my reputation suffered. I was never so happy to leave.

"Have you visited him in jail?"

"No. I know that makes me a bad person, but I just can't do it."

"Are you going back for the parole hearing?"

"Not if I can help it." Our gaze connects. "Dad still blames me for my brother getting caught. Like I somehow forced him to steal because I wanted to play ball. I hate being there when he doesn't get released. It was ugly the last time he got denied." Dad took his anger out on me. He tried hitting me, but I stopped him. Then I hopped on the first possible flight out of North Carolina. I haven't been back since. If I never stepped foot in that state again, I wouldn't cry.

"Did you ever seek counseling?"

"No."

"It wouldn't hurt to have someone professional to talk to. Maybe you wouldn't feel so isolated."

"Maybe one day. Until then, I'll avoid home as much as I can."

"I'm sorry."

"It's not your fault."

"No, but I'm still sorry people judge you."

"Story of my life." I step inside her space and watch her body tremble. I love knowing I caused that reaction.

"They don't know the real you."

"I'm not sure the real me is worth getting to know."

"That's not true."

"You once said when we met again, the timing would be better. But you were wrong."

"I once believed that. But I'm glad you're here."

"Me too." I dip my head lower, those pink lips too tempting to stay away. Her lips part and I'm so close to getting what I've craved ever since she left.

"Cassie," an annoying male voice calls out.

I quickly step back and watch her emotions shut down. "Your boyfriend's calling."

"He's not my boyfriend." Her whispered confession hangs in the air as the side door opens.

"Cassie?"

"I'm in here." She sidesteps around me, giving us distance.

Bobby walks into the room and stops abruptly when he notices me. Disapproval clouds his expression. "Is everything okay?"

I don't appreciate the accusation in his tone.

"Of course." There's a bite to her words. Cassie must not have appreciated his tone either. "I was showing Dalton the old '57. He's a pretty good mechanic. I figured he could tinker out here during his downtime."

"I'm good with my hands." I bite back a smirk when Cassie's cheeks pinken and Bobby's jaw hardens. I'm playing with fire, but let him think what he wants. Cassie handed me a small victory. I can't bask in it too long. She gives me the key to the building and leaves with her supposedly soon-to-be ex-boyfriend.

Cassie's voice echoes across the yard. I pick up a wrench, itching to work on this car and scope the inventory Coach has purchased. A funny feeling settles in my chest. Cassie gets me. Like really gets me. She knew I needed this outlet.

But is that a good thing? She has a boyfriend. One she doesn't love, but he obviously is still in the picture.

I have to get my act together and show her I can be boyfriend material. That I take baseball seriously. I may be a worthless fuck-up, but I do care about things other than myself. I just need to convince her and her dad that.

Until I can figure out how to make Operation Sainthood work, I may as well do what my legacy is—work on this blown engine.

CHAPTER THIRTEEN

DALTON

IF THERE WERE EVER A DAY I NEEDED A HIT FROM A BLUNT, today would be that day. But even I am not that brazen no matter how badly I need to calm the fuck down. Considering I'm standing outside the church and feeling like an imposter dressed in sheep's clothing, I don't think that will happen. However, I'm not claiming to be a false prophet, but a non-believer destined for hell, which can be just as dangerous.

This team requirement is pure bullshit. Not everyone belongs here. Take me, for example. Sure, the sign hanging on the glass doors may state *All Are Welcome*, but that isn't what they actually mean. That's apparent by each disapproving look tossed my way by the so-called *welcoming* congregation.

"Dalton."

I turn to where my name is called and face Carter closing in on me. He's dressed in a navy sports jacket, white button-down shirt, blue tie with tiny white polka dots, and matching navy dress pants. He blends, looking settled as if he's a member of the congregation. Where he fits in, I stand out like a sore thumb in my wrinkled khakis and a polo shirt.

"Why are you standing outside looking as if you could puke?"

"Just biding time. I rode with Coach. We got here forty-five minutes ago." I glance back at the doors and shake my head. "I couldn't go in there that early."

The asshole chuckles. I'm worried about lightning bolts striking me down, and he laughs.

"Come on. Attending church isn't that bad."

I grunt in protest but follow him in through the hypocritical doors. When my feet cross the threshold, I scratch my forearm and resist the urge to tug at my collar. The damn thing is too restrictive, choking me, and I'm sure I've broken out in hives. I suppose my personal suffering is better than lightning bolts flashing through the windows and catching the building on fire.

"You look like a fish out of water," Carter mutters under his breath. "Relax."

"Church isn't my thing." Walking to the back pew, I run my hands down the front of the only dress pants I own. We have functions that require us to dress formally, but I don't have an endless cash flow, unlike some of my teammates. I may have worked every summer since I was old enough to hold a wrench, but my dad never paid me. A roof over my head was sufficient payment in his eyes. The only money I received was from customers who slipped me tips when Dad wasn't looking.

"At least we don't have to volunteer for any other activities. Attending church won't be that bad."

"Says the person who blends." My murmur comes across as condescending while we take our seats, but I don't care. I don't want to be here. Soft chatter fills the air, and I can't help but search for Cassie. It doesn't take long to find her. She sits in the front row next to surprise, surprise—Preppy Boy Bobby. A snarl rests on my lips. My first priority is to expose his weakness. The only way I can win her dad over is to see where I have a chance. *But do I even have one?*

I know the answer to that question already. I just don't want to admit it.

I shouldn't want her. I should ignore whatever spell she has over me and focus on playing ball. But as I said, I'm a sinner. A weak mortal. When she peered up at me with those smokey-lidded eyes and a hitch in her voice, I was a goner. I'm so mad at how she handled everything, but that doesn't stop me from wanting her. It didn't stop me from taking my dick out and jerking off to the thought of her. And now my dick is springing to life. My eyes land on the large cross hanging at the back of the altar.

Yep, I'm pretty sure getting hard in a church is a direct ticket to hell.

Forcing myself to look anywhere but at her, I take in the typical A-frame altar. There isn't anything flashy about this place. I have no idea what denomination this church is—the ordinary white walls and muted rose colored carpet don't scream anything but plain, generic—but it hardly matters. I'm only here because Coach demands us to be. There should be a law against forcing people to attend against their will, but I get it. This is his team, his rules. We're here for discipline more than improving our craft, so whatever.

"Did you hear that team scouts will be at the next away game?" Carter asks.

This perks me up. "Oh, yeah?"

"Irongate gets most of their players from the top West Coast D1 schools, which usually draws the scouts, but with Coach's connections, they never miss our matchup with them."

I suck in a breath and try like hell to look passive. But with the pressure of the draft being over, maybe some teams will notice my talent. I hate not being a part of the Irongate team. I hate playing for the lesser one—the delinquents, as I've heard us being called. What makes it worse is fellow Cessna U teammates, Sean and Quinn, scored a spot on that team. The lucky bastards.

I glance at Carter and wonder what the fuck he did to be here. I quickly let the thought go when the mellow, sweet piano tone cuts through the silence, and a soft melodic voice I'd recognize anywhere follows shortly after. Cassie's voice fills me with warmth, conjuring memories of us on the shore. It was a time before I knew her real name. A time when I thought I got to know her while surprising her with a picnic and peering out at the ocean with the sun setting behind us.

A time when I foolishly thought we could be together.

After singing a few hymns, Mr. Greenburg steps to the pulpit and dives into the Bible teachings from 1 John 2.

"Whoever says he is in the light and hates his brother is still in darkness," his voice booms. I tune him out as he discusses sin and how we can choose against it. *What about not choosing to be here? Is that a thing?*

"Do not love the world or the things in the world. If anyone loves the world, the love of the Father is not in him. For all that is in the world—the desires of the flesh and the desires of the eyes and pride of life—is not from the Father but is from the world . . ."

I clamp my mouth shut. This sounds like pure bullshit. The kind of shit you tell people to keep them suppressed to follow your ideals.

"We can take these teachings and apply them to today's society. Look how often we covet our possessions. How often do we seek prestige, honor, and status? We need to stay humble."

I shift in my seat as I think about what I actually want. *Success* —that's what I want. Or maybe I should look at the reason behind wanting to succeed. It isn't for worldly possessions and approval— not at all. Being signed to a major league franchise is my ticket out of my hometown. Once I'm gone, I won't have to face my father and his heavy-handed parenting style—not that he can hit me anymore. I've filled out since leaving and tower over his shrunken frame. He can try to strike me the next time we're in the same room, but I won't hesitate to defend myself.

That's a fucking promise.

My eyes wander to the cross perched behind Coach. Where was God when each heavy-handed strike knocked me down? Or why did God abandon me along with Mom, who left without a care in the world? Mr. Greenburg stands and preaches about rejecting temptation leading to sin. Whether I reject the sin or not, it doesn't change a damn thing. God rejected me.

Crossing my arms over my chest, I sit and scowl as Coach continues. This earns me a side-eye glance from Carter, but he doesn't say anything. *Smart guy.* Rage races through my veins, and it won't take much for me to come unwound.

Coach stops preaching and steps away from the pulpit. He grins and looks at his daughter with admiration. No, I take that back. He's looking beside her at Bobby.

"And speaking about unselfish behavior. As you all know, Bobby just completed a four-month mission in Peru. He's in the final year of pastoral studies and took last semester off to help spread Christianity. I can't think of any more selfless act than giving your time and knowledge." Coach beams as if he's boasting about his flesh and blood. A sickening feeling settles in my stomach. "Come up to the podium and tell us about your experience."

What the ever-loving fuck?

Preppy Boy has been on a religious mission and wants to become a preacher? My hands tighten into fists. How the hell am I going to compete against a guy wanting to become a pastor? There's no way in hell Cassie's father would ever look at me the way he's looking at Bobby. The only selfless act I've done was train Shannon for her marathon. Even that came with scrutiny.

I grit my teeth as they roll out a slide show and dim the lights. I glance at the back of Cassie's head, wishing I could see her face. Maybe it's good that I can't. If she's eying this prick with the same amount of pride as her dad, it will kill me.

As Bobby drones on about all the good deeds he's done, I reflect on what I've been doing for the past few years at college—nothing too honorable besides playing ball.

Fuck.

Coach was right to snatch her away from Bellow Bay that summer.

I don't deserve this girl.

I never did.

But it doesn't stop the want I have for her. She may not be a

CHAPTER FOURTEEN

CASSIE

"I'm sorry, but I won't be able to go with you," Dad says as he rushes from the hallway and beelines to his bedroom.

Panic rips through my chest. Grabbing hold of the granite island countertop, I manage to squeak out, "Why?"

The backdoor slides open, and Dalton steps through. My gaze meets his, and the reason behind my increased heart rate now takes on a different meaning. Dalton stands shirtless with his tanned skin glistening from sweat. Those black athletic shorts sling low on his hips and showcase every ridge of his hard abdomen that I swear looks positively delectable. Tiny black ringlets peek from under his Cessna U baseball cap that he wears backward. That style drives my father insane, but I find it rather sexy.

Dalton makes his way over to the refrigerator and grabs a bottled water. I try not to stare, but it's hard not to. I like how he twists the cap off and takes a drink. The way his Adam's apple bobs up and down with each swallow.

What am I even saying?

I can't think of that right now. I have more important things to do, like pick up and deliver furniture to the storage unit by the church annex. I spent days getting this arranged. I don't want to reschedule.

"I know you need help. I'll take the car, and you can have the truck, but Mr. Barley's family called. He's taken another downturn, and they want me beside him."

I bite back a sigh. I understand their grief and need to hold onto their faith, but in the end, nothing will save him. Or maybe it's just me God gave up on. "That's understandable, but the truck does me no good if I don't have help."

I can feel Dalton's eyes on me. I don't dare look at him in front of Dad. Mr. Hawk Eye will see right through me.

"Call Bobby. He can drive you and help load the heavy things."

I flinch. Bobby is the last person I want to help me. I've kept my visits with Bobby limited. Heck, we've only seen each other twice since he returned, once when he demanded I plan a party for him and then again when he found me in the garage with Dalton. The fact I'm relieved instead of being upset tells me everything I need to know. I am not in love with Bobby—never was.

Regardless, I'm desperate, and Dad will ask about him when he returns. I pull up Bobby's contact and hit send as Dad grabs the keys to the Honda.

"Hello, Cassie. I can't talk right now."

"Oh, sorry. I was calling to see if you could help me with the fundraiser."

"No, I can't. I'm in Bethel helping the Two Brother's Church set up their bible study." Bethel is about thirty miles away from here, which isn't far. But there's no way Bobby would ditch helping their church. Helping to spread the Word is his calling or passion if you will, but what about helping me? When does all that volunteerism spill into helping yourself and your relationship with your girlfriend? Shouldn't that be important as well? I must've taken too long to answer because Bobby sighs. "I told you not to take on that added responsibility. It's overwhelming for you."

I bite down so hard I almost chip a tooth. Organizing this fundraiser isn't a burden at all. I've found it somewhat rewarding and satisfying. "You're right, but I did take it on, so it's my responsibility to follow through."

A hard thud snaps my attention to the kitchen. Dalton stands there, eying me with a death grip around the plastic bottle he placed on the counter with too much force. I give him a weak smile. I'm sure he thinks I'm being pathetic. He wouldn't be wrong.

"You'll just have to cancel. We'll do it in a few days."

"Fine." I don't remind Bobby this is the week I volunteered for vacation bible school. There's no point. I'll grab what I can and worry about the heavy furniture later. "Have fun at bible study."

As if on autopilot, my phone automatically rings the moment I hang up. I don't know what I have ever done without a phone before. "Hello."

My eyes flicker to Dalton. He stands as if he wants to say something.

"Cassie, can you bake three dozen cookies for the day you work vacation bible school?"

"Sure, Mrs. Dudley. I'll make chocolate chips."

"Oh, that would be great, but also if you can have another variety, that'd be wonderful. You know these kiddies enjoy choices."

"Sure thing." I hang up and glance at Dalton. He stands with his arms crossed over his chest, emphasizing pecs and biceps that have developed more since that summer we were together. He looks sexy. Well, except for the scowl currently occupying his face. He seems mad at me, but I don't understand why.

"What do you need me to do?" His clipped voice matches his mood.

"You don't have to—"

"Cassie," he interrupts, tone demanding. "What do you need help with?"

"Loading and unloading furniture into the truck bed. I have to transport a few items for the summer rummage sale."

He pushes off the counter. "Let me take a quick shower, and I'll help."

"Are you sure?"

He looks over his shoulder at me. "I'm never too busy for you."

Warmth spreads through me as he takes off down the hall. I draw in a calming breath. Being alone in the truck cabin with him may not be a good idea. If that's true, then why am I giddy like a schoolgirl being asked to prom by the star quarterback? Scratch that. Wrong sport. Giddy like a girl being asked out by a broody first baseman.

Yeah, that's better.

CHAPTER FIFTEEN

DALTON

I MUST BE A GLUTTON FOR PUNISHMENT BECAUSE I CAN'T SEEM to stay away from Cassie. The last thing I need to do is to be confined with her. Honestly though, how can I not volunteer? She needs help, and I want to spend time with her. I want to get to know her again. I can do that without falling harder for her and keep it casual until I prove myself worthy. *If that's even possible.*

She grabs the truck keys from the hook behind the cabinet and smiles up at me. "You're sure this isn't a bother?"

"No. Now come on, people are waiting."

"Do you want to drive?" she asks when we reach the truck.

"Why? It's your truck."

"I know, but you're the man."

I bite down on my bottom lip to stop the remark I want to make. One thing I've picked up on is how their church views women. They treat women like they're subservient. I may have been raised with an asshole father and had a mother walk out on me, but I still don't understand misogynist thinking.

"I can see that, but the truck is yours unless you'd rather me drive."

She shakes her head. "No, I'm just used to"—she shakes her

head—"never mind." Then she gives me a megawatt smile as she gets behind the wheel.

Yeah, this is a really fucking bad idea.

I clear my throat. "So, what's on the agenda?"

"We have some furniture to pick up and deliver to the storage unit next to the church annex. I could've gotten most items myself, but a dresser and a large chaise lounge were donated. I can't lift them by myself."

"Glad to be of service. I'm sure you can handle this on your own, but I'll be the added brawn when needed."

She gives me a side glance. A whisper of a smile ghosts across her lips. I don't miss the faint blush to her cheeks. My insides stir. Yeah, I won't have a problem falling deeper for her. *Liar.*

"Is Baytown where you grew up?" I ask more for a distraction than anything.

"Yes, I've always lived here. We moved into our current house when I started fifth grade."

I want to ask her where she'd been disappearing to at night, but I'm afraid the answer would be with Bobby. She assured me she's ending things with him, and she hasn't been as scarce, but I can't shake my curiosity. If she answers her boyfriend, I don't know what I'd do.

"So where have you been skipping off to?"

"I've been spending a lot of time with Nicole."

My hands unclench. I never realized how badly I was gripping them. "Is she still with her boyfriend?"

"The one she had when we visited Aunt Jan?"

"Yeah,"

"No, they broke up when she left for college. She has dated off and on but not anyone serious."

"Does she go to the same college as you?"

"Yes, although she's a year younger than me. That first year away was rough. I just wanted to be home with Mom."

"I'm sure your mom wanted you to go." I have absolutely no

idea, but I assume that her mom would want the best for her, given how close they were.

"She did. And even though I was alone, it was where I needed to be."

"Bobby doesn't go there?" I want to smack myself for bringing him up, but her comment surprised me.

"No, he goes to John LA Quad Faith University. It's in the next town over."

"That sounds like a cult."

She laughs. "You're not far off."

Wanting to lighten the conversation, I ask, "What is it you're studying?"

"Nursing."

"I can see that. You'd be good at helping people. Although, I picture you more in a management role overseeing a facility and making it run right."

She pulls into the driveway and turns toward me, eying me as if I've said the most beautiful thing in the world. Her surprise confuses me because she's so organized and rule orientated.

"Thank you."

A thought occurs. Back in Bellow Bay, we used to play "*what if*" but with our own spin on the game. It was our weird way to get to know each other better. I liked it even though I lost.

Pointing to the dresser by the garage, I lift the corner of my mouth to smirk. "*What if* we load this, and you tell me why you've chosen nursing as a career."

Her expression falls. "Then my answer will sound more like a confession."

I don't know what she means by that, but I have every intention of finding out. "Hold that thought. Let's grab the dresser."

The owner comes out of the house, and Cassie unbuckles her seatbelt. "Deal."

Once we maneuver the dresser into the truck bed and secure it with twine, we take off toward the next location.

"Ms. Willow's house will be the last stop."

It must be the chaise lounge she mentioned earlier. I give her a few moments, but when it's apparent she isn't going to volunteer the answer to my earlier question, I ask again. "Okay, why nursing?" I won't let her off the hook that easily, but when she takes a stuttering breath, I feel bad for forcing the answer.

"When Mom got sick, we were in and out of doctor's offices and the hospital. That solidified my calling to become a nurse. I want to help people. To make a difference."

"That doesn't sound too scandalous." Not enough for a confession.

"That's the version I tell everyone, and even though it's true, it's not entirely why. My reasons are more selfish."

"Meaning," I prompt when she pauses.

"I wanted a job where I would be self-sufficient. I didn't want to depend upon a man." She hangs her head as if this is something to be ashamed about. Scandalous even.

"That doesn't sound selfish. That sounds smart. A person should never be reliant on someone else."

Those electric blue eyes snap to mine. "That's not how I was raised. That sort of thinking goes against everything I've been taught since I could breathe."

"Your dad wants you to depend on a guy?"

"Not so much in those words, but essentially, yeah. A woman's place is to serve her husband."

I knew Coach Greenburg was strict. She told me that a few years ago, but I never knew it was incorporated into their beliefs. I don't know what to say. "You do know that's bullshit, right?"

"Somewhat. I mean, I don't mind having a man in charge, but I want to have an equal say." She looks ahead, studying the road as if in shame.

"That's how things are supposed to work. Relationships are a mutual joining." *Which is why I was so pissed when you cut me out.* I don't voice that because she has enough regret—that horse is dead, no need to keep beating it—but it's hard to see her so meek and timid. I miss the spunky girl back in Bellow Bay. She's more brazen when she's with me and away from the other men in her life.

She pulls into another driveway and turns the engine off before looking at me.

"You make it sound effortless."

"It's supposed to be."

The phone buzzes for the third time since we left the house. Cassie answers in what I've come to learn as her forced happy voice. I overhear another request for three dozen cookies, but this time they're for the social after church. These constant requests of her time shouldn't bother me, but when I see the tired expression haunting her eyes, I can't help but get upset. She gives so much of her time, and I hate these people taking advantage of her.

"Why do you stretch yourself so thin?" My tone comes across harsher than intended and causes her to flinch. I sigh and apologize. "It just seems like you're doing everything possible for everyone else, but not taking care of yourself. You're committed to what, six dozen cookies now?"

She stares out the window and nods. "I know. I should learn to delegate better or say no. It's just I'm trying not to make waves. I want this church rummage sale to go smoothly. A lot is riding on it. The proceeds go toward filling the food pantry. This year's goal is to raise fifty thousand. I have calls to various vendors. We get donations for the sale, but we also get a price match. This food pantry feeds several families in the surrounding community, so it's pretty vital to make it a success."

"That's a great cause and all, but who ran it before?"

"My mom."

Well, if that doesn't make me feel like an asshole. "I can see why you're so passionate about it."

"Before she passed, I told her not to worry about the rummage sale. I'd take charge." She gets a sad but almost dreamy look. "That seemed to relieve her. And my dad was actually proud."

"So you're doing this in her memory," I state rather than ask.

When she nods, I open the truck door. "I think it's honorable, really. But I want you to take care of yourself in the process."

"I will. I promise."

At her smile, I hop out of the truck. "All right, let's tackle this chair."

CHAPTER SIXTEEN

DALTON

I SCRATCH MY HEAD, STARING AT WHAT LOOKS LIKE SOMETHING out of a gentlemen's club back in early England. "This isn't a chair. It's a beast."

"It's a nineteenth-century Victorian Chesterfield chaise. The brown leather may be scuffed in places, but the walnut legs are in excellent condition."

"It looks heavier than the dresser." *And awkward as fuck.* At least with the dresser, we could remove the drawers to lessen the weight. This thing is top-heavy with the high Chesterfield back wrapping around the end where people sit. The backing tapers to within a couple of inches of where the feet go.

"Don't be such a wimp." Cassie smacks my arm playfully.

"Wimp? Not me. I was thinking about you and your scrawny arms." *Those rather beautiful arms that lead to delicate hands and fingers I want to wrap around mine and other parts of my body.*

She tips her head back in laughter. *Aw, there's that relaxed, carefree girl I knew back in Bellow Bay.* Ever since I arrived, she has been uptight. At first, I attributed that to my presence, but it never ceases and seems to worsen when her dad is around. It's as if she can't fully relax and be herself around him. I know the feeling all too well, but he doesn't seem to abuse her physically, unlike my dad.

"I'll have you know I can bench press fifty-five pounds."

"Now that I'd like to see." Any time she's sweaty and breathy, I'd like to see.

As if reading my mind, a nice rosy color flames her cheeks. I can't help but wonder if her thoughts are as dirty as mine.

She clears her throat. "Anyway, this particular piece is worth a heck of a whole lot more than the dresser."

"How much can this old thing be worth?"

"It should fetch us between ten to fifteen grand."

"Seriously?" I choke on my swallow, eying the old furniture with new respect. Personally, I don't see it. All I see are old Englishmen dressed to the hilts smoking their cigars.

"Yeah, that's why I saved this piece for last. I didn't want it to get damaged."

"No pressure or anything."

Her smile is catching. The older woman comes out with two tall glasses.

"Thanks, Ms. Willow," Cassie says as she takes the drink.

"You're welcome, honey." The woman turns to me and hands me mine. "I hope you like freshly squeezed lemonade."

"I sure do, thanks," I lie and hold back a chuckle. My gaze meets Cassie's over the rim of the glass. How ironic. I was so angry when I first arrived in town, thinking how sour my life was. It turns out making lemonade isn't so bad after all. Well, the metaphorical kind, that is. I force down a swallow. I still hate this shit.

"How nice that you have this strapping young lad to help you." Ms. Willow places her hand on my biceps and squeezes. "So strong."

Cassie's eyes grow wide. She holds her glass up to her mouth to hide her chuckle. "Yes, he's been a great help."

"Hmm, I bet." She gives me a once-over, lingering on my pectorals and arms. But not in the judging way most of the town has shown, it's more in appreciation. As in being checked out. When was the last time someone so blatantly checked me out? Scratch that. When was the last time someone over the age of seventy so blatantly checked me out? I don't even know what to think about that.

"Well, don't let me hold you up." She pats the chair's backing. "Hopefully, this fetches enough money to fund the food pantry for a while."

"Oh, it will. Thanks again. Your generosity is greatly appreciated."

We hand the glasses back to Ms. Willow. When the old flirt slips inside, we burst out laughing.

"Now that was fun to watch."

"Says you. I feel violated."

"Who knew you'd entice the old ladies?"

My confident smile slides into place, honing the dimples women seem to like. "I can get them at all ages, Choir Girl."

The effort achieves what I set out to do as evidenced by Cassie's shake of her head and eye roll. I laugh. She's so easily riled, which I love. She's her most genuine self when she tosses it back at me.

"Is that so?"

I give her a shrug.

"So, you think she'd still find you studly if I were to tell her that you're afraid of insects with eight legs?"

"Spiders are not insects." They're monsters. "And I'm not really afraid of them."

"Oh yeah? Then you may want to knock the one off your shoulder." She points to my right side.

"What?" I strain to look while swatting at my shoulder like someone just lit my ass on fire. Cassie holds her stomach from laughing so hard.

"It's not funny. Is it off?" A shiver races down my spine.

"I think you got it, Lover Boy." She swipes a finger under her eyes. "Let's tackle this beast."

"I'm going to get you back."

"Uh-huh. I can't wait."

She's still laughing as we lift the atrocity and carry it out to the truck. Or that's the intention. We don't quite make it. "Wait," Cassie huffs out.

I halt and lower my end to the ground while Cassie drops hers. "You okay, Miss I Can Bench *Half* My Weight?"

She gives me a stern look. "Yeah, just give me a minute. This chair is awkward."

"That's what I've been saying."

"Ha-ha." She shakes her arms a moment before repositioning them. With a nod, she says, "Okay, I'm ready."

We make it to the truck. Thank fuck I had the foresight to lower the tailgate. We set the beast on the pebbled driveway. I make the mistake of looking across the chaise to Cassie. She's bent over, arms resting on the foot end. Her cleavage spills forward, and I get a clear shot from the gap in her top. I gawk like some creeper, which I know is wrong, but I can't make myself stop. She's too damn tempting. I remember all too well having those breasts in my hands . . . their taste on my tongue.

"You think we should lift it by its side?"

"Huh?" My attention snaps to her face. Those cute little lines crease across her forehead.

"Side by side. You think that's the best way to lift it into the truck?" She stands up, but then she scoots to the side of the chaise and bends over. Those short shorts ride higher, giving a clear shot of side cleavage and ass cheek. Is she trying to kill me?

"Uh . . ." I try to conjure a response, but all my brainpower went to my dick. "I think you should stand by me, and we go end to end." Truthfully, her way is probably better, but I'm not being rational right now. All I'm thinking about is having her beside me.

"Really?" She starts to walk toward me.

"Yeah, then we can scoot it back."

"Okay, but we'll have to be careful with the legs . . . argh," she screams as her tiny frame stumbles.

I jump in front of her, but her momentum carries forward and knocks me backward. I pull her on top of me as we land on the chaise lounge. The neighborhood sounds fade to the background as I wrap my arms around those curves I've missed so much, my fingers digging into her flesh. Her sweet cucumber-melon scent encapsulates me. My teased dick springs to life, and by the small gasp leaving her mouth, she notices. Not surprised. There's only a thin layer of cotton separating us. I need to remember where we're at, but all I can focus on are her lust-filled eyes staring into mine and begging for a kiss. Or maybe that's my wish.

She bats her lashes and pulls away before I can follow through. Probably a good thing since prying eyes seem to be everywhere in this town.

"Are you okay?" I ask, finally finding my voice.

She scrambles off me, a pinkish hue coating her cheeks. She averts her gaze. "Mm-hmm."

She's so damn cute. She belongs to me—not some douchebag.

The team goes out of town tomorrow to play against Irongate. I'll pin Jason down and make him my best friend if I have to. I will finish that report. This is the only way to make Coach see me as more than a degenerate. I want Cassie in my arms permanently.

CHAPTER SEVENTEEN

DALTON

THIS IS A BAD IDEA.

Spinning my ring, I settle into the barstool in disbelief that I let Jason talk me into coming here. The thank-God-the-working-day-is-done crowd settles around us. Relaxed chatter fills the silence. Hands slap on friends' backs in cheerful greeting. Bottles clink as they hit the tabletop. All of it is in direct opposition to how I feel.

"What can I get you?" Jason asks as he signals for the bartender.

I purse my lips and study his candid features. His chin held high. His posture fully relaxed. He acts as if he couldn't care less if we're breaking a major team rule. I wouldn't care either if it wasn't for the fact of needing to improve Coach's shitty impression of me. Coach will be livid if he finds out we're in a bar, let alone drinking. This violates his drinking policy in ten different ways—not to mention how we're skirting curfew. But I can't help but question Jason's motives. Does he really want to talk, or is he trying to get me in further trouble? Legit intentions or not, I don't trust him.

"You look like a beer guy."

My hesitation must've taken too long because Jason orders two long necks before answering. I pull out enough cash to cover both drinks plus tip. I'm not letting this fucker get the upper hand. And what did he mean by *looking like a beer guy?* What the hell does a beer guy even look like?

"Loosen up, Boyd. Coach isn't going to find out. Are you *that* afraid of getting on his bad side?" Condescension lays thick in his laugh. "Hate to break it to you, but you're already there."

His words prick my skin like tiny patronizing daggers. I may be Coach's least favorite player, but I don't plan on holding that position.

"Despite what you heard, I do follow the rules." *When they're important enough.* And following rules is why we're here—not in the bar, but together, *bonding.*

The team rolled into town around three. After checking into the hotel, we met at the barbecue joint across the street. Coach received a phone call and headed back to the hotel early. Before he left, he gave strict instructions to head back to the hotel after eating. I asked Jason to stay and talk. He acted as if he was going to refuse but then changed his mind. He insisted we leave the restaurant and hop over to the neighboring bar. Carter and Javier tried their best to talk me out of going, but I want this discussion over with. It shouldn't take too long. One drink won't hurt.

Jason eyes me for a minute before letting out a resounding sigh. "What exactly do you want to know?"

The bartender places our bottles in front of us. Jason scoots the money toward him.

"I'll get the next round," he says as if there will be more rounds.

I tip the bottle back and take a pull, not sure where to begin. I'm unprepared, considering I didn't think he'd agree to talk. The fuck if I know what Coach wants me to find out. I place the bottle on the counter and state the obvious. "I suppose he wants me to know the reason you got into baseball."

Jason shrugs. "Like every other guy, I suppose—for the love of the game."

"I'll drink to that." I take another swig before asking, "Did you always play first?"

"No, I started as a pitcher, but my fastball wasn't fast enough." His jaw tics, and I suspect there's a story there.

"Is pitching your favorite position?" I prod.

His jaw tics again, but he shrugs. "It doesn't matter. I play first base. My dad coached the high school team and told me that's where I would play."

"Sounds as if you have a supportive parent." I'm fishing. The inflection in his voice makes me think he wanted to pitch and his dad is a dick, or he is better suited for first, and his dad did him a solid.

"Yeah, you know how it goes." His eyes cloud over, voice devoid of emotion. He takes his first swig of the beer.

No, I really don't. I try to picture my dad in the stands rooting me on. It was a dream I envisioned back in my tween days. The closest Phil Boyd ever got to the stands was when he came to practice drunk and pulled me from the field to go home and fix Mrs. Clancy's car. That caused a visit from social services. My brother and I had to pretend our dad was top-notch while the kids on my team made fun of me. I never dreamed about Dad being in the stands from then on. But I don't mention any of that and just nod. Because even though Jason says the right words, I don't think he believes them. It's in the subtle way his lip curls up or the way his fingers clenched the bottle tighter.

Maybe we're more alike than I thought.

"I suspect your old man was as pissed off as mine was by your not getting drafted?" he asks.

My eyes flash to him. I don't know what compels me to confess. Maybe it's because I'm tired of hiding the truth or living this continued lie that everything is okay, that none of this bullshit bothers me. The truth is, I want out from the burden of my family. So, I suck it up and tell the truth. "No. He'd rather see me fail, so I go home and run the family business."

Jason's eyes widen. His mouth opens to speak but gets cut off by three guys approaching us.

"What do we have here?" The taller guy in the middle looks from me to Jason before landing back on me. His Irongate baseball hat sits proudly on his head. Isn't this nice. We face these fuckers in tomorrow's game—the one where scouts are rumored to be and I can't screw up—and they're here stirring up trouble.

"You must be the worthless delinquents from Baytown," he continues when neither Jason nor I speak.

My eyes narrow at the one speaking's familiarity. "What's it to you?"

Jason's back stiffens. If he really thought we'd stay under the radar by coming into this bar, his plan just backfired. Neither one of us is getting out of here unscathed. These boys came looking for trouble.

"Just surprised to find you tucked away in a bar. Doesn't Daddy Greenburg have a rule against drinking?"

The stooges next to him laugh while the ringleader's mouth transfixes into a smirk. No matter how badly I want to be the one to wipe it off, I won't let his taunts affect me. He can try to rile us up all he likes. It won't work.

"We're just here to have a conversation." I tip my bottle toward Jason and then take a drink. My eyes never stray from the guy. Then it dawns on me how I know him. He's the prick with the hard slide into Garret, our shortstop, toward the end of the season. Garret was fine, but the slide was dirty, and this prick knew it. We exchanged a few choice words that ended with me being tossed from the game.

"I'm not surprised to see you since you never got drafted. You were the weakest link on the team." The prick laughs. "You couldn't keep your temper in check. It's no wonder you ended up on Greenburg's team. That's where the rejects go."

Jason pops out of his chair, fists clenching. I place my hand up to stop him. "He's not worth it, man."

The asshole has the audacity to laugh again. "Oh yeah, tomorrow's going to be fun." He drops his voice. "I'll be sure to have my cleats extra sharp."

The muscle in the side of my jaw twitches as I grind my teeth. It takes everything in me not to engage. I want to pummel this guy, but hell, he probably already cost me one draft. I won't give him the satisfaction of ruining this year.

He steps to the side, and I think he's leaving, but then he turns back to me. There's an evil gleam in his eyes as the corners of his mouth curve upwards. "Are you staying away from that daughter of his? I heard you're the lucky bastard staying at the house."

My fingers ball into fists as anger worms its way through my veins. I straighten my back and try desperately to keep my face passive—it's hard telling what he'd do if he found out about my relationship with her—but I'm a bit of a hothead. I hate Cassie being disrespected. She doesn't deserve that. I don't know if I can hold myself back.

"I've seen her once. She's a fine piece of virginal ass. I'd like to tap that," the prick says, eying me the entire time. I can feel the muscle in my jaw tic, but my feet stay planted. I hate myself at this point. It feels wrong not to defend Cassie.

"I bet she's a real wildcat between the sheets," the stooge to the left says.

"Preachers' daughters usually are," the other stooge says, laughing.

My heart pounds in my chest. I'm so pissed.

"Or she may be a frigid bitch." The words no sooner leave the prick's mouth, and my fist connects with bone. No one disrespects my girl that way, and I mean absolutely no one. Consequences be damned.

The big guy stumbles back. His posse catches him before his ass hits the floor. Then it's on. Punches fly everywhere. I hate to pull Jason into the mix, but he throws his fair share of hits. At least, I think he is. It's hard to tell in this chaos. One stooge picks up a chair. He raises it as if to hit Jason across the back. Fucking asshole. Fight like a damn man if you're going to start something.

"Jason, watch your back."

He turns and blocks the bigger blow. I turn to face my prick, and pain splinters across my left eye socket. The fucker got in one good punch. Rage takes over as I unload.

Police sirens wail in the background, growing louder, but I couldn't care less. I'm tired of people telling me I'm not good enough. I'm tired of feeling inadequate. But most of all, no one will disrespect Cassie that way. This fucking asshole is getting what is due to him.

CHAPTER EIGHTEEN

DALTON

"Jason Fowler. Dalton Boyd. You're free to go."

The buzzing sound reverberates off the block walls, along with the locks releasing. I push to my feet and wait for the door to slide open. Is this how my brother starts his mornings? I never thought about it from his perspective. But standing here confined in this small space, I can't imagine. It's a rather shitty feeling to start the day. Guilt seeps into my bones. Dad's right. I've been rather selfish.

"How pissed do you think the coach is going to be?" Jason asks.

"Pissed beyond words." But I can guess who he'll direct that hatred toward. It won't be the star pupil beside me. However misguided Coach's anger will be, I'll take it. I deserve it. I'm the one who screwed up and let my emotions control my actions. Would I do it again? In a heartbeat. That disrespectful bastard got what he deserved for what he said about Cassie. There may have been a better way to handle it where I didn't have to drag my teammate into my mess, but it was satisfying putting the prick in his place.

"I'm sorry, man. This is my fault. I was just trying to get you drunk so that you wouldn't play well." The mortification on his face rings true.

"I figured as much. Just our luck, the biggest asshole on the planet showed up."

We reach the booking area and they shove the release papers in front of us. Once the forms are completed, we turn in the vouchers for our personal belongings.

"There must be bad blood between you guys by the way he ragged on you."

"He slid in hard at second, taking out a teammate in the process. Fucker knew what he was doing. Luckily, nothing serious came of it, but he's a dirty player. He wasn't going to stop until I punched him." *And I walked right into that trap.*

They hand us our personal belongings. I fish around the bottom of the bag and finally relax when my fingers land on Gramp's ring. My mother's dad had given it to me when he found out he didn't have long on this earth.

A fifth of bourbon was drunk the night Dad found out. Dad thought Steve deserved the ring instead since he was the oldest. Dad made an ass of himself when he confronted Gramps drunk. That's when Gramps told me to keep it in a safe space. I wondered at the time if I should call the ring *Precious* since it turned people into greedy monsters. It had already made Dad angry, and he wasn't even wearing it.

The ring is made from hammered black zirconium with a center inset of black diamonds. I'm sure it's valuable, but that's not why I keep it close to me. Gramps had told me not to let anyone take it from me. And by anyone, he meant Dad. He wanted me to have something special. I think the old man knew what was going on in our house. I resented him for not stepping in but loved him for the normalcy he provided. He just didn't stick around that long.

We finally make our way to Coach, who stands with his arms crossed. The glare he tosses our way makes my balls shrivel. His face is the deepest scarlet I've ever seen on anyone, and that includes my drunken father. He doesn't speak a word as he pivots and heads outside. Jason and I exchange a look before following

Coach out. The TikTok sound "I fucked up" plays through my head. The moment the night air touches our skin, he unloads.

"What were you doing in a bar?"

Jason shifts on his feet, clearly not speaking up.

"We were talking, sir," I manage to say through the thickness in my voice. I doubt I can talk my way out of this mess. "I, uh, wanted to get to know him better so I can finish the report you asked for."

Coach's steely eyes glare at me with disappointment. Sweat breaks across my brow. He turns his attention back to Jason. "Is that true?"

"Yes, sir."

"Were you drinking?"

"Yes, sir." Jason's voice cracks. He drops his gaze to the ground as if in shame. It was his idea to have the beers, which he conveniently leaves out.

"Let me get this straight." Coach shifts his gaze back to me. Through gritted teeth, he asks, "You somehow finagled my player into a bar, ordered drinks, and got into a fistfight?"

It's funny how he assumes I'm the one who instigated all this. Yes, I did want to talk, and I knew better than to go into the bar, but I'm not solely to blame. When will I ever make good choices?

"Yes, sir," I say.

Jason's eyes dart to mine, but I don't pay him any attention. I'm too busy holding my own with Coach.

"Tell me right now why I shouldn't ship you back to North Carolina?"

How the hell do I answer that? The facts are stacked against me. He *should* ship my ass away. I'm nothing but a fuck up, and from the looks of it, that's never going to change.

"I just wanted to get to know my teammate better. I wasn't thinking about the consequences, nor did I anticipate a fight. I didn't initiate it."

"So you never threw the first punch? I believe the police report says otherwise."

I bite my tongue to keep from cursing. Sure, it looks bad on paper, but I didn't instigate the fight.

"It was my idea to go to the bar. It was a slip in judgment on my part." Jason's confession surprises me. He doesn't have to say anything. This is his chance to get rid of me and slide into my position. A funny feeling settles in my chest. I peer at him, and he gives a slight nod as if to suggest he has my back. No, that's bullshit. I shut that line of thinking down. No one ever has my back except my ex-roommates at Cessna U.

"It was your idea?" Skepticism drips in every syllable. Of course Coach wouldn't believe him.

"Yes, sir. And I ordered the drinks."

"You're not lying to cover up for your teammate are you?"

"No, sir. That's the truth. Like I said. It was a bad judgment call on my part."

Coach scrubs a hand over his tired face. His weary eyes turn to me. "I didn't have high expectations for you, but you"—he points to Jason—"I didn't expect to disappoint me."

I suppose I shouldn't be surprised, but do I have to keep proving everyone right all the time? I straighten my shoulders and try not to look like his words affect me. On the other hand, Jason looks as if he's about to toss the barbecue pork up. He's a little green around the gills.

Coach lets out a disgruntled sigh. My stomach knots. I've done it this time. He's going to ship me home. I barely breathe, waiting for him to continue.

"I can't send both of you packing, and it wouldn't be fair to just send one." Coach points a shaky finger at me, while his words make me want to drop to the ground and kiss it like a seasick tourist coming off a four-hour fishing expedition in the choppy Atlantic. "I won't forget that you threw the first punch, and you're lucky the charges are dropped. Don't think you're getting off scotfree. You'll have to pay for the bar's damages."

I wince. I have no idea where that money will come from. I'm flat broke, but I stand there and nod like it's no problem. Coach has me by the balls, and he knows it.

"There is never a valid reason to settle arguments with a fist."

"The other guys were talking smack about your—"

"Team," I interrupt Jason before he mentions Cassie's name. There isn't any reason for her name to be dragged into this. She would be mortified if what they said got back to her. She deserves way better than to be made into a sick joke. That shit ends with Jason and me. If I have to sacrifice myself, then so be it. She's worth it.

"I have to pull you from the game." Coach stares me in the eyes.

"But the scouts—"

"Things you should've thought about before disturbing the public." He shakes his head as if disgusted. "Come dressed, but you'll be warming the bench indefinitely."

Jason's eyes bulge as if he's pleading for me to speak. I'm surprised he cares. This is a good opportunity for him. He's getting what he wants. I shake my head. I'll tell him to keep the part about Cassie quiet. In the meantime, I'll put my nose to the grindstone and be the All-American Rule Follower poster boy.

CHAPTER NINETEEN

CASSIE

I GRAB FOR MY CROSS PENDANT ONLY TO COME UP EMPTY AS THE waiter takes away my empty plate. One would think I'd be used to the fact my necklace no longer resides on my chest. But it's a habit I picked up whenever nerves took hold. I watch the waiter take away Bobby's plate, and I know my time is up. I must end things with him tonight. He can't keep thinking we're an item.

"You're quiet tonight. I think I know why."

My gaze meets his. "You do?"

"Yeah, you're still upset with me for not helping with the fundraiser. I'm sorry you're upset."

But not sorry about not helping. Got it. This right here is why I can't be with him.

"That's not the reason. I already told you Dalton stepped up and helped. We delivered the furniture. I accomplished what I needed."

Bobby's face draws to a scowl. "I don't want you alone with that guy."

"He lives with us. That's virtually impossible."

"I don't like it."

I ignore his attempt at machismo and press forward. "We need to talk about the future and our goals."

His eyes narrow. "Our future is set."

"No. I know you talk about missionary work, but as I've said before, that's not what I want to do."

"What do you mean? It's all we've ever talked about. I'd become a preacher and you'd obtain your nursing degree. We'd be a great team spreading knowledge and Christianity."

I bristle. The worst mistake I made was not speaking against the idea when Bobby first brought it up. But I was at a low point in my life, and anything that took me away from here sounded good, but things have changed. My thoughts and goals have changed. My mom's death taught me life isn't guaranteed, and we need to be happy. But how do I explain to him without coming across as one of the people he wants to save? Spare me that lecture, please.

"That has never been my dream. I've tried telling you that before."

"Nonsense. Once you go, you'll see that it's your life's calling. You want to do more than sit around and plan parties for the church."

I lean back in my seat and stare at him. That comment feels like a direct slam to my mom. She was the church's event coordinator. "That may not be how I wish to spend my time, but that job is every bit as important."

"Cassie, relax. I just meant you're more than that."

That's still a backhanded compliment.

If only I could redo everything, I would, but Bobby was there during Mom's illness. He got me through my grieving process. I can see now that I leaned on him too much, which wasn't fair to him.

I hate letting people down. I pride myself on doing for others. I can't bear to see the hurt in his eyes. But when I look back at him, there's only determination. He doesn't seem to be hurting at all.

"It doesn't matter. What matters is that my goals have

changed, and I no longer want to do missionary work. I think it's best if we go our separate ways."

"That's your nerves talking. I was nervous for my first mission trip too."

"No, Bobby, that's not it. We're too different. I like helping people. That's why I went into nursing school, but I want to help patients here in the States. I have no desire to spread God's Word." *Especially since I stopped believing in the concept of religion.* There, I voiced it, if only in my head. I've been so lost for so long. I can't fathom the idea of preaching every day in a foreign country. Why can't he see our goals and wants are miles apart. Why wouldn't he want to break it off?

"I think I know what's best for you, Cassie. You're like a delicate flower. You'll wilt without support. Once you graduate, you'll have more confidence. Trust God. It's his will."

I bite my tongue so hard I taste blood. God's plan for me isn't to go on a religious mission. God doesn't have a plan for me at all. He gave up on me.

My fingers dig into my thighs, the need to scream at him for not listening claws at my throat. If we weren't in public, I would. This discussion should've been held privately, but there wasn't any way I'd get him to come over with Dad being gone on the baseball trip. And I need to break things off with him.

"You're not listening to me." My voice is low and steady as I study the white linen cover. I'm trying hard to rein in my temper. "I'm breaking up with you."

"No, I hear you, but you're confused. I think that the delinquent you have staying at your house is messing with your head."

I snap my chin up. "Dalton isn't a delinquent. He's a good guy."

The condescending look Bobby shoots my way fuels my anger. "If he's such a good guy, then why did your dad have to pick him up from jail last night?"

"What?"

"Yeah. Your *good guy* got into a bar fight. So not only was he out when he shouldn't have been, he was in a bar drinking and fighting."

No! That can't be right.

My heart pinches. Scouts were supposed to be at that game.

"How would you know that?" I ask. I haven't talked to Dad today. And it's not as if I can text Dalton. I stole his number off Dad's roster and programmed it in my phone—not that it does any good. I can't do anything with it since Dad checks my texts and call logs.

"Your dad told me when I called to ask permission to take you out tonight."

I let the fact that he still asks for Dad's permission even though we're in our twenties slide. Learning about Dalton is more vital. "There has to be a good reason. He wouldn't jeopardize his career."

"I'm sure he doesn't care about his career since he threw the first punch." Bobby scoffs. "It's pretty selfish of him, considering the team needs to win these games."

"He really didn't play?" I ask more to myself than Bobby. I sit back in my chair, defeated. Dalton missed performing in front of the scouts. I suddenly feel sick. I thought whatever fueled his anger was under control. He had been ducking into the outbuilding a lot, which I assumed meant he was taking his frustration out on the car. I guess I was wrong.

"Of course he didn't play. Do you think your dad's going to reward sinful behavior?" Bobby's haughty tone boils my blood. He's always so smug.

"There has to be a reason why he went off like that. Especially with everything riding on this game," I quip.

"People like that are just bad. They don't think like us. Their morals don't line up."

"You don't know that. You don't know anything about him or his home life."

"And you do?"

I can't exactly say yes, so I tap-dance my way around that question. "I'm just saying you're making assumptions."

"Having a hard life doesn't mean you have to make bad choices. I just spent months in a desolate country. Now those people have a hard life, yet they're choosing God."

"No doubt they're underprivileged, but a hard life is a hard life. It's not a contest."

He tosses me another condescending look. "We're fighting over something hypothetical. I think it's time to stop."

I push to my feet. "Take me home."

He sighs. "I'll allow it for now."

"That's good because I'm leaving with or without you." I don't wait for a response and head toward the parking lot. I have to get my head straight before Dalton comes back home. I need to know why he would do this. I can't imagine any reason behind sabotaging his chance at making a good impression or risking angering my dad. I'm equally surprised Dad didn't send him packing.

When I reach the car, I fire off a text. Consequences be damned.

Me: *This is Cassie. What happened last night?*

Dalton: *It's a long story. Some guys from the other team were talking shit.*

Me: *Are you okay? I know my dad must be livid.*

Dalton: *I'm fine. It's all worked out. You're not getting rid of me that easily.*

I take a relaxing breath for the first time since hearing the news. I hate that he missed having the scouts see him, but at least he isn't leaving.

Me: *Good, because what if I like keeping you around?*

Dalton: *Then I'm never leaving you ever again.*

Warm fuzzies fill my chest. This is silly. He doesn't really mean it. He'll have to leave to go back to school. At the end of summer, we'll go our separate ways. But this time is different than last. We have a way to communicate. I'm done leaving things to fate.

I lean against the car and wait for Bobby to come out. He's more than likely paying for the meal. I suppose I should've paid for my half, but he wouldn't have let me. He won't let me break up. What makes me think he'll let me pay for a meal? This is my second attempt to break things off, and he still thinks we're together. I have to fix this.

For the entire ride home, I don't say a word. I'm lost in my thoughts. When he pulls up in front of my house, I clear my throat.

"I'm not sure I got my point across earlier, but I'll always consider you a friend. You got me through the hardest times in my life. But that's all we'll ever be. I can't be your girlfriend anymore."

His jaw sets hard. His eyes grow cold. I take that as his acceptance. I step away from the car. Right as I push the door closed, he mumbles, "My party will fix everything."

He drives away, leaving me perplexed. What does he mean by that?

CHAPTER TWENTY

CASSIE

"Bellow, I'm leaving you in charge of warning me if Dad comes home. Do you understand?" I crouch to the ground and stare Bellow in the eyes. Those sugary brown irises peer up at me. He yelps and wags his tail. "Good enough."

I squeeze the water bottle—my excuse for going to see Dalton —and stand to my full height. I zero my sights on the outbuilding where Dalton's been ever since his run. We haven't had a chance to talk since their return late last night. I still haven't learned what caused the fight, but I plan on resolving that now. His last text said he'd never leave me, which he hasn't technically done, but he isn't quite here with me either. Our conversation feels unresolved.

It's not as if I could've sent any more texts demanding him to talk. I already have to come up with an excuse for the small exchange. Dad doesn't realize I know he checks my call log. One day, I walked up behind Dad when he had the app open on his phone. The screen revealed phone numbers along with a time-stamp. Talk about an invasion of privacy. I wanted to confront him, but he would've taken my phone away. Rule number two-hundred sixty-six, never *ever* talk back to elders. There isn't any way I could explain a text sent late in the night to one of his base-ball players. I took the risk yesterday after supper. I should purchase my own cell phone plan, but there's this tiny problem of paying for it. Dad refuses to let me get a part-time job. Money equals freedom. One more school year, and I'll make enough money to leave.

It can't come soon enough.

I push open the side door, and once I round the corner, it's like I stepped into an episode of *Overhaulin'*. The car hood is propped open. Various car parts clutter the countertops and floor in a chaotic, orderly fashion. The only thing missing is the mechanic. A hint of a smile creeps across my lips. He must've dived right into this project.

"You know I can't do that." A frustrated sigh follows.

The sharp bite in Dalton's voice pulls me forward. I lay the bottled water on the counter and step around the car. I find him behind the trunk near the far wall. His backside faces me. He holds a phone to one ear while his thumb spins his ring on the other hand. The ring spinning is his tell for when he's nervous or frustrated.

I soak in every detail. His rigid stance. Those taut biceps the sleeveless tee showcases so well. It is wrong to check him out while he's frustrated, but I can't help myself. Those ripped jeans he loves to wear fit his backside nicely. And even though I know he's irritated, I can't help but think dirty thoughts. I would follow this man to hell and back if it weren't for the fact, I'd bring him down with me.

"I know I wasn't there the past two times. I'm a little committed."

Pause. Another huff.

I inch close enough to hear the shouts coming from the phone. The longer Dalton listens, the more agitated he becomes. I have a feeling the other person is his dad.

"We've discussed this before. I'm committed to my team." Another long pause. "Steve understands."

Steve. I rattle that name around my mind a few times. I'm positive he has a brother by that name, which confirms the other person is his dad. A shudder skates across my spine. I can still picture the way his dad smacked him. I feel smothered by my father, but I never doubted his love. I know Dalton must question that all the time. His mother abandoned him, and his father mistreated him. Has anyone ever shown him affection? Has anyone ever stuck up for him and fought his battles?

"Do me a favor, Dad. Get some help." The yelling grows louder. Dalton looks up to the rafters and slams his fist against the wall. I shift, trying desperately not to go to him, but it's hard. My heart breaks. It's no wonder he's been so broody with shouldering this burden along with everything else. If his dad is giving him problems, this could be the reason he was so quick-tempered.

I take another step forward, this time not as quiet. His body whips around. Those dark eyes full of anger soften a moment before growing cold. I bite back my gasp from the bruise encasing his left eye. So it is true. He really did get into a fistfight. Disappointment flutters my stomach. I can't make Dad see Dalton's potential if he isn't willing to help himself. *No, don't jump to that conclusion. That is everyone else's assumption—not yours.* I believe there is an underlying reason for his quick temper, and I have every intention of finding it.

"I'll be back at the end of August." Dalton ends the call and stares at me. "How long have you been out here?"

"Long enough to overhear your dad yelling."

He lets out a resonated sigh. He mutters in a barely recognizable voice, "Sorry about that."

"There's nothing to be sorry about. You can't control your father."

He looks away. I step to within a few inches and lean so he faces me. "I'm serious. Is it his drinking? Has it gotten worse?" *Is he still abusing you?*

That's the real question I want to ask. He may not be present to strike him physically, but abuse comes in multiple ways. I don't dare ask. He won't be confessing anything tonight with that invisible shield covering his eyes.

"Is he the reason you're struggling?"

"I'm not struggling." His hands clench as I watch his jaw set with determination. Or maybe it's stubbornness. Either way, I struck a chord.

"You have a black eye that says otherwise." I'm a non-confrontational person by nature. I never stick up for myself, except when I'm around Dalton. For some reason, he brings it out in me. I feel as if I can say what is on my mind.

"Don't you have a boyfriend to get back to?"

Did I mention that shield he has built is made of ice? I shiver from the coldness in his stare.

"I told you I broke up with him."

"Funny, because on the way home, your dad told me all about the date you had last night. He made sure I knew just how much in love you two are."

"I assure you I broke it off. It isn't my fault he hasn't come to terms yet." I don't clarify who *he* is. I technically haven't broken the news to Dad. Unlike when I'm around Dalton, I don't get to be myself when it comes to my dad. That will be a different battle to fight. But I need Dalton to understand it's over between Bobby and me. I erase the distance between us and place my hand on his biceps. I ignore the size and strength beneath my palm and soften my tone. "Tell me what's wrong."

Dalton stares at my hand a moment before he caves. "You're right. Dad's drinking has gotten worse. He wants me to come home."

"What! Now?"

Dalton gives a quick nod.

"But it's midseason."

He lets out a humorless laugh. "As if that matters. He doesn't care about me playing baseball. He only cares what I can do for him back home."

"Doesn't he realize how talented you are?"

The look Dalton pins me with screams "get real" and "are you kidding" at the same time. "He doesn't know shit about me other than I'm not home running his shop."

"Is that the real reason for wanting you back? So you can run his shop?"

"That and among other things. He's still harping on me to be back for Steve's parole hearing."

"Does it help when you're there?"

He shrugs. "I suppose it couldn't hurt, but my presence never helped before. I've missed the last two hearings."

"Are you feeling guilty?"

His stare holds a vulnerability he rarely shows. I briefly wonder if the ground is wet from his shield's meltdown.

"Yes, but for the wrong reasons. I don't want to go. Don't get me wrong, I want to support my brother, but I can't stand to be around my old man. It's the reason I've stayed away."

"Last week when you blew up in the dugout, was it because of your dad?" He never did tell me the reason, but the picture is coming together.

He studies me, and I can see the pain buried deep in his eyes. The muscles beneath my palm tense. I want to pull him even closer and embrace him—to comfort him—but I can't go there, not fully. It doesn't matter if I ended things with Bobby, I'm still not good for Dalton. The power Dad wields over him hasn't lessened. Dalton may not realize, but he'll face further repercussions in tomorrow's game. I have no doubt that Dad will test him.

"It was because of him, wasn't it?" I prod.

Dalton licks his lips. "Dad had called right before game time."

I can tell he's uncomfortable talking about this. Whether he wants to admit it or not, that conversation threw his game off, and he needs to discuss it. He carries too much weight on his shoulders.

"Is this the underlying reason you got in that fight the other night?"

"Part of it."

"What does that mean?" I prod. He needs to give me something to work with. I can't help him if he doesn't tell me.

"It means not to worry about it."

"Not to worry about it?" I screech, backing up. My hands fly to my hips. I tip my chin up and glare. "You threw the first punch. That looks really bad, Dalton. What prompted you to do that?"

"I had my reasons. Just leave it at that."

He's beyond frustrating. Here I thought we were making progress. "There aren't any excuses for starting a fight. This makes you look bad."

"You weren't there." He steps into my space. The heat radiating off him licks my skin.

"Then tell me what happened," I practically beg.

His eyes smolder as his body hovers beside me. I feel trapped. Not by the physical sense—he'd move out of the way if I shoved him—but more from emotions. Is there such a thing as an emotional trance? If so, that's what he has me in. I just want him to answer. More importantly, I just want him to be safe. I can't be the reason another person loses their career.

"Tell me what was so important you'd risk ending your career."

"What does it matter?" He presses his body against mine. Tension sizzles between us. And not the agitated kind from earlier. This is the kind that makes me want to do naughty things. The kind I haven't felt since leaving Bellow Bay.

"Because I care." My voice comes out breathy. He's so close I feel every intake of breath and the rapid beat of his pulse. That smoldering gaze drops to my mouth. I don't have time to think before those lips I've dreamed of since leaving Bellow Bay are touching mine. Then they move in a way that is everything I remember plus more. The kiss is exhilarating and passionate with a hint of desperation. Okay, there's a lot of desperation. Our arms fumble for placement until his hands land on my waist. Our tongues collide, reuniting as if we're each other's source of survival. I lose myself in his touch and in the deep, guttural sounds he exudes. In everything about him, because, oh my goodness, I feel alive for the first time since hearing about Mom's diagnosis.

I push the thought of Mom aside and focus solely on him. My hands cup his face, the slight stubble tickling my palms. He deepens the kiss, and it's just me and him and no one else. That is until barking cuts through the bubble we created.

Wait, barking. That must mean Dad's home.

We pull away in haste, and I pray Dad isn't nearby. By the way our chests heave and the lust buried in what I'm sure is both our eyes, Dad would figure out what we did in a heartbeat.

Dalton leans closer, cupping my jaw and running his thumb across my lips.

"You belong with me, Cassie. No one else. I don't know how, but we *will* be together. Mark my words."

CHAPTER TWENTY-ONE

CASSIE

"ARE YOU GOING TO TENSE UP EVERY TIME YOUR BOY STEPS TO the plate?" Nicole asks.

I feel Nicole's crooked smile on me, but my gaze doesn't stray from the batter. My nerves are frayed. "Dalton needs to have a good day today. He can't afford any more misfortunes."

This is the first home game they've played since the bar fight. We're in the bottom of the seventh, and Dalton's having an incredible game, going two for two with three runs batted in. I'm not surprised Dad started Dalton, given his natural talent, but I keep waiting for the moment he tests him. I know it's coming.

"Did you find out what caused the fight?"

"No. From what I gathered, the guy from the other team must've talked smack." Although Dalton never said, I pieced together that conclusion from what Bobby had told me and what I overheard Dad say. I have a suspicion there is more to the story than Dalton let on. Something the guy said triggered him that night. I just don't know what.

I suck in a sharp breath as the opposing team's pitcher winds up and throws the ball. Dalton swings and misses. My groan comes out louder than intended.

"Relax. He's two for two and had an excellent defensive day. Did you see the split he did when he made that one out?"

"Uh-huh. But he needs this hit." I know my dad. The minute he messes up, Dad will yank him to see if he'll keep his temper in check. That's just how my dad is. I've heard him talk about his strategy multiple times throughout the years. He may have sent me away every summer after the one that shall not be named, but he always talked about his tactics on reforming his players. He is harder on the players staying at our house. The poor sap becomes Dad's pet project.

Another pitch is delivered, and Dalton connects with the ball but sends it foul.

"Have you told your dad about your breakup with Bobby?"

That question earns Nicole a glare. "What do you think?"

I divert my gaze back to the field. *Come on, babe. You got this.*

"He's going to find out. I'm surprised CC hasn't called and told him yet."

"Bobby hasn't accepted it yet."

Dalton takes ball one.

"What do you mean?"

"I keep telling him we want different things, but he won't let me break it off."

"Won't let you? You simply say, 'I'm breaking up with you. We're done.'"

"Every time I say that he tells me that's not what I want." I clamp my mouth shut as irritation lights a fire inside me. Every time I visualize his condescending smirk, I want to scream. "I'm so tired of men controlling my life."

"That's because you let those men gaslight you too much."

"More like steamroll me," I mumble.

Dalton sits on ball three. With a full count, things just got interesting. I lean forward as if that position helps me see better.

"That's your fault and no one else. You let that boring bastard dictate to you for far too long. Tell him you're done and then quit talking to him. Have you answered his calls?"

The pitcher sets and looks back at the runner on first. I will him to hurry so I can get out of this conversation. I don't want to talk about Bobby.

"He hasn't called since we went out to dinner. His party is in three days and I won't have to talk to him after that."

"It doesn't sound like it's going to be that simple."

Smack.

"Oh." I stand and watch the ball sail into left field, officially shutting down the Bobby topic. A roar echoes from the crowd as the runner takes off from first. The ball drops between the left and center fielders as Dalton rounds the corner at first and looks over at third base. The running coach motions for him to stop. He retreats to first and pumps his fist in the air as the runner from first lands safely on third. "Yes! Three for three, baby."

"Now can you relax?" Nicole shakes her head but wears a huge smile.

"Yes! Barring no errors, he should be safe."

Except he isn't.

At the top of the next inning, our pitcher shows signs of waning. I watch my dad motion for relief and signal for a double switch.

"No," I whisper-shout.

"What's wrong?"

"Dad's doing a double switch."

"What does that mean?"

"How are you even related to me?" I roll my eyes. "Dad's calling for a new pitcher along with another position player."

"That doesn't sound bad."

As Jason stands and heads out of the dugout, my answer is a groan.

Nicole gasps when she notices the new position player. "Oh, it is bad."

My breath stills. *Please, please, please maintain your cool*, I silently beg. There isn't any reason for Dad to take out Dalton. No reason at all other than to be a dick. And yes, I just called my dad a dick, but he's being one. I bite my lower lip and watch Dalton's expression. Irritation flashes across his face, but he quickly masks it. When Jason reaches him, Dalton taps his glove against Jason's and *smiles*. He actually smiles.

My pulse begins to slow back down. When did they become friends? Okay, maybe the term *friends* is a stretch, but Dalton gave him an honest to God real smile.

I think Dalton just passed my dad's test, and I know exactly how to celebrate. The problem will be implementing my plan.

"Nicole, I need your help."

CHAPTER TWENTY-TWO

DALTON

"WHAT A WIN. I'M STARVING." CARTER PATS HIS STOMACH AS WE step from his truck. We just won the game, and everyone is pumped. We're heading to the pizza parlor. I should be ecstatic. I had an incredible night and played the best ball I've played since arriving here. Coach rewarded me by allowing me to go out with the guys and gave me an eleven o'clock curfew. That's nothing short of a small miracle, considering he's still reeling over the fight I got into. I'd like to think I'm gaining some of his trust. It was nice of him and all, but I'm not feeling it tonight.

"What's the matter?" Carter asks when I don't respond. "Are you pissed you got pulled from the game?"

"No." I may be able to lie to Carter, but I can't lie to myself—I wasn't happy and admittedly a bit surprised—but I knew Coach was pressing my buttons. "Jason deserved playtime." *I suppose.*

"Then celebrate. You're finally allowed to party with the guys."

I'd rather celebrate with a short blonde. I saw her in the stands. It was hard knowing she was there, and I couldn't look at her. The few glances I stole weren't enough.

A white Hyundai Kona pulls up along the curb and honks, drawing Carter's and my attention. I recognize the driver right away. She's alone.

"Get back in your truck and follow me."

Carter's eyes grow wide. "Who the hell is that?"

I smirk. "We're right behind you."

"We are?"

I slap my new buddy on the back. "When a gorgeous woman tells you to do something, you comply."

We get back into Carter's truck.

"I sure hope the hell you know her."

"She's Nicole, Cassie's cousin."

"Cassie? As in rule number one, keep-your-hands-off-my-daughter Cassie?"

"The very one."

Carter pulls behind Nicole, and we take off down the road.

"This is a bad idea, bro."

"It's a great idea."

"*Please* tell me you don't have a thing for the coach's daughter."

I contemplate telling him how we met back in my hometown, but I don't. That information needs to stay private. The fewer people who know about it, the less chance Cassie will be in trouble with her dad. But how do I answer this question? I don't want to lie because I have a very big thing for her. And that shared kiss only proved it never went away. She tasted divine.

Carter groans. At first, I think I spoke about how she tasted out loud, but then he shakes his head.

"You do, don't you?"

"You can't let anyone know."

"You're playing with fire. Why chance it?"

"It's a long story."

"I've seen you around campus. You're not short on girls."

I wince. It shouldn't matter what I did in the past, nor should it matter what she's done. We weren't with each other, but damn if I don't regret my choices after not finding her. I honestly thought I'd never see her again. And I sure as shit hate the thought of her douchebag ex's hands touching her.

"Whatever you do, don't mention the other girls."

"Come on, I'm a better wingman than that. All I'm saying is to watch it. He'll send your ass packing if you get caught."

"We won't get caught," I say reassuringly but recognize the risk. It doesn't matter. I can't stay away from this girl.

"Whatever, man. They better have food."

He's quiet after that. We follow Nicole into the next town over. She pulls into a park, and there sits Cassie, waiting on a bench. Her face beams when she sees me.

Carter notices and gives me a side-eye glance. He doesn't say anything but shakes his head knowingly. Yeah, I'm not following any rules when it comes to her.

Nicole exits her car but leaves it running. She walks over to where we're standing after we parked and tosses an arm around Carter. "Okay, big guy. You're taking me out for dinner."

Carter's eyes bulge again at Nicole's directness. He looks back at me, shrugs, and then hops into the truck.

"Hi," Cassie says, eyes sparkling.

"Hi," I return. I want to devour those lips and give her a more proper greeting, but I don't know whose eyes are upon us.

"Okay, you two lovebirds, be back by ten. You don't want to turn into a pumpkin."

"Wait." I jog back to the truck and grab my jacket along with a candy bar. I may need this later if we don't go for food. Like Carter, I'm starving.

"Thanks, Nicole." Cassie gives her cousin a grateful look.

I can't help myself. When I approach Cassie, I reach out and grab her hand. "See you later." Then I tug Cassie to the car. If our time is limited, I want every precious minute alone I can get.

When she drives out of the park, I ask, "Where are we going?"

Her eyes slide to mine. "Somewhere we can be alone."

And just like that, my cock is hard and all promises to be good get left in the park. There's no way I can keep from touching her.

CHAPTER TWENTY-THREE

CASSIE

"So where are we going?" Dalton asks as I drive us out of town.

"It's my secret escape spot."

He raises an eyebrow. "Oh?"

"My college isn't too far away. I found this spot one day when things got to be a little too much." It was right after Mom had a bad episode, and I couldn't get home. I was numb, feeling helpless. Dad sent Bobby to check on me. I didn't have any fight left in me at all. We essentially started dating. It was all too much. I needed an area where I could escape reality and reminisce about everything I mourned—not being with my mom during her illness, not being with Dalton. Just everything. I never showed Bobby this spot.

"Thanks for taking me there."

Silence chews up the next few moments. "You had a great game."

"It felt good. Tonight, we meshed as a team should."

"You know my dad only took you out to test you, right?"

"Yeah, I figured something like that was going on."

"You passed."

"It's a little sadistic, don't you think?"

"That's my dad. Preacher by day, hypocrite by game."

Dalton laughs. "I think everyone is a little hypocritical."

"Maybe. I wish I had given you a warning, but you handled it well."

"I may be losing my bad boy status."

"You were never bad."

"That's not how I'm perceived."

"They're wrong. They don't know you at all."

He's quiet for a moment. The ocean comes into view. I pull into the designated parking spot and kill the engine.

"I packed a picnic for us."

"Are you stealing a scene from my playbook?"

"Maybe."

When I visited Bellow Bay, we had to sneak around my aunt Jan's back. It seems to be our forte. Anyway, Dalton took me to a beach. He surprised me with a picnic. That was one of my favorite days. It's no wonder why I would want to recreate it.

Dalton grabs the bag while I grab the blanket. We take off down the path leading to an overhanging cliff. Dalton halts in his tracks and takes in the view.

"Wow. This is incredible."

The waves crash against the rough, rocky terrain below, drowning any civilization. The sea stretches for miles, but it's the enormous rock formations that steal the show.

"I've always preferred the northern coastal ranges, but this state has some amazing landscapes." I smirk. "Wait until the sunset."

"I can finally collect then?"

"It's three years too late, but yes."

He lowers to brush a kiss against my lips. "It's never too late."

When we were at the beach in North Carolina, I had promised him a sunset. "I'm happy to deliver."

We settle into the blanket and dig into the sandwiches I brought. He bumps his knee against mine.

"I'm glad you brought food. I'm starving."

"I thought you would be."

After he eats a sizable portion of the sandwich, he asks, "How's the planning for the rummage sale coming along? Ms. Willow ask for me yet?"

"Okay, now you're just fishing for compliments." The twinkle in his eye makes me smile. I take a drink and continue, "The rummage sale is pretty much done. I expect a few more items to trickle in, but everything else has been uploaded and priced. I think we're ready."

"That's good. We don't have a game until later that evening, so I can recruit a few teammates to help in the morning."

"Really? That would be great."

We finish, and I collect the trash and toss everything into the bag.

"Come here." He pats the small space between us, and I snuggle against his large frame. He leans down to kiss the top of my head as he drapes his arm around my shoulder.

"I'm telling my dad about breaking up with Bobby after the welcome home party this Sunday."

"Do you want me there when you tell him?"

"No, I'll be okay even though he won't take the news well. I swear, most days, he loves him more than me. And as much as I'd love to have you there, this is something I need to do myself. But could you be there for the party?"

He gives me a side glance. "Of course. Whatever you want."

Whatever you want. What I want is for us to be together without any restraints. That will never happen. I know Dad, and he'll never approve. I hesitate. "You know, even after telling Dad about Bobby, we still can't be seen together."

He blows out a breath. "We can sneak around if you want, but your dad isn't my end-all. He doesn't have that kind of power."

"But he does. You don't know what happened."

"What are you talking about?"

I take a deep, pained breath and close my eyes momentarily as I summon up the strength to tell this story. "There's a reason I got sent away every year during summer league. Back when I was four-teen, Malcolm Darrius came to stay with us. I was infatuated with him. Not too many boys ever paid attention to me. Plus, Malcolm thought I was sweet."

Dalton's body becomes rigid. "Are you telling me an eighteen or twenty-year-old came on to you?"

"No! Nothing like that. Malcolm was nice to me. Dad warned me to stay away from the players. Told me never to talk to them, and I never did until Malcolm came and stayed with us."

"What made him different?"

"He was a little rough around edges. He had tattoos and sported an attitude but was friendly to me. He never tried to make any moves, but I couldn't stay away. I was enthralled."

"Should I be worried that your fascination with me is just a carryover from this Malcolm dude?"

I playfully smack his arm. Dalton laughs but catches my hand and entwines his fingers with mine.

"Hardly. But you do enthrall me. More so even."

"I take it your dad came unglued when he saw you talking?"

I hang my head and stare out at the waves. "I ruined that guy's chances. He told me how badly he wanted this baseball career, his scholarship, and how he needed it all to work out. I felt sorry for him. He looked so sad talking about his parents. I thought he needed comfort. Whenever I got sad, Mom would always hug me. So I did what I thought would comfort him. I hugged him. And that's when my dad walked outside and saw us." I shiver from that memory. The yelling. Me trying to explain the innocence of it, and Malcolm pleading his case. I never felt so low in my entire life. Well, that's not true, but it was close. "My dad made him leave. He never played baseball again and lost his future. I ruined that guy's career all because I didn't listen to my dad." I turn to face Dalton with tear-streaked eyes. "I can't be the reason you lose your base-ball career."

"How do you know he never played?"

"Dad told me. After taking Malcolm to the airport, he returned and said I cost that kid his career. He told me his contacts would take care of everything."

"Jesus. You don't believe that, do you?"

"Of course! Why wouldn't I?"

"Because your dad probably said those things to scare you."

"No, he wouldn't lie to me. That's what I was being punished for—breaking the rules and lying about it."

"Sweetheart, think about. You don't have a television, so you don't have access to any sports stations. You don't have the internet. You wouldn't be able to search for him. Don't you think it's possible your dad lied so that you would leave the future guys alone?"

"I-I . . ." I'm stunned. I've carried that guilt around for years. Surely Dad wouldn't lie and let his fourteen-old-daughter carry the burden of costing a guy his scholarship. Would he sink that low? "I suppose, but he knows a lot of people, including the president of the NCAA."

"Let's look up Malcolm Darrius and see what happened to him."

I bite my lip as he types Malcolm's name into the search bar. "What college did he attend?"

"Cessna U."

His eyes flick to mine. "Interesting." Then he resumes his search and smiles. Showing me his phone, he says, "See, this shows the dates Malcolm Darrius played on the Wildcats and the year he graduated. You didn't cost him his scholarship at all."

"Huh." That makes me feel somewhat better, I guess. "But that means my dad lied to me."

"According to his stats, he played his junior year for the Baytown Crushers and must've transferred to an amateur baseball league not sponsored by the NCAA."

"What about the majors? Did he make it professionally?"

He shakes his head, and a part of me feels deflated. "I don't think so. I can't find any more stats." He looks up, and he frowns at whatever's on my face. He nudges his shoulder against mine. "My guess is he graduated and is working somewhere."

"Thanks for trying to make me feel better."

"Look at me." Those dark soulful eyes peer down at me. "I know you're worried about me, but if anything happens, it wouldn't be your fault. I'm big enough to know what I'm doing. Any risk I take falls on me."

"I know. I just . . ." *Love you.* "Don't want anything bad to happen to you."

He kisses the top of my head. "I already told you. I'm not going anywhere."

We say nothing as we watch the sun dip lower into the ocean. The waves crash against the rocks. The salty air fills my lungs. Sitting with him reminds me of when we were in Bellow Bay, when everything was new and exciting. But the thing is, being with him is still as exciting. And I hate that what we feel for each other is a secret. I want to shout that Dalton and I belong together from the highest rooftop. But that's still too risky.

"You were right," I say.

"I usually am." That earns him a pinch in the side. He chuckles. "Okay, okay. About what?"

"Our timing *is* off."

He backs away just far enough for those dark brown eyes to peer into mine. Without a doubt, he knows what I mean.

"No, Choir Girl, I was wrong. There's no such thing as bad timing when it comes to you."

"But—"

"Listen to me. I don't know what I did to have you in my life, but it must've been something spectacular. Because I must admit, I don't deserve someone like you. I certainly never expected it. But I was drawn to you the moment I saw you. And you are so much more than what your *boyfriend* or even your dad makes you out to be."

My heart beats like a caged wild animal. Dalton has always gotten me. He sees me. Every other male in my life wants to control and suppress me. They don't care what I want or see my potential if I do their bidding and toe the line. I've been drilled on Paul's letter to the Ephesians about wives submitting to their husbands as to the Lord, and the husband is the head of the wife as Christ is the head of the church. Deprogramming myself will take time, but it's a lot easier with Dalton by my side.

His arm still draped around me tightens its hold for a moment before tracing its way along my side. My body catches like it's on fire. Desire, lust, and full-on need stake a claim, and I can't think a coherent thought. At least that's my excuse when I blurt, "Bobby and I never had sex."

Dalton's body stills. I watch the slide of his Adam's apple. Those dark hues meet my blues. Surprise mixed with disbelief coats his expression, but there's an underlying current of something else. Horror maybe. Or regret.

"That doesn't matter. I mean, it's none of my business."

"I know, but I thought . . . I don't know what I thought, but we've barely kissed."

"How? You were exclusive, right?" He shakes his head as if that would give him some clarity.

"Sex should be between two joined in union under God's eye."

"I can see not having intercourse, I guess, but kissing? How could he resist your lips? They're delectable."

How indeed.

"So you've only . . ."

"Had sex the one time with you." I fill in when his voice trails off.

His eyes darken, but they're overshadowed with regret. "I'm not so innocent, but I *am* sorry I gave up on us."

Sorrow laces the edges of his tone. I can't fault him for being with others. I just hate that it couldn't have been us this entire time. "That doesn't matter. Remember, we were supposed to live."

He nods as eyes full of intensity stare down at me. After a beat, he says, "I remember not liking that phrase when you said it all those years ago."

"It's in the past. What does matter is we're here now."

His move is lightning fast, and I find myself lying against the earth with Dalton hovering over me. "You know what else I'm not?"

I smile. "What?"

"A saint."

Thank the heavens. But then his lips crash upon mine, and my thoughts are anything but heavenly. They're pure sin.

And I'm down for every forbidden taste.

CHAPTER TWENTY-FOUR

DALTON

NIRVANA. PURE FUCKING NIRVANA IS THE BEST WAY TO DESCRIBE Cassie in my arms with my lips on hers. And that includes being picked up by the majors. Holy shit, I am not this guy. I don't let girls get in the way of my dreams. I don't pick the righteous path. I don't do religion. So why do I want to do right by her? Why does this girl bring me to my knees with one bat of her eyelashes?

"I've thought of you so many times these past few years," she says, breath heady. My lips dip along her neck as her fingers knead along my back and sides. It's as if she can't decide where to touch, so she's covering as much territory as she can. I breathe in her fresh, clean scent. It's cucumber crisp and melon sweet—a powerful combination.

"What were you doing while you thought of me?" A wicked smile crosses my lips when Cassie's breath hitches. Damn, I missed this girl. I thought I'd lost her and would never see her again. But I got a second chance, and I'll be damned if I don't take it. Cassie's mine. I won't let her go this time. "Tell me, Choir Girl."

"I-I was pleasuring myself."

Fuck, that's hot.

She bites her lower lip, but I nibble at it to make her stop. It isn't my intent to do anything but talk—not here, not now—but

I'm being driven by pure emotion in search of any nugget she's willing to toss my way.

"Does that embarrass you?" I smile at her nod. She tries to duck her head, but I'm not letting her off that easily. I whisper in her ear, "Don't let it. Do you know how hot hearing you say that is? Your name already passes through my lips, but you touching yourself is what I'll picture from now on every time I beat off."

"Oh, goodness," she moans.

The honorable thing to do would be to slow down, but I can't seem to make myself. The only way I could stop was if she told me to. And the way she's panting and gyrating her hips into mine says anything but slow down.

I plant small kisses to the underside of her jaw while one hand slips behind her neck and the other skims along her side. When I reach the hem of her shirt, I brush my fingers against her skin, gauging her reaction the entire time. She's so damn responsive to every touch, to every kiss. That's the thing about each stolen glance and every hidden conversation we've had over the past few weeks. They've fed into the anticipation of what is to come and fueled this prolonged foreplay session.

My fingers glide underneath her shirt and work their way up her body. Once her breast fills my hand, I brush my thumb across her nipple. It hardens into a tight bud underneath the lacy fabric. Her moan comes out half satisfied and half pleading.

"Please," she pants. "I want you so bad."

"Babe, I want you too, but we're out in public."

"I don't care."

I chuckle. "Don't worry. I'll take care of you."

My dick strains against my shorts, obviously not caring if we got caught. I, on the other hand, need to keep my wits. I do a quick scan of the area. We're completely alone. Cassie was right about this area's seclusion. I frown, thinking about her coming here by herself, but then let it go. She's not by herself now, and I have three years' worth of orgasms to attend to.

I retake her mouth. Her stomach quivers as I brush my fingers along her hourglass-shaped curves. I slip my hand beneath her skirt and trace my fingers along her thigh and up to her ass. I lean back enough to catch her eyes, surprised by the lack of material.

"You're wearing a thong under this skirt?"

Blush coats her cheeks. "I wore it for you."

I don't recognize the sound that leaves my mouth. It's low and carnal and highlights everything I feel. I want this woman more than anything. I can't believe she's here with me. I capture her mouth with mine and shove the strip of fabric aside. My finger slides into her pussy, and I about lose it when wet warmth greets me. She's ripe. So goddamn ripe. And tight. Her back arches against my body, and the moan she emits is full of heat and desire. It's as if she was sexually starved for years. I guess it's been three. Damn. Three years to think about sex. To imagine it. I have some big shoes to fill while I compete against a fantasy.

Fueled by desire, I bite through her shirt and nibble on her nipple. I want nothing more than to shove the shirt out of the way, but we're still outside. The twilight hour may be approaching, but she's still exposed if anyone happens to come upon us. Keeping part of this PG-13 will have to do for now.

I keep working my finger back and forth at a slow pace. Her breath increases as her body starts to writhe. Her walls clamp down on my finger, and . . . oh shit, she's close. I pull out, not expecting her to be there that soon.

"What are you doing?" she protests.

"Don't worry. I'll finish you off, but I have to have my dessert." I'm three years too late. I scoot down, taking her thong along for the ride. I reposition between her legs which she greedily spreads for me. I shove her skirt up farther, and, ah, yes, her pink pussy glistens just as I remember. Fuck it if anyone happens to see. I hope they enjoy the show because I sure will.

She squirms as I run my tongue from top to bottom. The moment her sweetness hits my taste buds, I come unglued. She tastes so fucking good. I've missed doing this, missed the scent of her arousal. I may have had my share of sex these past three years, but I've tasted no one else. That was a hard limit. Doing this with anyone but Cassie would have broken me.

I reach up and palm her breast while I slip a finger inside. Continuing with my pumps, I flick the tip of my tongue against her clit and slip another finger inside. Her fingers weave through my hair, tugging and pulling the longer I lick circles on her sweet spot.

"Oh, God. I'm not going to last. This is . . ." Her voice shifts into a moan as her body starts to convulse. I work my fingers faster, harder, which sends her over the edge. She comes undone under my palm, letting her moan free. I watch her face as the orgasm takes over.

She's so beautiful.

My dick is painfully hard, but he'll have to calm down. I guarantee the image of her fingering herself will play like a movie reel over and over in my mind later while I release this tension.

When she comes down from her high, her face is flushed as those gorgeous eyes stare down at me. I lick my fingers and moan. "Sweet. Just as I remember."

Her hand reaches up and covers her face. "Oh, God."

"Nuh-uh. No hiding or getting embarrassed. That was long overdue."

She peeks through her fingers at me. "It's hard."

"That it is."

"Oh. Oh! I can take care of that." She goes to move, but I stop her.

"No, today was all for you. I couldn't have you going around with lust in your eyes."

She smacks my arm. "You're such a jerk sometimes." But then she gives me a soft smile. "Thanks. I really missed you. The worst mistake I made was deleting your number from Nicole's phone."

"I missed you too. But your crazy fate theory worked. I found my way back to you."

Her smile grows wider. "That you did."

I replace her underwear, and she snuggles up against me. We

spend the rest of our time talking. She catches me up on her college, and I tell her about my teammates and friends. We keep this up until the sun dips and bursts into fiery golds and reds on the horizon. Vibrant hues of amber clouds streak across the yellow canvas in a blazing display of fire and heat. The picture is surreal. Or maybe it's just being with her again.

"You were right," I say. "West Coast sunsets are magnificent."

She sighs and leans her head on my shoulder. "I don't want to return home."

"Neither do I."

But I know what needs to be done. I snuck around with her the last time. I don't want a repeat. This time around, I want to show her off and tell the entire world she's mine. That starts by being honest with her dad. He still doesn't trust me, and I have an uphill battle to gain his respect, but I have to try at least.

CHAPTER TWENTY-FIVE

DALTON

"Tell me why you talked me into staying?" Carter asks. We're standing in the back of the church annex as people mill around the room, chatting with each other. Tables lined up in rows like in a cafeteria. A big, gold-lettered welcome home banner hangs above the food serving table. Church let out about fifteen minutes ago. Carter could've split along with the other teammates. I had no choice but to attend.

"You love me," I deadpan. I try to act like I don't care, but truthfully, I'm grateful. I don't want to be here—especially when the only person I care about is currently off-limits—but Cassie has asked me. And speaking of my girl, Cassie emerges from the hallway carrying a deli tray. I try not to keep staring, but I can't help it. She keeps walking back and forth from what I presume is the kitchen. It's as if she single-handedly runs the show. Anger starts to take hold because what the fuck? Why does she bear all the responsibilities? But the moment her gaze raises to meet mine, all reasons to be mad are forgotten and replaced by flashes of memories from the other night. Of how sexy she looked when she came on my mouth. The way she moaned my name. My body stirs to life, recalling every detail, wanting an encore. A blush coats her

147

cheeks as if she could read my mind. She dips her head and adjusts the tray before pivoting and rushing back toward the kitchen.

"Never mind. I know exactly why I'm here. To keep you from making a colossal mistake."

My gaze pulls from Cassie's retreating backside and lands on Carter. "I'm going to talk to her dad after this party."

"And tell him what?"

"That I respect his daughter. That I care a lot for her."

"As in asking permission to date her?" Disbelief oozes through each syllable, and I can't say I blame him. Coach hasn't hidden his daughter away all these years to have another tattooed bad boy fixate on his pride and joy. *Fuck.* What am I thinking?

"Something like that," I say, but I'm not too convincing.

"That's not a good idea. He'll never approve."

"I have to try." And I should confess how we met three years ago. Come all the way clean.

"He'll send you packing."

I wince. Carter's more than likely right, but if I don't confess now, it'll only be worse later. "I don't have a choice. I can't hide these feelings I have for Cassie for much longer."

Carter studies me for a moment. "You think she's worth it?"

Of all the questions to ask, why does everyone pose that one? *Of course she's worth it.* She's more than worth it. The truth is, it's me who doesn't measure up. I know she is too good for me. But I also know I am too damn selfish to let her go. Cassie is the sweetest, most caring person I know, and she's mine. When we're back at her house, I plan to make my intentions known. It's the first step to gaining Coach's approval. He demands honesty. Well, I'll be nothing but truthful. Honest fucking Abe here. I don't want to spend the rest of the summer sneaking around that man's back.

Cassie comes back out, carrying a tray filled with sliced desserts individually wrapped on single-serving plates. She unloads each dessert onto the table. When she is down to the last one, her eyes find mine. One corner of her mouth tips upward as suggestion swirls in her stare. My dick stirs to life. Her mouth parts ever so slightly, and damn if she doesn't run her tongue along her teeth. Damn temptress. She knows how much I like that tongue of hers. The way my dick wakes up, he remembers fully too. Her smirk grows bigger as she turns and trots down the hallway.

"Okay, you better tell the man something because if he sees that eye-fucking you two gave each other, he'll figure it out in no time."

His words barely register as I take off after her.

"Where are you going?"

"I'll be right back."

"Don't do it, man. You're playing with fire."

But I don't listen. I only have one thing in mind as I slip down the hallway. It has nothing to do with Coach or Bobby's party and everything to do with a certain temptress disguised as an angel.

The hall is long and narrow. The two doors to the right sport male and female signs, which I presume are bathrooms. I slink inside the one marked for males. It's a single-occupancy bathroom, thank God. I don't know what I would've done had someone else been in here. It's bad enough I'm hanging by the door and waiting for my girl like a creeper. I don't need witnesses.

Cassie emerges from the kitchen carrying a bag of rolls. I find myself once again thanking God for small favors. My plan would never have worked if she was carrying another large tray of desserts. When she nears where I stand hidden behind the door, I grab her by the arm and whirl her into me.

She lets out a small yelp before it registers who I am. "Dalton, we can't be in here." Her arms wrap around my neck as she presses her body against mine. My hands run along her curves until resting on her hips. This girl feels so damn good in my hands.

"Your mouth says no, but your body is saying something completely different."

"My body is a traitor."

"Your body knows exactly what it wants," I practically growl and draw her into a kiss. She hesitates momentarily before her body melts against me. My entire world rights itself as we steal this moment together. Her mouth on mine and her fingers weaving through my hair are all innocent. I have no intention of taking this further. Just one stolen kiss to get through this god-awful party is all I need. Carter is right. I am playing with fire. I'll end up burned, but with her beside me—those tender lips on my mouth—I'm ready to walk across fiery coals.

I force myself to break away before the congregation decides to immolate me. "You better get back out there."

"Meet me in the garage when we get back home."

I study her blue eyes that plead for more and nod. This seems to satisfy her. I don't mention how I'm talking to her dad afterward. The less she stresses about today, the better. "I'll be there."

She smooths her hair down and flashes me a bright smile. With a glance down the hall, she slinks out of the room with confidence in her stride that was absent before. I wait a few minutes before exiting.

As I make my way over to where Carter still stands, I catch Bobby watching me. I tip my chin to him. His eyes narrow, and his gaze lingers a beat more before directing his attention toward Cassie. He works his jaw as if he's trying to figure something out. He can prove nothing. I'm allowed to use the bathroom.

Carter and I sit through the dinner without any issues and listen to Mr. Sainthood himself thank everyone. He mainly talks about his efforts of spreading the Word and how he can't wait until next year when he can be there for longer periods of time. He seeks out Cassie and motions for her to join him. While she walks to him, he glances at her dad with a knowing smirk. Her dad nods.

Uh-oh. A funny feeling settles in my stomach. I don't like this at all.

Cassie forces her fake smile and stands beside him. I don't understand how no one can see how devoid of emotion she is when she's around this douchebag. It's so obvious.

"I wanted to make an official announcement," Preppy Boy says.

My hands clench as he grabs hold of her hand, and she doesn't pull away. *Pull away, damn it.*

"As you all know, I've known Cassie practically my entire life. We grew up together and have remained friends."

"Uh-oh," Carter mimics my sentiment.

"And then we started courting a couple of years ago."

Courting? What is this, the sixteenth century? Who uses that term these days? What guy would? He really is a douche.

Bobby looks down at Cassie as collective "ahs" ring through the room. I want to barf.

"Since we'll be graduating at the end of this school year, it's finally time to announce that Cassie has accepted my marriage proposal." He whips out a ring. Cassie's fake smile flattens to a look of astonishment.

"Uh, what's going on?" Carter leans over, his voice so low, I barely hear him over the applause. Or maybe it's due to the swishing in my ears from the sudden spike in my heart rate.

She said yes? Is this a joke?

Cassie stands there as if too stunned to move.

Deny it.

Is she not moving because she never expected him to announce this now? Was she playing me the whole time? Why doesn't she deny it?

Bobby slips the ring on her finger and holds her hand up to the crowd. A constellation of light dances off the diamond. I would make fun of the size but fuck if it's not bigger than anything I could afford.

Deny it.

Pain slices through me and punches me in the gut when she smiles at the crowd. I haven't moved a muscle. Hell, I don't think I've breathed.

Why is she smiling and not denying it?

Her dad walks over to them and pats Bobby on the back.

"Let's give these two lovebirds a round of applause," Coach says.

It's the warm smile he tosses Bobby's way that gets me.

"Son, welcome to the family."

I digress. It's when Coach calls Bobby son, I lose it. Carter doesn't say a word when I bristle beside him. Cassie's gaze meets mine, her smile wavering, but she doesn't deny a thing.

I storm out of there and run.

CHAPTER TWENTY-SIX

CASSIE

HOW DARE HE. MY BLOOD BOILS AS PEOPLE WHO HAVE SEEN ME grow up, celebrated my baptism, and comforted me through my mom's death peer at me with satisfied gleams. This can't be happening. No one tells me who to marry. My proposal won't be an ambush where the only choice I have is to say yes.

Do they actually think this is the way proposals should go? With Bobby deciding the answer for me?

He slips something cold and rigid on my finger and lifts my hand to the receptive crowd.

I'm too stunned to react.

The smug look on Bobby's face. My dad's knowing smile. *Dad knew.* Of course he knew. Bobby wouldn't have gone through with this without getting Dad's approval. He knew Bobby was going to blindside me, and he didn't have the decency to stop it.

I feel betrayed and ambushed at the same time. I fight the tears pricking my eyes.

Dad calls Bobby his son, and it's like a knife straight to the heart, but it snaps me out of my trance.

My gaze seeks Dalton's.

Dalton.

What is he going to think? He's the one I want to be with. He's the only one who never thinks for me. He's the only one who makes me feel and challenges me to stand up for myself.

When our gazes connect, it doesn't take long to figure out what he's thinking. He's pissed. He has every right to be, though he's not as pissed off as me.

I want to cry out that this is a sham. To not listen. I want to run over to him. I *need* to run over to him. I shift away from Bobby, but his grip on my wrist tightens.

Manipulative asshole.

A flash of pain haunts Dalton's stare right before he runs out the door. I move to chase after him, but Bobby halts my movement and pulls me closer to him.

"Don't think your little friend liked the news," he whispers next to my ear.

I turn to him while Dad's speech fades to background noise.

"Oh, you didn't think I was stupid, did you?" His eyes grow cold, calculating. "I know all about your secret."

My heart skips a beat. Did Bobby find out about me taking Dalton to my spot? He doesn't know about my place. Did he follow us? Or did he see Dalton and me in the hallway? Or the overall secret that Dalton and I met three years ago?

"What secret?" I manage to squeak out.

There's a calculated response to his laugh. "Smile, Cassie. The congregation is watching."

No! I'm done being manipulated by him and my dad. If Dad doesn't want to pay for my college, so be it. I'll be like everyone else and take out more loans. It will be worth it. What I won't do is agree to be married off to this manipulative bastard.

"I will *never* marry you," I spit out between clenched teeth.

"We'll see about that."

Yes, we will.

And as soon as the last person leaves, these two men who have controlled every minute of my life get an earful.

CHAPTER TWENTY-SEVEN

DALTON

THE FRONT DOOR SLAMS SHUT, FOLLOWED BY SHOUTS. I STEP OUT of the bathroom and stare at my bedroom door, contemplating what I should do. If I duck inside, I won't have the chance to talk to Cassie. And I *need* to speak to her. I thought about her reaction to Bobby's bullshit announcement during my run. The lack of her warm smile that she usually wears was proof enough that she hadn't known what he was going to do. She shut down and became that shell of a person she is when he's around. Once I got out of that stuffy room and pounded the pavement with my loafers, it was evident to me.

"You're being irrational. That boy is going places. He'll take care of you."

"I don't need someone to take care of me, especially if that someone is Bobby Pickler."

I glance at her door and think about waiting for her in there. Coach never checks on me. But if I get caught in Cassie's room, it'll be disastrous. Although thinking about it, he hasn't once come to her room since I've been here. They hardly interact at all.

Bellow's barking cuts through my thoughts. He's not used to hearing this kind of ruckus.

Their argument reinforces my early assessment—they blindsided her. She doesn't want to marry Bobby. That realization should make me happy, but it doesn't. It only fuels my anger. They treat her like a piece of property. That's just wrong.

"Don't be ridiculous. A woman's place is—"

"Don't preach to me. For once, can you just be a regular dad?"

"It doesn't work that way. I'm head of the church."

"Regardless of what you think, I can and will take care of myself. I broke up with Bobby over a week ago. Is that who you want as a son-in-law—some deranged psycho who can't take no for an answer?"

"Bobby isn't like that. You had plans. You need to honor them."

"No, Dad. You and he had plans. I never wanted to go to Peru. That has never been my dream. And I told him that multiple times. He just doesn't listen. Apparently, controlling women is a dominant trait among males."

"I have spoken!"

A hush descends over the house from Coach's outburst. Even Bellow's barking stops. He lets out a small whimper before retreating to his corner.

"I may be your daughter, but I'm not like Mom. I don't have to listen. I'm twenty-one years old. I can move out."

"You have no money. Where on earth would you live?"

"I'd find a way."

"If you leave, you'd never get another dime from me."

"I'd rather live on the streets and work as a sex worker than to marry that guy."

Slap.

Oh, hell no. I burst down the hallway, ready to fight. No way will I allow him to raise another hand to her. Cassie holds the side of her face with tears pricking her eyes. Coach stands in bewilderment as if he can't believe what he just did. I place myself in front of Cassie as a shield. If he's going to hit anyone, he can hit me— Cassie's off-limits.

"You need to calm down, sir," I say.

Coach draws his eyes from his hand and directs them to my

face. "I-I . . ." He closes his eyes and hangs his head in shame. He doesn't say a word as he pivots and heads to his bedroom.

Once he disappears behind his door, I turn to Cassie. "Are you all right?"

She nods. I remove her hand and assess her face. Welts are starting to form, but she shouldn't bruise. I walk her to the edge of the kitchen.

"I'm going to grab a bag of frozen peas." I don't leave her side until she nods. With the bag in hand, I place it against her cheek and guide her to her bedroom. She's silent the entire way.

I walk her to her bed. She sits on the edge with such a dejected look on her face it kills me.

"I'm sorry. I should've come out sooner." I should've protected her. Instead of giving them space to air out their grievances, I should have gone to her.

"I wouldn't have said the things I needed to say if you were there."

"Do you want to talk about it?"

She shakes her head.

"It's okay." I hold her tight. Even though their argument was heated, her dad does love her. The man is strict and can be an overbearing asshole, but he'll never abandon her, no matter what he says. He'll always be there for her. I see the adoration in his eyes every time he looks at her. He just doesn't show it through actions.

"I should get back to my room."

"Don't go." She clutches me tighter.

"I won't." How can I leave her? I can't. If she needs to hold me all night, I'll be here for her. I would worry about her dad checking in on her, but I doubt he'll leave his room before morning. He may have been remorseful, but he's also too proud to apologize tonight. Cassie's arms haven't left my waist while she leans against me with tears spilling from her eyes. The sound of her ragged breath fills the silence. We remain like this until her sobs slowly fade.

I glance around the moonlit room until I find a T-shirt draped over her desk chair. "Let's get you into something more comfortable."

She remains quiet as I slip her sweater combo off. I leave the bra intact. I don't want to take that big of a risk. After changing, we lie on her bed, and she snuggles next to my body. As we lie there spooning, I trace circles on her bare arm. After tonight's fiasco, there isn't any way I can talk to her dad. If I want to be with her, I'll have to continue sneaking behind his back. What choice do I have? I can't not be around her. She's everything to me. And I'll do anything to be with her.

Her breathing slows to an even pace until she eventually falls asleep.

"It'll be okay, Choir Girl. It may not seem like it, but your dad would never abandon you." Her soft snores let me know she didn't hear a word I said, but those thoughts lay heavy on my mind as I drift into memories I'd rather forget.

"Dalton, do you need a ride?" Marty's mom asked. Marty was my best friend.

I shook my head because Mom should be here soon to pick me up. She was late, but she always ran late on the days she and Dad fought. Mrs. Johnson frowned, but she shuffled Marty away.

I waited and watched as the other kids got picked up one by one. Where was she? The last school bus pulled away, and she still hadn't come. I never watched the buses pull away before. I went and sat on the stairs. I hugged my knees, trying to hold back tears. Tears were for pussies. That was what Dad said. But I made him mad. And I made Mom mad. She said it was always my fault.

"Dalton, is your mom coming to pick you up?" the principal asked.

I looked up at Ms. Jenkins. She has kind eyes, even for a busybody. That was what my mom called her.

"She'll be here. She's just running late." I clutched my backpack tighter and waited.

And waited.

But she never showed.

CHAPTER TWENTY-EIGHT

CASSIE

THE HEAVINESS FROM AN ARM DRAPED ACROSS ME COCOONS ME in heat as I stir awake. It takes a moment to register the soothing, woodsy scent mixed with a hint of spice. Then it hits. Dalton slept all night in my bed. My eyes pop open, but as his features come into focus, the panic abates.

Those slightly too thick eyebrows that always seem drawn in concern are relaxed as if he hasn't a care in the world. The jaw that is always hardened smooths as if the weight of the world that burdens him has lessened. Gone is the edginess his expression usually holds, and in its place is nothing but innocence. Or maybe it's because all I see is the little boy inside the man that yearns to be loved even though he would deny it.

My gaze drops to the tattoos he once said don't mean anything, but the recent addition of the school mascot must. I wonder if he finally feels as if he belongs. But then again, something had to be amiss since he's here.

As his soft breaths fill the silence, a war brews in my mind: snuggle closer—which I admit it feels incredible waking up in his arms—or freak out because holy smokes, Dalton Boyd is in my childhood bed.

I choose to burrow deeper.

The freak out can come later. Or not at all. It's not as if I need to worry about Dad bursting through the door. He has stepped foot in my room maybe five or six times since we moved here twelve years ago. And after last night, he wouldn't dare come near me.

Last night.

The events replay through my mind and land like punches in a boxing match: *the jab*—the confidence Bobby wore when he brought me in front of the crowd, *the cross*—the smug look he exchanged with my dad right before dropping the bombshell, *the lead hook*—the look on Dalton's face when Bobby announced our engagement, *the rear hook*—the argument that pursued after I told Bobby under no circumstances would I ever marry him, *the lead uppercut*—the even greater argument with Dad, and then there's the rear uppercut or in this case, *the knockout punch*—the slap across the face.

Not once has Dad ever raised a hand to me. But then again, I've never given him cause. I was always the obedient daughter. Little Miss Rule Follower. But I can't be here anymore—not after he crossed a line by trying to marry me off.

"Your body's tensing. Are you thinking about last night?" Sleepiness coats Dalton's voice and makes me smile. He isn't one to mince words. He certainly doesn't sugarcoat them. So this gentle, softer side he displays pulls at my heartstrings.

"How'd you know?"

"It doesn't take years of growing up together for me to know what your dad did is killing you." He begins to trace circles on my back. Even with the barrier of the T-shirt, his touch is soft and caressing. I start to relax. "Has he ever hit you before?"

"No." My answer must appease Dalton because he lets out a relieved sigh. Then, those dark brown eyes that make me melt open. Indecision swirls in his gaze.

"Your dad regretted slapping you the moment it happened. I could see it in his entire demeanor."

"That may be so, but he still did it."

"I know. I'm not trying to make excuses, and your dad's remorse doesn't negate the act, but at least he showed regret, unlike . . ."

"Unlike your father?" I guess when his voice trails off.

He glances away as if in shame. "I don't want to lessen your abuse by comparing it to mine." He lifts and brings his arm around to find my hand. Lacing our fingers together, he whispers, "I can't believe they ambushed you."

"You and me both." I think of my mom and wonder what she'd say about this. There isn't any way she would go along with this scheme. She may have been the perfect preacher's wife and dedicated her life to the church, but she wouldn't have agreed to that.

"You're tense again. Now, what are you thinking about?"

"My mom." My confession seems to startle him, but he recovers quickly. "I miss her."

"Tell me about her."

"She was a trooper. She volunteered for every cause within a hundred-mile radius. I used to tease her that she stretched herself too thin. But she was the most caring, generous, loving mom. Where my dad was the authoritarian figure, she was lenient. She used to fight my battles. I wanted to go to the homecoming dance my senior year. Dad was dead set against it. I already told you I couldn't date. Well, that ban extended to school dances as well. She told him since I was a responsible young lady, I deserved to be rewarded. It was his moral responsibility to trust that I knew how to act properly and decently." I chuckle, remembering the way Dad's face twisted with rage at how she backed him into a corner.

"Your mom sounds like a badass."

"Every once in a while, she could be. But she mainly served Dad and the Lord. I watched Mom suffer toward the end and wondered if she had been happy. Outside of being with me, I don't remember her acting happy." I reach for the necklace, but my fingers come up empty. I wore the necklace religiously but took it off after Mom passed. "I haven't been to Mom's grave since returning home from school. I can't make myself go."

"Maybe you should. It may help clarify some things. I've heard it can be therapeutic."

"Yeah, maybe. Do you believe in God?"

His breath hitches right before his lips flatten to a thin line. He's quiet, and I can practically hear his skepticism as he contemplates how to answer.

"It's okay if you don't," I say, rushing my words.

"It doesn't matter what *I* believe, only what you believe. If believing in a higher power gives you the peace you seek, then that's all that matters."

"I don't know what to believe anymore." Silence stretches between us before I finally admit, "I'm mad at God."

"Because of your mom?"

"*What if* it's his punishment?"

"Then I'd have to question, for what?"

"I broke the rules, and Mom got diagnosed with cancer. If I hadn't been rebellious, maybe God wouldn't have punished me and taken her away." My voice cracks at the end. I've never told anyone —not even Nicole—these thoughts. But they're what haunt me ever since I came home that summer. They're what make me doubt everything I've learned ever since I was old enough to comprehend. This doubt, this anger, is what made me take off the cross pendant. What kind of hypocrite would I be if I kept wearing a symbol that gives me nothing but doubt?

"No, Cassie, that's not—" He kisses the crown of my head and lets out a resonated sigh. "Are you referring to us having premarital sex?"

I close my eyes, knowing how bad this sounds and knowing that my self-doubt tarnishes our memory. "I don't want to ruin that memory, but part of me believes it's God's way of getting back at me."

"Cassie, plenty of people have sex, lots of sex, and bad things don't happen to them. You're taking way too much blame when nobody is at fault."

I nod but still find his words hard to accept. God failed me, but I failed him first.

"Look at this way. Your mom got diagnosed while you were gone. Chances are, the cancer was already taking hold before you even left. Before you met me."

My gaze meets him. "I didn't mean to imply that you were the reason."

"Shh." He cuts me off, but I know he feels hurt by what I said. I can tell by the slight shift in his demeanor. "I already knew I wasn't good for you."

"Stop. That's not what I meant at all. I made my choice, and I don't regret it. I regret God. Yes, I failed him, but he failed me too. The one time I needed him to come through for me, he failed."

"Is that why you took off your necklace?"

"Yeah. I didn't want to be a hypocrite. Daddy has all these plans for me. They all involve the church in some shape or form. But after I fulfill my commitment to Mom with this rummage sale, I'm done. After I graduate, I'm moving far away and working toward building my own future. One where I take care of myself. I hate this world that views men as superior and women as submissive."

"I picked up on that."

I suppose his statement shouldn't surprise me. The congregation's viewpoints are obvious to outsiders. That's the thing. I never thought about questioning their beliefs since I grew up with them.

"Yes. Who dares question the hierarchy? Even though that line is disgusting. Daddy believes it's the woman's right to cook, clean, and take care of the husband. Women were placed on the Earth to serve their leaders. Only men can be spiritual leaders, as said in the Bible."

"Uh, as much as I like the 'taking care of the husband' part, you know that's pure bullshit, right?"

"It's what I have been taught ever since I was a little girl."

His eyes widen as he opens his mouth, closes it, and then opens it again. "I can see how that message would mold your thinking, but

I don't believe that's true. I mean no disrespect to your dad, but I believe people cherry-pick passages and steer them into their line of belief. There are too many parables in the teachings to know the messenger's original intent. I don't believe that you must conform to some guy's will because you're a female. That's pure bullshit."

"It's hard to shift that thinking. I feel so weak."

He places my knuckles up to his mouth and kisses them, his gaze never straying from mine. "Do you realize you're the strongest person I know? There isn't a submissive bone in your body when it comes to me. You always stand up to me, and whatever crap I spew, you toss right back. What you need to figure out is why you can do that with me and not with others."

"Because when I'm with you, I can be myself. You let me just be me."

"You deserve to be happy. Don't let others knock you down."

I love this man so much. Leave it to me to fall for the guy with the most challenging path. But he's right. I'm done kowtowing to others. From this point forward, I'm going to start living for myself for once.

Bellow's bark vibrates through the door pulling me back to reality. "I better let him out."

"Should I sneak back into my room?"

"Stay. I'll let you know when Dad leaves. He'll be gone most of the morning."

A slow, easy grin crosses his face. "Don't forget about me."

"Wouldn't dream of it." I have plans when I come back that consist solely of Dalton.

CHAPTER TWENTY-NINE

CASSIE

I STEP FROM THE BATHROOM AND HEAD TO THE KITCHEN. I know Dad will be tied up with church duties this morning, and I want to get back to Dalton. Perhaps it's ill-formed to think about the naughty things I want to do to Dalton while Dad leaves to officiate Mr. Barley's funeral, but I've been a rebel lately. I may as well keep the streak going.

Bellow greets me when I step into the kitchen. The house is quiet—no sign of Dad.

"You need to go out, boy?" Bellow trots to the slider and wags his tail. I freeze as the creak from my bedroom door sounds down the hall. My gaze darts toward Dad's bedroom, but the door remains closed. I don't release my breath until I hear the bathroom door open and close. One crisis averted. Relaxing, I head to the patio door. "Here you go, Bellow." I step into the morning air and startle when the clink of glass sounds to my right.

Dad.

The grim expression he wears stirs my stomach. I have no idea what he's thinking. Regret? I somehow doubt it. Dalton seems to think so, but I haven't witnessed my dad regretting much of anything. He's more of a fire and brimstone type of leader. That must be nice to go through life without regret, equally so for having every demand followed. It's a certain privilege I would never know.

Only because you allow it.

Man, my inner critique can be so mean.

I turn away without saying a word and wrap my arms around my midriff. I wait for Bellow to do his business as last night's tension hangs between us.

It's suffocating.

After what seems like a lifetime, Dad sighs. It's just long enough and holds the right amount of guilt to draw my attention. Dad scrubs a hand over his tired face, and that's when I see it. The remorse Dalton was talking about.

"I owe you an apology for last night."

I stay quiet, not sure what part he's apologizing for.

"I should've never laid a hand on you and for that, I won't forgive myself."

I quirk an eyebrow, waiting for the rest. He sighs again.

"And I'm sorry for the stunt Bobby pulled. I thought I was doing you a favor."

"By forcing my hand in marriage?"

"I thought you loved him. I thought I was helping."

Maybe I should cut Dad some slack. I never voiced my intentions. From the outside, it appeared that I liked Bobby. Otherwise, the entire congregation wouldn't have been so happy and congratulatory.

"I haven't been the best at keeping up on your needs. I've been stricter than normal lately. Your mom would keep me in check. Without her around, I . . ."

"It's okay, Dad."

"No, it's not."

"You're right. It's not, but I should've told you I didn't love Bobby. I was never going to marry him. I did try telling him, but he wouldn't listen. But I should've been more open with you."

He pushes to his feet. "I have to leave for Mr. Barley's funeral. If you need anything, call. I'll be gone most of the morning."

"I'll be fine. Give my condolences to the Barley family."

He gives me a curt nod and stalks away. I let out a breath. I hadn't expected Dad to apologize, but it does make me feel better. *Somewhat.* Perhaps, we're making progress. Time will tell.

Bellow trots back to me. "You all done?"

That question earns me another bark and more tail wagging.

I chuckle. "All right, let's go inside."

Dad's gone by the time I step into the house. The bathroom shower is going, and a plan sparks to life. I double-check to make sure Dad's truck is gone. Once I'm in the clear, I march down the hall with determination.

Steam greets me as I push open the bathroom door. I close the door behind me and waste no time peeling off my clothes. I let them fall to the floor beside Dalton's shorts he had slept in last night. He'll never know how much I appreciated the way he took care of me. It was a small gesture, but sometimes the smallest acts of kindness have the biggest impact. I needed him last night, and he more than came through.

Naked, I step toward the shower, my stomach churning like those slushy machines in convenience stores. I think if I drank one right now, I'd throw up. I'm out of my element and feel perverted standing outside the linen shower curtain. I don't know what to do. Do I invade his space, slide the curtain open, and be like, *surprise, here I am?* It feels weird since we've yet to have sex since we reconnected. Well, the penetrating kind. Is it okay to have shower sex first? Does it matter if it's here or in a bed? I'm such an amateur at this. Why can't I be bold? Instead of surprising him, I settle on clearing my throat. Loudly.

CHAPTER THIRTY

CASSIE

"Cassie?" The curtain whips open. Dalton's expression goes from puzzled to a holy-cow-there's-a-naked-woman-in-front-of-me level of shock to pure appreciation. It's the latter look I love. I don't have a model-worthy body. I'm short and curvy. But I feel like the sexiest woman alive when he stares at me like that.

So what do I do? I wave lamely.

My seduction skills need some serious sharpening.

"I, uh, thought you might want some company."

His gaze peruses my body, and I watch his dick go from semiflaccid to hard. My breasts grow heavy. I've given a lot of thought to what I'm about to do. Maybe too much thought. But three years is a long time to think about repayment. I owe him this.

"Are you sure?" He looks past me and to the door. "I take it your dad left?"

"Yes, he'll be gone for a couple of hours."

His cocky grin slides into place as he pushes the curtain wider. "Hell yeah, I'll take some company."

I step into the tub, wishing we had a fancy walk-in shower that featured a bench and a wide-open space. Things I never thought of before. I never even cared. But that was before Dalton's large frame ate up the real estate. He's everywhere. He's consuming. And he's standing right in front of me, naked.

I suck in my bottom lip as water sprays upon his back. Dalton stares down at me with an intensity, I swear, clenches my insides and gives me all sorts of feels. But what I want to do isn't about me. I want this to be about him. Instead of moving, I stand still as he lowers his mouth to mine and kisses me with a yearning I feel in my soul. There has always been something magnetic between us. That's why I believed so vehemently about fate. When two people have this strong pull toward each other, how can destiny not be real? I may have given up the idea along the way, but each kiss, each stroke of his tongue, each brush of his fingertips solidifies my belief. Dalton and I are meant to be together. It's the how we have to figure out.

Before I lose courage, I drop to my knees. I never got the chance to do this to him back in Bellow Bay, and I always regretted it.

"Babe, you don't have to do this."

"But I want to." He has no idea how badly I want this.

Dalton sucks in a sharp breath when I cup his balls and wrap my lips around his dick.

"Seriously, I don't expect you to do this." His voice cracks when I pull back just enough to run my tongue around the tip and then take him deeper in my mouth. His head lolls back as the most delicious groan erupts from deep inside.

He weaves his fingers into my hair. My gaze flashes to meet his. Lust and desire greet me. He wants this despite his politeness.

I pull back just long enough to speak. "You don't know how many times I've pictured doing this." *Or how many times I researched how to give good blowjobs.* I must've known deep down that we belonged together. How could we not? Our appearances may be different, but our emotional scars are more similar than not. We're two lost souls that somehow found each other through the crazy.

"Jesus, this feels so good."

With his balls still in my palm, I squeeze a little tighter and then take more of his length. His hips buck, but I think more out of surprise than anything.

"We're really doing this?" His words come out breathy. My answer comes in the form of pulling back and then sucking in more. I work my tongue against his cock, keeping up the pacing of his thrust. He leans forward, bracing one hand against the shower wall while the other holds my head.

Warmth tingles in my belly. I never realized the natural high I could get from this, but it's a freaking turn-on knowing I'm bringing him to the brink of ecstasy. I bob my head back and forth, taking as much as I can as he fucks my mouth.

His groans. His forward thrusts. I love it all. I take a deep breath, adjust my jaw, and swallow his length.

"Holy shit, Cassie."

I pull back and massage his balls as I take a breath and then swallow him back down. The sound of water hitting the porcelain tub provides the background for his groans and heavy breathing.

"Babe, I'm going to come, and I really want to be inside you."

My thighs clench because I *really* want that too. But this wasn't supposed to be about me. It was for him.

He tugs my hair so I'll look up at him. "You wouldn't happen to be on the pill, would you?"

I nod.

He stills. "You are?"

I want to laugh at the disbelief in his voice, but my mouth is currently occupied. I'm the last person anyone would peg for taking birth control. Everyone besides Dalton thinks I'm a virgin.

I pull back and replace my mouth with my hand. "I take it to control my periods."

Dalton pulls me to my feet and flips me around. "Place your hands against the wall."

I do what he says.

His mouth lowers to my ear while he runs a finger along my seam. "You deserve to be fucked properly on a bed, but we're pressed for time. Is this okay?"

"Yes." Waves of anticipation ripple through me. This is more than okay. This is better than any fantasy I've concocted.

"Now spread those legs for me."

His fingertips brush against my clit, sending another shock wave through me.

"You have me so worked up that this will be hard and fast. Is that okay?"

I answer, "yes," but it comes out so jumbled. I nod to erase any doubt. He isn't the only one turned on. He grabs my hips and positions them to his liking. I gasp as he enters me in a swift motion. Even though I expected it, his swiftness caught me off guard. Good grief, does this feel full.

"You okay?" His voice strains as if he's holding back. As if he's afraid I'll break if he continues. I don't want him to hold back. I want him to move. I want it hard and fast as he promised.

"Yes. Don't hold back." Our first time started slow, and it worked then, but that isn't what I want.

He lets out a guttural moan, and then he moves, quick thrusts in and out. His hands reach for my breasts and cup them as I press my hands against the tile for dear life. He's so tall and I'm so short, I have to reposition myself until we find that perfect position. And once we find it, he drives in faster and deeper until I'm nothing but sensation and heat and putty in his hands. The man could ask for anything, and I'd hand it to him on a gold platter as long as he never stopped. It feels that good.

"Cassie, I'm not going to last." His words turn to moans as a chorus of grunts and skin slapping against skin fills my ears. His fingers work lower until they reach that special place that sends me over the edge. The slaps get louder. The moans get deeper. And then we're both climaxing and reaching that high. A few more pumps and swirls are all it takes until my body explodes into tiny molten pieces. His body jerks a few more times, chasing the last of our orgasms.

"That was . . ." His voice trails off. His breathing labored.

"Unexpected?"

"Incredible." He slips out of me, pulls me up against his torso, and rests his head on my shoulder. "You're fucking perfect, you know that?"

I shake my head. "No one's perfect."

"You're perfect *for me*."

I like that he added the phrase *for me*. I like that a lot. "We're perfect for each other."

He spins me around and kisses me. It's a soft kiss but an intimate one and says so much.

"How much longer do we have until your dad comes home?"

"Maybe another hour."

He lets out a tortured moan. "I want you for longer."

"I know, but Dad does have an all-day retreat on Thursday."

Dalton shoots me a wicked grin. "That's why he canceled practice."

The water turns cold, causing us to jump out of the spray. Dalton turns off the water and I screech.

We're laughing as we grab towels. Our eyes meet, causing me to pause. It's in the way he looks at me that stirs my insides. Without a doubt, I'm truly in love with Dalton Boyd.

CHAPTER THIRTY-ONE

DALTON

"You were a beast." Carter slaps his gloved hand against my shoulder as Javier high fives me.

The roar of the crowd fades in the distance as we walk further into the tunnel leading to the locker room. It's Wednesday night, and we just won our fifth game in a row.

"The look on the pitcher's face when you hit the three-four pitch and it sailed over the fence was priceless," Carter says.

"He totally wasn't expecting that," Javier says.

"He underestimated my strength, but I showed him who's boss." It's a cocky statement, but I reserve the right to make it. I had one hell of a game. I brought the team to victory. No, back up. I *helped* get the team to victory. Everyone played their role well. "You had a great game too," I tell Carter. "That throw you made to second base was masterful."

The play was close. The runner pushed off first to steal the base, but Carter snagged the wild pitch and threw to second with razor-sharp accuracy. The runner wasn't too happy with the call, but he was out.

"Thanks. I've been working with the coach, and he has helped hone my skills. I can't wait till we start the Wildcat season. We're kicking ass this year."

I smirk. It'll be tough without Braxton and the crew, but we should hold our own. "We'll show off our talent."

"Damn straight, we will."

The spirits are still high once we've showered and dressed. I reach for my phone and notice a missed text from Shannon.

"You coming, Boyd?"

I glance at Carter. "I'll be right behind you."

Shannon: *Heads up. I'm coming Saturday. You better be ready.*

I can't stop the smile from breaking across my face. I could use a dose of Shannon. I could get her advice on my situation with Cassie's dad. She knows most of our story, but she'll tell me how to approach Coach.

Me: *Sounds great. I'll send you the address when you get here.*

Shannon: *Awesome. See you Saturday.*

I place the phone in my pocket and step out of the locker room, but raised voices echo down the hall, stopping my progress. That's new. No one starts arguments on this team—not where Coach could overhear. Intrigued, I march down the corridor with every intent to put a stop to it before Coach finds out. But as I round the corner, it's not two teammates going at it. It's Jason and an older version of him. A woman stands off to the side looking uncomfortable. I duck back behind the corner before either of them notices me.

"We didn't fly in to watch you sit on the bench. You're better than this. What the hell happened?" The guy, which I'm guessing is Jason's old man, is clearly upset, but his face isn't red and blotchy, like my old man. Jason, though, he is devoid of emotion. Is that what I look like to most people—jaw clenching, wanting to stand up for myself but the unwilling to do so since the consequences are worse? But I have no way of knowing if his dad is the same level of asshole as mine.

"Coach usually plays us both. This was the first game I didn't play."

"And it just happened to be the game we watched?" He scoffs as if Jason's lying. But Jason is telling the truth. We usually do share playtime. I was surprised Coach kept me in the entire game. My bat may have been on fire, but that hasn't stopped him before. My chest tightens as a foreign feeling capsizes my gut. Why the hell am I feeling guilty? I don't ever feel guilty for getting playtime. This is Coach's fault for making me care.

"Should I cancel our flight for Saturday? There's no point in coming if you're nothing more than a bench warmer."

"I'll get to play."

"Are you putting in one hundred percent? I told you not to lose focus. This isn't a time to slack. You need to—"

"Dad, I've put in the work. I'm trying here, okay? I'm doing my best."

"Try harder."

There's a pause before I hear a frustrated growl followed by, "I'll meet you at the hotel." Footsteps pound against the concrete, but I only hear one set. A female sigh resonates down the hallway.

"I know you have his best interest at heart, but must you be so hard on him?"

"He has wanted to play ever since he could hold a ball in his hand. He's talented. I'm just trying to make him live up to his potential."

"But you're pushing him away from the goal, not closer."

"It's the only way I know how to be with him."

"I know it's hard, but sometimes you need to tuck the coach in you away. Remember, you're a dad first, then a coach."

"I just want him to succeed."

"And he will. Or he won't. It's on him."

"You're right. I'll talk to him."

Fuck, his dad really is a good one.

My insides clench at the obvious regret in his long exhale. Jealousy mixed with a hint of intrigue consumes me. Not once has my dad ever shown remorse. Jason has no idea how lucky he is.

I don't know what comes over me. An illness maybe? Or have I lost my damn mind? Yeah, that must be the reason. Temporary insanity is the only sensible explanation for turning around and marching straight to Coach's office. But I know what it's like to be a constant disappointment. I know what it's like having a dick of a father. I know how it feels to not be loved by the guy you're supposed to look up to. Jason may not realize it, but that isn't what he is going through. He has a decent father who obviously cares but just goes about it wrong. His dad wants him to succeed. And these reasons are why I'm not surprised to find myself knocking on Coach's door.

"Come in," the gruff voice belts through the door.

Yep, I've completely lost it, I think right before I walk in.

"Dalton, what can I do for you?" Coach hides the surprise on his face and motions for me to sit. I oblige.

"Can you start Jason in Saturday's game?"

He leans back in his chair and tosses his pen on the desk. "Is there an injury I'm not aware of?"

I clench my teeth as I straighten my stance. Asking for this favor is a lot harder than I realized. I could fake an injury as a cop out, but then I risk Coach catching me in a lie. There have been enough of those floating around. I go with the truth. "His parents will be here to watch him play. It would mean a lot to him if he was to start and ease the tension from his dad."

Silence stretches over the longest pause in history. I'm not the fidgeting type. Usually, nothing bothers me, but Coach's constant assessment has me needing to refrain while tiny sweat beads break across my forehead.

"You know scouts are going to be present?"

I take in a long, deep breath and slowly release it. I did not know that, and now, I want nothing more than to take back my words, but this is beyond me right now. Playing in Saturday's game would mean everything to Jason. He needs a shot. The same shot I need, but I'll get another opportunity. I hope.

"That would be even better for him. Not to mention how it would make his dad feel." *Which better be nothing but pure joy.*

Coach's eyes widen in disbelief. "I have to say, that's highly unselfish of you. And I'll take that into consideration."

"Our opponent's record is on life support. I doubt we need my bat." What am I doing? He gave me an out. I did my part. Why push it?

"I'm impressed you did your homework." Coach tilts his head, his gaze growing more intense. "I'm proud of you."

There it is. That stupid fluttering in my gut. It doesn't last long. Coach wouldn't be proud if he knew his daughter's mouth was wrapped around my dick last Monday. But as generous as I feel today, I'm not confessing. "Thank you, sir. Jason's a good guy."

"That he is."

I turn to leave. With my hand on the door handle, he adds, "The same can be said for you."

For the first time in my adult life, tears prick my eyes. I swallow back my emotion and mumble, "Thank you, sir."

And then I get the hell out of there.

CHAPTER THIRTY-TWO

DALTON

IT'S THURSDAY. CASSIE'S DAD LEFT EARLY THIS MORNING FOR the all-day retreat while Cassie had to help her cousin and aunt clean out their garage—a commitment she had forgotten about when she made plans for us. I didn't mind her going. If anything, I was relieved. Not that I don't want to have sex—quite the opposite, actually—but since I've yet to talk to Coach about getting his permission to date Cassie, I feel guilty. He told me yesterday he was proud of me. Sneaking behind his back when I'm starting to gain his trust seems wrong. It isn't settling well with me.

We need to slow down until I can talk to him. But what if he says no? And face it, he more than likely will. Will I have the willpower to stay away? Essentially, that's what I'd have to do. And that answer is a huge hell no. But damn, it would be nice not to sneak around. I hate having to hide the fact that I want her.

This boxed-in, cagey feeling had me so worked up I took an extra-long run. It hadn't eased my mind any. I had to find something else to distract me, which was why when Cassie came back home, she found me in the garage with my ass in the air.

"Now that's a view I can get used to." Her melodic voice causes me to smile.

"Like what you see, huh?" I glance over my shoulder and

chuckle at the blush coating her cheeks, but I don't miss the heat brewing in her eyes. I turn my focus back to the car and tighten the bolt a couple more turns. As much as I'd like to ditch the project right now, leaving it loose would be problematic.

"There'd be no denying that."

"I feel objectified," I tease and then straighten back up, tossing the wrench onto the nearby bench. I turn to face her and lean against the grill.

She smiles. "Should I apologize?"

"Never. You can do whatever you want with my body. I'm all yours." *So much for taking it slow.* My gaze drops to her body as she saunters toward me, determination etching her features.

"That's good. Because I can think of a few things I want to do."

"Yeah?"

She stops within a foot and nods. Her gaze glances behind me, seemingly pausing the seduction scene as she takes in the car.

"Wow, you've made good progress with this car."

Pride swells in my chest. I take in the '57 beauty and smile. For the car that has caused irrevocable harm to my family's reputation, it pleases me to rebuild the engine. "There isn't much left to do. Thankfully, your dad had all the parts and tools."

"Does it run?"

"I'll be able to test that after a few more man-hours. But your dad's garage is a mechanic's dream. He has everything, including the portable hoist." There isn't any way I could've dropped the engine in without it. My dad would split a nut to own one of those.

"You're so talented." Appreciation coats her gaze. My chest tightens from the sincerity in her delivery. She believes that. Believes in me.

"I just finished what your dad started."

"All my dad did was disassemble everything. You're the true brains. Brawn and brains. What a powerful combination." She steps closer, heat flaming her blue irises.

"You're not giving your dad enough credit." I'm pushing my

limits by teasing her but toying with Cassie is fun. And she doesn't disappoint.

Cassie unbuttons her blouse, starting at the top. Holding my gaze, she says, "I don't want to talk about my dad."

"No?" A slow seductive smile creeps across my face. My girl's patience is running out.

"Nope." She reaches the last button and slides the top off. Her red lacy bra exposes those generous tits, and my dick thickens. He obviously doesn't have any scruples.

"What do you have in mind? To talk about, I mean?" I haven't made a move toward her. I kind of like this seduction scene she has going on. She has no idea how sexy she is right now.

"I think you know exactly what's on my mind. And it doesn't involve talking." She proceeds to unzip her shorts and slide them over her curves.

Holy shit, there's no denying her—not when she stands before me in nothing but matching lingerie. I tug my T-shirt up and over my back. My heartbeat hammers wildly in my chest. Cassie closes the distance between us and wraps those dainty arms around my neck. When she stretches to her tiptoes, our mouths collide. All my nerves and guilty feelings dissipate as if they were a forgotten memory. The fight between right and wrong no longer exists. Her lips upon mine feel too damn good for this to be wrong. There's a hunger to her kiss—a desperation as if we're each other's last breath. Each other's lifeline. And maybe we are.

I lift her by her ass. She weighs practically nothing as her legs wrap around my hips. I nip at her bottom lip. She runs her hands through my hair, grinding against my rock-hard cock. It's so fucking solid that I'm surprised it hasn't ripped through my jeans.

I can't wait any longer. I have to be inside her. I carry her to the backseat of the car. It's less than ideal, but it's the only viable flat surface.

"Would you rather go to your bedroom?"

"No. No more interruptions. No more waiting. I want you now."

I smile at my greedy girl. "One day, we won't be rushed. Soon, we'll have all the time in the world."

"I like that. But right now, all I want is you."

"You have me." Kissing the underside of her jaw, I work to remove her bra. My fingers never leave her skin. The soft brush of my fingertips leads to slight teasing. Her nipples pebble, the peaks too tempting not to suck. I give her breasts the attention they deserve while skimming my hands along her sides.

God, I love this woman. She has no clue what she does to me. It was an instant attraction when I saw her for the first time. But the more time I spend with her, the more I know she's who I want to spend *all* my time with. My fingers slip beneath the edges of her underwear, and I tug them down. If I'm going to fuck her, I need to get her ready. I slip a finger inside her. Holy shit, she's soaked already. Yeah, there's something to be said about anticipation.

"Babe, you're so wet." *And wanting.*

"All I thought about the entire morning was your dick."

"I-I . . ." I don't know what to say, so I don't say anything and shove another finger inside her. Talking is overrated. And far be it for me to make her wait.

She gives an appreciative moan. I start pumping faster and lower my lips to her clit. I brush my tongue against the sensitive spot, and an orgasm hits her without warning.

"You needed that, huh?"

"Uh-huh," she mumbles, clawing at the zipper of my jeans. "I need more."

"You got it." I climb out of the car and toe off my shoes. I remove a condom while unzipping my jeans. I was reckless the last time by not using one. I can't make that mistake again. The last thing I want to do is thwart her future. There are enough men in her life dictating to her. She doesn't need any more people in her life trapping her.

My jeans and boxer briefs join the floor. Standing in nothing but my socks shouldn't be that sexy, but the way Cassie stares at me makes me feel like I deserve a cover spot on *GQ*.

I climb back on top of her and settle between her legs. "You mean the world to me, Cassie." Before she can answer back or question what I mean, I enter her slick wet heat. I have to stop to catch my breath. She feels incredible. She feels like home, but a good home with chocolate chip cookies and genuine love. Jesus, why am I thinking about cookies while being inside her?

I press my lips to hers and get lost in the way we feel together. I move in and out, each thrust a silent promise to be a better person for her.

I hold her stare as I take in her flushed cheeks, the want in her eyes. My need for this girl is layered in so much more than heat and passion. I want a lifetime with her. To obtain the happily ever after she dreamed about since she was little. And I promise to give it to her. She deserves every little fantasy she has concocted in her gorgeous head.

Her leg slides up my back, and that slight move brings me back to the gorgeous girl beneath me. I rock my hips forward, increasing the speed. I want her to come with me, but I'm not in a good position to touch her clit.

"Show me how you pleasure yourself."

She gasps at my demand but snakes her fingers between us and does what she's told. *My avid rule follower.* But damn, if she isn't hot.

"Yeah, just like that. You look so damn sexy."

Her eyes grow darker and heady with want. I can tell by the uptick in her panting she won't last much longer. The pressure continues to build until neither one of us can take much more. She comes undone beneath me. I bring my mouth to hers, chewing up her moan. I slip over the edge and ride out the orgasms as her pussy squeezes and milks every last drop from me until there's nothing left to give. I remain on top of her, refusing to pull out just yet. I wrap my fingers around her neck and trace my thumb along her cheek and jawline. I want to stay in this blissfulness forever— me inside her, her staring up at me as if I hung the fucking moon.

CHAPTER THIRTY-THREE

CASSIE

"I'LL NEVER TURN DOWN HELP FROM A FINE YOUNG MAN SUCH AS yourself." Ms. Willow's flirtatious vibe reverberates off the block walls inside the church annex, drawing Nicole's and my attention. We stand slack-jawed in the back of the room, watching in awe as the seventy-five-year-old openly flirts. Dalton picks up the floor lamp she more than likely doesn't need and flashes her a smile. She pats his arm, and . . . wait, did she just bat her eyelashes at him? I *knew* the old lady had a thing for him when we picked up the chaise lounge.

I glance at Nicole, and we burst into giggles.

"You better watch it. Someone's gunning for your guy," Nicole singsongs.

"Who knew taking out a floor lamp would be grounds for getting hit on? Poor guy." The morning rush from the rummage sale has passed, and Dalton's muscle has been a tremendous help. Well, he and a couple of guys from the team he recruited to help. I contribute a lot of today's success to Dalton. Without his help, I wouldn't have gotten people checked out as fast. The other guys left to prepare for tonight's game, but Dalton stayed behind, waiting for his college friend to arrive.

"I'm not going to lie. Lover Boy does look rather sexy."

My gaze peruses Dalton's body as he enters the annex through the glass door. It isn't the clothes themselves that make him sexy. It's how he carries himself. He's relaxed and exudes confidence. Sure, it doesn't hurt that the heather gray T-shirt fits snug across his broad shoulders and biceps. Every time he lifts something, I want to run my hands along his corded muscles, knowing how they work to please me. Nor does it hurt that those ripped jeans I love are slung so low that I want to push them farther down and devour what I know they hide. Warmth floods my cheeks when my gaze meets his. Thinking dirty thoughts of what I can do to him while doing God's work goes against everything I'm taught. No wonder lust is a deadly sin. But that doesn't negate how my body buzzes with a need he can more than fill. That desire bubbling inside couldn't care less where we're at. It just wants him to satisfy it.

"Looks like Lover Boy is coming over."

"Mm-hmm," is all I manage to say.

"Girl, you have it bad. You better not be in the same room with him when your daddy's around. There is no hiding that lustful look you've got going on."

"You're insane." I bite my lip and straighten the scant pile of clothes scattered across the table. I need to keep my hands busy. Otherwise, I'd fidget, and Nicole would make fun of me even more.

"I don't think so."

"There isn't a special look." But as the words leave my mouth, my eyes betray me as they continue to watch Dalton's approach. I get lost in his features. He's so handsome. But then, he notices me staring and smiles. All of that physical appearance disappears, and I'm left seeing the little boy who just wants to be loved. But I also see the man who turns me into the best version of myself. I love that he demands that I stand up for myself. No other man in my life has ever done that.

"Where do you need me next, boss?" There's a slight tease to his tone.

"Ms. Willow finally release you?" My lips twitch.

"She hinted for me to go home with her, but I politely refused. Although, I'm sure she could use some help getting the lamp inside the house. The lamp's taller than her."

"She wanted help, all right," Nicole says. "But it wasn't for the lamp."

I choke on a laugh. "Nicole!"

Dalton's grin widens.

"What? He's probably the only reason she showed up today."

"She might've mentioned something along those lines." Dalton stands taller and puffs out his chest.

"Who would've thought a seventy-five-year-old would be my competitor." My eyes bulge at my admission. I glance around to see if anyone heard while Nicole laughs.

Dalton leans down to grab a rogue sweater from the table. The movement places his mouth by my ear. "When it comes to you, there's *no* competition."

Chills chase down my spine.

"Nice save, Lover Boy." Nicole pats his arm as she walks by. "I'm going to get the boxes from the car. We don't have too much to pack up." She turns to me out of his view and wiggles her eyebrows. "Have fun."

"You were right. This was a madhouse." Dalton straightens to full height and looks around the annex.

"The community's very supportive. But thanks to social media, our reach extends a few hundred miles. As you can tell, we sold most of what we had, including the furniture. We should surpass our goal."

"I'm impressed, Miss Greenburg." He steps into my space, closing the gap between us. My heart rate kicks up a notch. I should back away. If anyone saw us, what would they think? But instead of creating the much-needed distance, I stay stagnant as his stare holds me captive.

"The summer will be smoother from now on. There won't be so many distractions."

"I can think of a few distractions."

My cheeks flame again. "Hmm, maybe working together is a bad idea."

"Why's that, Choir Girl?"

"I'm not doing a good job hiding what you do to me." *Or what I want you to do to me.*

His breath hitches. "What am I doing to you?"

Making me think dirty thoughts while in church. Well, while on church grounds, but all the same. The air around us ignites. The noise level drops to a low hum. A streak of red flashes down the hall, but I ignore it. No one else matters right now. "I have a feeling you already know the answer to that question."

"*What if* we went and found an empty room?"

Tempting. So darn tempting.

"Then I'd be scandalized if caught."

"I'm willing to take that chance if it means stealing time with you." His gaze drops to my lips, and I swear my undies are soaked all the way through. What this man does to me. It's positively sinful.

I'm about to cave and take him up on his offer when a female voice shouts, "Dalton Boyd."

Dalton steps back as if caught stealing signs from the opposing team. Our heads snap to a tall blonde whose arms are tossed in the air as she runs toward Dalton.

Dalton steps toward her. She practically leaps into his arms, and he swings her around. This must be Shannon, the college friend he told me about. When he mentioned their friendship, he failed to mention how close they were. An uncomfortable pressure swells in my chest. It's as if I'm jealous. Which makes no sense. I don't have any right to be, nor do I have a reason. He told me they were friends. It's just, I didn't expect her to be so tall and pretty.

I've been living each moment as they come and haven't looked past this summer. But it won't be long until Dalton will leave. He'll be back at college, surrounded by girls. Lots of girls who'll come in all shapes and sizes, including tall, pretty girls like her. My stomach lurches. Suddenly our future seems very bleak.

After a quick exchange of *hellos* and *how are yous*, they break apart. Dalton seems to remember me standing there.

"Cassie, I want you to meet Shannon Smith. Shannon, this is Cassie Greenburg."

"It's so nice to meet you finally." The girl pulls me in for a hug, and my saucer-sized eyes shoot toward Dalton. He smirks and shrugs unapologetically. "I feel as if I know you already. Dalton talks nonstop about you."

"Oh," I manage to say. I really don't know how to respond. *He talks about me?*

"It's not that often." Dalton looks around. "And you may want to keep your voice down."

"Sorry. I got carried away. I'm just so excited to meet you and to see this thug." She turns and smacks Dalton on the arm. "I just wish you were playing."

"You're not playing?"

Dalton gives a hard glare to Shannon before turning back to me. "I'll explain later. Come here, Shannon. I need to show you something." He whisks her away before I can ask why he isn't playing and why he hasn't told me. He's never kept secrets from me. At least, I don't think he has.

"Can't you see what being with him brings?"

I whip around to the voice and come face-to-face with Bobby. "Where'd you come from?" *And what did you hear?*

"I wasn't going to miss your big day."

Then why did you show up toward the end? I clamp my jaw closed tight to keep from vocalizing my thoughts. He actually has the audacity to look offended.

I ignore him and glance behind me. Dalton has stopped to show Shannon the chaise lounge. It sold, but the couple who purchased it didn't have a truck. They're coming back on Monday to pick it up. Shannon laughs at whatever Dalton says. I have to admit, they look comfortable with each other. It's obvious they know each other well. To an outsider, they seem like a couple. They certainly look good together.

"Don't you get it? People like him don't have the same values as us: family, faith, core values. They will always choose themselves over anyone—even God."

"Quit trying to pretend to know him. You know nothing about him," I huff and move to the next table to condense the piles. Where's Nicole with those boxes?

"I know his type. You'd do yourself a favor by realizing the truth before you're left tainted."

"Tainted?" I repeat. "What does that even mean?"

"You're a good girl, Cassie. Act like it." Bobby shoves past me and heads back down the hall.

I scowl at his retreating red shirt. Maybe I should warn Dalton that he overheard us. I turn to walk over toward him, but he's already gone without so much as a goodbye.

I chew on this fact. Am I trading one dependency for another? Will Dalton choose himself over me? Will he leave me? Is he even the type that could settle down?

Gah, I'm letting Bobby's words and my insecurities grab hold. Dalton isn't completely selfish. And the part that is he can't help. Who wouldn't be given his circumstances? He has good inside him. I know it. He's just caught up with a familiar friend. I can't fault him for that.

CHAPTER THIRTY-FOUR

DALTON

"OH MY GOD, DALTON. SHE'S WAY TOO CUTE." SHANNON LEADS me to her car. We just left the church annex. I hated leaving Cassie behind with the mess to clean up, but the baseball game won't wait. It sucks I won't be playing, but I still need to be dressed and ready in case Coach decides to put me in late.

"Did you like her? I know it was brief." It's not that I need anyone's approval, but Shannon's opinion means a lot to me. Out of all my friends from Cessna U, she's the only person who knows me. And she still doesn't know me as well as Cassie does. Cassie knows all my family's dirty secrets. The ones I've kept hidden so well from my friends.

"I do. I'm pretty good at reading people." She gives me a side-eye glance as we hop into her car. "I read you pretty well back when we first met."

A smile stretches across my face. "I did like driving your brother and Noah crazy. How are they, by the way."

She waves me off. "They're fine. I don't want to talk about them. I want to talk about your new love."

I laugh at the way she draws out the word love. "There's not much to talk about."

"What's the address to the ballpark? I'll type it into the GPS."

I rattle off the address. "Sorry about having to head straight to the ballpark. I wanted to stay at the rummage sale and help as much as I could."

"That's fine. You know the ball field is my second home." She smirks. Having a brother and a boyfriend in the minors solidifies that statement. She grew up watching them play ball. "Quit changing the subject. Spill. What's been going on? I take it by the way you guys acted, her dad still doesn't know?"

I shoot her a glare. Miss Big Mouth almost blew our cover. "You've heard the rumors. He'd rather shoot first than ask questions later. So, yeah, it's on the down-low for now. But I want to talk to him and ask his permission to date."

"Hmm. How do you think that will go?"

"Terrible." My laugh turns into a groan. "He's going to fucking kill me."

"And you still want to try?"

"I don't think I have much choice." It'd be different if this were a fling, but I want it to last beyond summer. Just like I wanted the last time.

Shannon purses her lips as if in thought. "Cassie's good for you."

"Oh, come on. There's no way you can tell from that brief encounter."

"No, I'm serious. She's totally right for you. You've changed."

"I've changed?" Skepticism edges my tone. I haven't changed.

"Yeah, you're more at ease. I don't know. You seem happier." She turns when the GPS tells her to. "It's a good look on you."

"You're nutty." I may reject her words, but I know they hold truth. I am happier. It's as if the darkened state I've been living in is lightened somehow.

"How are you going to approach her dad?"

"That's the million-dollar question. I'm not sure how, but I want to confess everything to him. Even the part about knowing her before coming here."

"You think admitting that would be a good idea?"

The question hangs in the air right as we drive by the church. It's as if the universe is sending me signs. I hold in a laugh. Cassie's rubbing off on me, having me believe in fate and serendipity moments.

"It's the only way to have a future with her."

"Is that what you want? A future with Cassie?"

I shouldn't. I don't see how it could possibly work, but it seems so dark and cold when I picture my life without Cassie. She breathes life into my existence. Can I have fun without her? Of course. Playing ball has always fulfilled me. Do I want to have fun without her? Hell no. I've tried both ways. Life is way better with her in it.

"Yes. I just need to convince her dad that I'm worth it." *When we both know that I'm not.*

"You never told me why you aren't playing today."

A smile edges its way in. "Is that a question?"

"I'd like an answer," she says, laughing.

"The other first baseman's parents are here this weekend. His dad didn't get to see him play the last time he was in town. I overheard them talking, and his dad sounded upset. I figured if he started today's game, his dad would be happier."

"And you told this to the coach?"

"More or less. I asked him to start Jason since his parents would be here. I left out the part about his dad being upset."

Her face softens, and I can't quite read her. "Then he already knows how good of a person you are despite his preconceived ideas."

"I don't know if it's going to be enough."

"Do you love her?"

"Yeah, I do." It feels wrong admitting that to Shannon when I haven't told Cassie yet. But it's how I feel.

"Then I guess she's worth the trouble."

That she is. I just need to come up with a way that we all win in the end.

Needing to redirect the subject from me, I ask Shannon about her summer. "So tell me how *Glamour Project* went." *Glamour Project* is LA's version of *Project Runway.* The show aired a special edition where they picked one representative from the art department of colleges across the United States to compete in their show. Shannon represented Cessna University.

"It was amazing,' she beams. "Even though I didn't win, the experience I had and the connections made are surreal. I met some of the top designers. I'd name them, but you wouldn't know who I was talking about."

"Yeah, you're right. Nike and Under Armour are about all I know."

"Those are brands, not designers." She rolls her eyes. "Anyway, there's one who really liked my designs. He offered me an internship at his company next summer. And it's a paid internship, so not a free labor type deal."

I laugh. "That's great. I'm so proud of you."

Her smile drops. "Yeah, the only problem is it's in Paris."

My eyebrows raise to the roof. "France?"

"Yep."

"What does Noah think about this?"

She scrunches her nose. "I haven't told him. I'm not committed to the job yet."

"But that would be a waste to turn down. And it's only for a summer, right?"

She winces. "To start. He made it seem like it could lead to greater things." She gives me a side glance. "I have a year to think about it."

I wonder what I would do in Noah's position. If Cassie were offered a fabulous opportunity in a foreign land, I'd be excited for her but also sad to see her go. Long-distance relationships suck, but it's something I'll have to get used to, given our situation.

"It's great they saw your potential."

"I know, right?" Her smile is back in place, but it doesn't quite reach her eyes. "I can't wait for school to start. I'm ready to get back at it."

I sit back in my seat as she pulls into the stadium. The end of summer is fast approaching which means saying goodbye to Cassie. I'm not ready to leave her yet. And that reinforces my need to talk to her dad. I just have to come up with the right approach and let the consequences fall where they land.

CHAPTER THIRTY-FIVE

CASSIE

"SHANNON IS REALLY NICE." THE BASEBALL GAME ENDED, AND we're leaving the pizza joint after saying goodbye to his friend. It's been a successful day. The rummage sale raised about three grand more than our goal, and to top off the day, the Crushers won. The only downside was watching Dalton sit on the bench for most of the game. I met Shannon in the stands, and we had a heartfelt talk. I can see why Dalton likes her, and it's obvious how much in love she is with her boyfriend. I was stupid to let Bobby instill doubt. It's like Nicole said, he doesn't have my best interest at heart, only his.

"She really liked you." He nudges his hand against my leg and rests it there.

"Yeah? She surprised me at first. I didn't realize she knew who I was."

His eyes avert mine as he glances out the passenger window. "I, uh, may have mentioned you to her a time or two."

Oh my goodness. I'm not sure what I like more, the fact he mentioned me to her or the way his dimple just popped. Hands down, he has the cutest boyish grin. I love bringing out this softer side from an often brooding man.

"She talked about her brother and boyfriend quite a lot. It's cool they're both playing in the minors."

"Yeah, Braxton and Noah were my roommates. That's how I got to know her. Noah grew up next door to them. The three have been connected forever." His hand fans out across my thigh. I try not to melt under his touch, but it's too hard to ignore what he does to my body.

"That's sweet. It seems they're pretty serious."

"Oh, yeah. Shannon's a year younger than us, so she still has two years left at Cessna U. I bet as soon as she graduates, he'll put a ring on it. Maybe before."

"I'm sure Braxton is thrilled." I mean that in a good way but Dalton's low deep chuckle suggests Braxton may not be.

"He is now, but it hasn't always been that way."

"What do you mean?"

"Noah wasn't a guy Braxton deemed good enough for his sister."

"What?" My eyes widen as I turn left onto our street. "But she makes him sound so perfect."

"He is, but Braxton had a front row seat to Noah's hookups. He never took any girl seriously, except when it came to Shannon. He had a weak spot when it came to her. That was obvious the first day I saw them together. How Braxton didn't see it, I'll never know."

"So Noah never acted on it?"

"No. He stayed away mainly because of Braxton. He had other reasons too, but he didn't want to ruin his friendship with his best friend, which is stupid."

Stupid?

"What do you mean? I'm sure Braxton was like a brother to him. Shouldn't he put family first?" Our house comes into view, and Dalton slips his hand away. I miss the warmth of his touch.

"Not when it comes to getting what you want. Family lets you down at some point."

Hmm. I concentrate on pulling into the driveway. Bobby's

words replay in my head. *"People like him don't have the same values as us. They will always choose themselves over anyone."* I thought those words were plain bullshit, but hearing Dalton confirm what Bobby said doesn't settle well. I open my mouth to ask what he means but stop when I notice Dad in the front yard examining the roses. He hasn't paid attention to Mom's rose garden since I've been back.

"How was the pizza?" Dad's voice beams.

"Good as usual." I smile back at Dad, a little perplexed by his good mood. It must be due to the win.

Dalton holds up the leftover box. "We brought you home some."

"Thanks, if you could place it in the kitchen, I'll be in a few minutes. I was just looking over these roses. They need a good pruning."

My eyes dart across the front yard to the two years' worth of overgrown shrubs, the weeds popping through the rocks, and the rose bushes housing too few blooms, probably due to the lack of pruning. A pang of sorrow pinches my chest. Landscaping was Mom's job until she could no longer take care of things around the house like roses and gardening. I glance around the landscaping and try not to cringe. Things looked nicer when Mom took care of them. Maybe I should've come out here more to help.

I swallow past the lump in my throat and nod. "It'll be waiting for you."

"What's the matter?" Dalton asks the moment we're inside. He always picks up on my mood shift.

"It's silly." I grab the pizza box mainly to have something to do and place it on the island.

"It doesn't seem silly if it's upsetting to you."

I sigh. "It's just, Mom used to tend to the landscaping. The bushes and flowers always looked pristine. Now, it's . . . different."

"Hey." He pulls me into a hug, and I let him. I'm so confused. How can he not care about family, but yet show me so much affection? Doesn't he realize that I would become his family if things progressed between us? I'm jumping ahead of myself and overthinking. Dalton is good underneath. I know this. I'm giving Bobby's words too much real estate in my mind.

"Hey, look at me."

I tip my head back far enough to meet his eyes. He tucks a curl behind my ear. The brush of his fingers grazing my skin sends chills down my spine.

"Life changes, but what matters is what is in your heart. That's where the memories are kept."

And he always says the sweetest things.

"Can you sneak into my bedroom tonight?" I blurt out. I'm not asking for sexual reasons, not really. I mainly want him to hold me. I want to wake up in his arms.

He hesitates. "I should talk to your dad first. We've been lucky so far, but—"

"We can talk to him tomorrow," I interrupt. "Please? I just want you to hold me."

His eyes hood over, and he squeezes a little tighter. "You know I can't resist you."

He's about to kiss me when the door handle jiggles. We quickly break apart before Dad enters. It's going to be a long evening. But Dalton's right. We need to talk to Dad. I can't stand hiding what I feel about him. It's not fair to either of us. Dad isn't going to be happy, and I have no idea what he'll do. That's why I want to wait until tomorrow. I want one last night of him holding me before my dad tells me to stay the rest of the summer with Nicole. Dad isn't going to be happy, but he won't stop me.

CHAPTER THIRTY-SIX

DALTON

THIS IS CRAZY. MY HEART POUNDS AS I WAIT FOR THE SLIDE OF the patio doors. Coach will take Bellow out, which creates the perfect opportunity to sneak into Cassie's room. Once the door slides shut, I dash into her bedroom. I close the door behind me and fidget with the handle, trying to find the lock.

"There's no lock." Cassie's voice says through the darkness. *That can't be good.*

"You're positive he won't come in here?" I step toward her. I know sex is on her mind, despite what she said, but my only reason for being here is to hold her. I promised myself I wouldn't touch her. I was serious about wanting to talk to Coach before doing anything else. The guilt is tearing me up. When we came back from the pizza joint, he seemed the most relaxed I'd ever seen him. He also never left our side all evening, so I exited to my room early. But he's finally treating me like a normal human being. I don't want to jeopardize that until our talk.

"Quit worrying. He never comes in here. The missing lock is a safety feature in case of a fire." The night light cast a soft glow over Cassie's silhouette. Her hair shines. She stares up at me with dark and sultry blue eyes. My dick comes to life. My promise is only hours old, and it's already in jeopardy.

I move to her bed and pull back the covers. I hold back a groan when I discover she's naked. All my blood runs south. *Shit.* This isn't good.

"Just to hold you, huh?"

She blushes. "I changed my mind."

"I just don't want to get caught. Not until we talk to your dad." I slide in beside her.

"We'll talk to him tomorrow, I promise." She sidles up against me. "But no one said we have to be saints until then."

"Cassie, I—" I stop speaking when she grinds against me. My dick hardens to full mast, pressing against my shorts. I can't help but tug her closer. My hands run along her silky skin. It's a good thing I didn't bring a condom. There's no way I'd restrain.

"Shh. No more talking." Her lips press against mine, and my will snaps. Kissing isn't bad. I can handle kissing. I can even satisfy her if that's what my girl wants.

The kiss starts out slow and sensual. I explore her body with my palms, perusing every inch, every single curve.

"I want you." She goes to lower my shorts, but I stop her.

"I don't have a condom." This causes her to pause.

"You didn't bring one?"

"No." What I thought was an ingenious idea turned into the worst decision since the Cubs traded Javier Baez. I mean seriously, who gets rid of their team's spark plug?

"Hmm, it's a good thing I have some."

"You do?"

"Yeah, Nicole set me up."

Fuck me.

She backs away and slides her bedside table drawer open. When she pulls out a strip of condoms, I can't help but laugh.

"You're going to be the death of me." I pull her back to me. "Come here, you little vixen."

Our mouths collide, and it's not soft. This kiss holds heat and desperation. I shove my shorts down, glad to be going commando.

I tug the shirt over my head and toss it on the floor along with the shorts.

When she's back in my arms, I take my time exploring. I do love her, but it's way too soon to tell her. I made that mistake last time. I don the condom and pause, staring into those gorgeous eyes full of heat and want.

"You know I can't deny you. I'll give you anything you want." And then I slip inside her and all the worry, all the pent-up frustration, and all the negativity leaves. This right here just feels right. I can't explain it. She feels like we're always supposed to be. I shift to move. Slow pump in. Slow slide out. She's perfect. And she's mine. When I told her about family always leaving, I meant my family. I could never leave her. The way she's looking up at me, I know she wouldn't leave me either. We'll figure out a way to be together. I suck on a breast, her back arching to give me more. I take it because I want more. I want her everything. I want to be her everything. We haven't talked about what happens at the end of summer, but we'll figure it out. We have to.

"Dalton." My name is a whisper on her lips. Emotion swirls in her eyes. I continue my pumps. I swirl my hips. She feels so damn incredible. I weave our fingers together and press our hands into the mattress. This connection we have is more than real. It's hard to explain what I feel for this girl.

Heat starts building in my lower belly, and I know I won't last too much longer. I lower my free hand and rub her clit. She lets out a moan.

"Dalton, I'm going to come."

I get lost in the way her body writhes beneath me that I don't hear the slight knock on the door. I'm too busy chasing her orgasm with mine to notice the jiggle of the door handle. I'm so high on Cassie and post orgasm bliss to register the creak of the door.

"What the hell are you doing?" the deep baritone voice booms across the room.

Aw, fuck.

I slip out of Cassie and make sure she's covered. Her body quivers as she shrieks. "Daddy, what are you doing in here?"

"You"—he points a finger at me—"get packed. I can't believe I trusted you."

Cassie's saucer-sized eyes look at me. I mouth "I'm sorry," as I pull away. *Fuck. Fuck. Fuck.* The look on Cassie's face is so stricken I want to fix this, but I don't know how. I sweep the clothes from the floor and hide my junk with the condom still on. Coach's eyes stray to me, and I swear steam flares from his nostrils. I really did it this time. I hold my head down and move to pass.

When I brush past his shoulder, he murmurs, "Pack your things and book a flight. You leave tomorrow."

I don't say a word and nod.

I royally fucked this up.

Once I'm in my room, I grab my phone and search for tickets. I know what needs to be done, but the fuck if I don't like it.

CHAPTER THIRTY-SEVEN

CASSIE

I'VE NEVER MINDED GOING TO CHURCH. IN FACT, I RATHER enjoy it, or I had for most of my life. But not today. Today, I couldn't wait to get back to Dalton. He hadn't joined us. I didn't think he would. But he hadn't left his room all morning which means we haven't had a chance to talk. I owe him an apology. He wanted to wait until we talked to Dad, and I didn't listen. I put my selfish needs first and ruined another person's career, just like I did to Malcolm. He may have graduated, but my impact wasn't positive.

Dad pulls into our driveway, and I dart from the truck the moment Dad slides the gear into park. I no longer care what Dad thinks. My only goal is to talk to Dalton. I fly through the front door and glance around the kitchen and living room. Empty. Why am I not surprised? But the house is completely silent. A sinking feeling edges its way inside. I beeline down the hallway and knock on his door.

More silence.

"Now, Cassie, don't think you can defy me. I order you to go to your room."

Orders me? I am not some little girl. He doesn't get to order me around anymore. I wrap my hands around the door handle and shoot Dad a glare. Then I burst into Dalton's room.

But I don't get far before the emptiness hits me. My stomach lurches, the small muffin I forced myself to eat threatening to cough back up. My gaze flits to the area where his suitcase had been laid and then to the bed that was made for the first time since he arrived. Realization hits, but I refuse to accept it.

No, no, no. He couldn't have left.

I scan every inch of his room in search of a note—for some sort of goodbye—but find nothing.

"I forbid you to . . ." Dad doesn't complete that sentence when he registers Dalton's absence.

"You forbid me? I'm a grown adult, Dad. I can do what I want."

"Not while you're under my roof. You will not defy the Word or me."

"Save it. He's gone. Are you happy?" I toss my arms up in the air like a lunatic. I shove past him and march to my room. Maybe he left a note here? A certain sentiment? Anything? He wouldn't have left without saying goodbye, would he?

Family or friends always leave at some point.

Bad boys never stay. They don't have the same morals.

Warnings flash through my mind, pieces of truths I want to reject. Dalton wouldn't do this. Would he? How could he? He said he would never leave.

"Cassie, listen to me. Can't you see what happened here? You tossed your relationship with Bobby away over some unruly boy who will never amount to anything."

Back to Bobby? I thought I made myself clear on that point.

"You don't know what Dalton's capable of. You've seen his talent. You've seen his potential. He just needs a freaking break." My bottom lip trembles as I shove my shaking hands through my hair.

"Don't raise your tone with me."

I scoff. "Or what? You'll force me into a marriage I don't want?"

"Know your place."

"Oh sure. My place. And where is that exactly? Following some God that teaches not to judge people? I think you should heed the advice you spew out every Sunday. You stand up there every week and preach about love and respect, but you don't apply it to people in actual need. You know nothing about Dalton. You sent him packing and home to an unstable environment. His dad abuses him. Did you know that?"

"Come on, Cassie. Wake up. The boy would say anything to play upon your emotions. His endgame was to get you to bed."

"You're wrong. My endgame was to get him in bed. He tried talking me out of it."

My dad cringes. "That's because he manipulated you with a sob story. You have a kind heart, and he took advantage of it."

"A sob story? I *witnessed* the abuse with my eyes! He tried making excuses, but I saw the bruises. I saw the hard slaps. I heard the foul language belittling him, and you sent him back there. If anything bad happens to him, I'll never forgive you."

I push past him and head straight to the garage. The garage is my last hope of finding Dalton. Tears sting my eyes. I can hardly breathe. I dial his number on the way, but it goes to voicemail. *Don't freeze me out. Not like what I did to you.*

"Cassie, wait," Dad says, trailing behind me.

I shoot him a glare that says, don't mess with me and step into the garage.

Darkness greets me, and I want to scream. He's gone. He actually left without saying goodbye. A vice grip constricts around my heart. I fight back the threatening tears and flip on the light. The '57 chevy sits in the middle of the room, gleaming under the fluorescent lights like it just came off the assembly line. Pristine and put together. He must've come out here last night and finished it. My heart squeezes a little more.

On top of the hood sits the keys. No note.

I turn and glare at my dad. He stands there slack-jawed. "Yeah, he's a real selfish bastard."

CHAPTER THIRTY-EIGHT

DALTON

I HITCH THE STRAP OF THE TOTE BAG HIGHER ON MY SHOULDER and stare at the rundown house. A sickening feeling swirls in my stomach. Not much has changed since I've been here, other than the yellow paint has faded and chipped away more. I grab the handle on my suitcase and proceed forward. I may as well face my dad now.

Quietness greets me, followed by a raunchy stench. I don't miss being here, that's for damn sure. I bypass the dirty dishes filling the sink and scattered across the counter and head to my old bedroom. I never wanted to step foot in this house again. But I should've expected it. When you're a colossal fuckup like me, it's bound to happen.

It doesn't take long before I hear the old man stumble inside. Great, he's already drinking.

I tried going somewhere else. I got a hold of Garret last night to ask about his parents' house, but they're on vacation. The old job I held between summer league ball and school wasn't available to me this year. Without money to stay in a hotel, my only choice was to come home. I should man up and call Cassie to check on her. But I don't. I can make excuses all day long—her dad would find out I called and get her into more trouble, or she's better off without me—but the truth is, I'm too chicken to find out if another person I love abandoned me. She surely realizes by now how better off she is without me in her life. I don't think I can stand knowing she wouldn't want me around. So, I took a page out of her notebook and blocked her number, even if the move gutted me.

I change into my running gear and step out into the living room. Dad startles when he sees me.

"What the hell are you doing here?"

"I'm back."

He scoffs. "I always knew you'd blow your chance."

My hands ball into fists, but I press them into my thighs. My jaw clamps tight. Talking back now would only fuel the fire. It wouldn't help.

"Yep, give a man enough rope, and he'll hang himself." He laughs menacingly. "I'm not surprised. You screw everything up."

I want to say not everything. I want to tell him about fixing the '57 Chevy he supposedly broke. It wasn't Dad's fault, but fixing the car that ruined the already broken family gave me some sort of restitution. It felt good having accomplished something. If all fails, I guess being a mechanic won't be so bad. I don't necessarily have to work in my dad's shop. There's a need for mechanics all over the country.

"It doesn't matter. I'm back now. You got your wish."

"You're worthless."

"Yeah, well, I'm here." I breeze past him and head out the back door. The door slams behind me but not before I hear Dad mumble to himself, "I knew he'd screw up sooner or later."

My feet hit the pavement, and I run. I try to clear my mind with the wind on my face, but every repressed memory crashes forward. The houses blur as I remember Steve picking me up at school and walking me home. He tried making it seem like it wasn't a big deal that Mom was late. But then we walked into the house, I learned what a big deal it actually was.

"This is your fault." Dad's face turned red as spittle flew from his

mouth. I'd seen him angry, but I'd never seen him this angry. He pointed a finger at me. "If you weren't a little bitch boy, she wouldn't have left."

"Dad," Stevie pleaded, but his attempt to calm Dad down only fueled Dad's anger.

"Don't you try and coddle him too. That's his whole problem. That bitch coddled him ever since he was born." Dad leaned down and got in my face. Pure disdain etched his features. "Look at ya. Red, swollen eyes. You're nothing but a little pussy. You've always been needy. You're the reason she took off. You drove her goddamn crazy."

"Dad, that's not—" Steve didn't get to finish talking because Dad smacked him aside the head like he did Mom. Steve stumbled back a few steps, his eyes wide with fear.

"I said shut up."

I couldn't help the tears that slid from my eyes. I tried to hold them back, but the harder I tried, the more I couldn't. I drove Mom away. I made Dad mad. I couldn't do anything right.

"Look at you cry. You disgust me."

That was the first time my dad hit me, but it wasn't the last.

CHAPTER THIRTY-NINE

DALTON

It takes great restraint not to tug at my polo shirt as I wait to visit my brother. Dressed in my Sunday school best, I spin my ring to keep my mind occupied. Fidgeting around armed guards would be frowned upon, I'm sure, and the last thing I want is to draw any more attention than necessary. Part of me wonders what I'm doing here in the first place.

A week has passed since I left Baytown. I haven't reached out to Cassie. I wanted to. I wanted to apologize. But what can I say? Her dad will never accept me, and despite what she thinks, she will never leave him. She loves him wholeheartedly. He's the only family she has left, and I won't be the one who steps between them. *No regrets. No remorse.* I won't let Cassie choose between her family or me. Whether or not she realizes it, she'll regret that decision and end up leaving me anyway.

My body tenses as the correctional officer steps into the room. I raise my head in anticipation, but he calls some other family member. I close my eyes and take a deep breath, but it's useless. I'm too keyed up. I haven't laid eyes on my brother for two years. Guilt sinks in. I've been on the approved visitor's list since Steve's incarceration, but I've never utilized the privilege. I never intended to until now. I need answers as to why he's in here. I need to find out if the reason he's in here is because of me. If Dad is correct and he did this all for me, I need to apologize. I haven't heard from the Wildcats coach. I can only assume I'm off the team, and I can kiss my scholarship goodbye. And that means everything my brother did that landed him in jail was for nothing. I close my eyes to the tan block walls surrounding me. A tiny baby cries in the corner of the room. The mom leans over and whispers coddling sounds. The seconds on the wall clock tick by. I tamp down the jittery feeling clawing up my spine. It's almost time.

"Mr. Boyd, you can come this way."

I stand and follow the correctional officer to the visitation room. It's another sterile place with tables set far enough apart for privacy. The officer shows me to my seat. Once settled, my eyes draw to my brother approaching the table. Nothing could have prepared me for the sight of him dressed in orange. Guilt washes over me. Shame for taking advantage of my life while he spends time staring at these block walls. Not that I haven't worked hard, but I certainly never gave any thought to his living conditions. Both times I've seen him, he wore a suit to his parole hearings.

His face has hardened, but emotion swirls in his eyes when they connect with mine.

"Brother," Steve says as he sits.

I swallow past the sudden lump of emotion lodging in my throat. I've lost my train of thought as to where to begin. It's not like I can ask how he's doing. How fucking lame would that be?

"It's been a long time," I state the obvious.

Lines form between his brows. "Why aren't you at summer ball?"

Our gazes connect. I hadn't expected him to be so . . . I don't know, aware? But here's my big brother still putting me in my place. I swallow hard.

"I messed up." *To put it lightly.* I want to blame Cassie. If she hadn't asked me to visit her that night or if she hadn't begged me for sex . . . If, if, if. But the truth is I wanted her. I could've refused her if I didn't want to risk it. Regardless of whether Coach caught us, the fault wasn't hers. It was mine. She hadn't forced me into anything. I took what I wanted willingly. No one is to blame but me. These revelations were all things I worked out while on my jog.

"Is it fixable?"

Steve doesn't ask what I have done. He just jumps to the solution. I've missed that about him. Too bad he couldn't fix his own situation.

"I don't know. I'm still waiting to hear from the school. Once I talk to my coach, I'll know more." I drop my gaze to the table. "I, uh, slept with the coach's daughter."

Steve lets out a long exhale and shakes his head. "Of all the available girls, why her?"

"I love her."

"Then that's what you lead with." He sits back in his chair and eyes me. "But what is the reason for coming? I doubt it's to seek relationship advice."

I let out a humorless laugh. "No."

"Then what is it?"

"Was I the reason you stole those items?"

His eyes narrow. "Why would you think that?"

I don't want to answer him. I don't want to admit that he's strong, and I'm still weak, letting Dad get under my skin. Steve saw me run to my room and cry too many times than I like to admit. After Mom left, the tears dried up, at least until I was alone in my room. "I need to apologize."

"For what?"

"For failing."

"Dalton, I only want to see you succeed. You know that, but there are other things to do if college isn't your thing. You're good in the garage."

"Yeah, but if I get cut from the team, that means you being here was all for nothing."

"What do you mean?" He narrows his eyes again. Earlier, I

thought he was just trying to goad me, but I don't miss the confusion written on his face this time.

"Dad said you were stealing to raise money to pay for my college."

"Is he still on your case?"

"Things haven't changed." That's mostly true. He hasn't tried to hit me. I overshadow him. I've gained muscle while he drank his away.

"Listen. I made my choices. They had nothing to do with you."

"But—"

"No." He puts his hand up to stop me. "Being in here is all on me. I was in it for the thrill and the escape. You're not the only one Dad mindfucked. Stealing had nothing to do with your college. That's just his excuse to try and justify my wrong."

"I miss you, Steve." I hadn't meant to say it. I didn't want to say anything that would make him feel worse after our visit. But the words flew out of my mouth before I could stop them because, damn it, I do miss him. His words should be freeing, but they're not. I still feel like shit.

"I miss you too, bro. More than you know."

"Why does Dad hate me so much?" The lump in my throat sits there, garbling my speech. Steve's mouth flattens to a frown as defeat coats his eyes. He looks conflicted. It's as if he knows but doesn't want to tell me. I stay still, barely breathing, while anticipating his answer.

"I've had a lot of time to think while being locked up, and I have a theory." Steve pauses as I watch the war brew inside him on whether or not to tell me. He must see the desperation on my face because he closes his eyes momentarily before speaking. "I wonder if he thinks you're not his."

I wasn't ready for the blow to my chest. It's as if the burly guy over to our right kickboxed me in the chest. The more the thought festers in my mind, the more it makes sense. He's hated me ever since I can remember. He rode my ass more than he ever has Steve's.

"If that's true, then why did Mom leave me with him?"

"I assume because she had her own demons to fight."

My mind fogs from too many entities tugging at me. I can't think clearly. Maybe Cassie's right and I do need to talk to a shrink.

CHAPTER FORTY

DALTON

THE WAVES CRASH TO THE SHORE, BUT THERE IS AN EERIE stillness in the air. It feels like the moment before an impending storm where the air is charged with palpable energy. The kind of storm that leaves no one in its wake. Steve's earlier assumption about Dad weighs heavily on my mind. I lean against the pillar under the dock with my friend Marty and try wrapping my head around everything: Cassie, baseball, Dad—if he's even my dad. What if he's not? Would it make a difference? I somehow think not. It may even be a relief. I was going to confront him when I got back, but I found him passed out in his recliner. It made sampling him easier though. The fucker never even moved when I swabbed him.

"You want a hit?" Marty asks, pulling out a blunt. I almost smirk. Leave it to my friend to never change.

"Sure." *I have nothing to lose.*

"Have you heard anything from your coach yet?" Marty's referring to Coach Callahan from Cessna U.

"No, but I'm sure they kicked me off the team." Although I find the radio silence strange. I figured my old coach would've called by now to let me know either way. His silence is killing me slowly.

"So what now?"

"I guess I'll become the 's' in Boyd's and sons." If the parental testing kit I sent off comes back as a match, that is. Otherwise, who the hell knows?

Marty winces. "Isn't there something you can do? Some open tryouts or something?"

"What's the point? I may have had excellent stats, but my attitude kept me from getting drafted. Do you think getting kicked out of summer league improved that image?"

"That sucks, man. You don't have an attitude. Not really."

I laugh and take another hit before passing it back. "Yeah, but I wasn't a team player either." If Coach Greenburg taught me anything, it was that I certainly didn't get along with teammates.

Laughter from a volleyball game draws our attention. It isn't lost on me that I was standing here the first time I saw Cassie. She was a vision. I had no idea how much that girl in a French bikini would impact my life. I think back to the day I went for my run and crashed into her. Our first conversation was her scolding me. Then she got on that ridiculous bike. She was so damn cute. Her charm entranced me that day, and I've been hooked ever since. I glance up at the overhead boards. I miss her smile, the way she sasses back at me, and how she always sticks up for me. I miss the blissfulness on her face after she orgasms. That sight never gets old —especially the last time. Anxiety plows into my chest like a freight train thinking about our last night. Reality hits. I'm never going to see her again.

"Bro, you don't look so well. You that worried?"

"Nah, it is what it is." I'm fucking crushed, but as much as it kills me not to play ball, it's nothing compared to the hurt of losing Cassie. The thought completely terrifies me. I can't admit that to Marty though. He wouldn't understand.

"Or does it have more to do with the girl?"

Damn observant asshole. "Nah. That's a lost cause."

"But you love her."

"What do you know about love?"

"Me? Nothing, but you? You gave up everything for that girl—your college of choice, the opportunity to have a killer year, and now your baseball career. You seriously going to tell me that you don't love her?"

"Yeah, you're right. I do love her."

"And you're willing to let this setback stop you from being with her?"

"I don't have a choice." My pitch rises higher. I don't mean to get mad, but what is he getting at? That I'm purposely choosing not to have Cassie in my life? I can't be with her and she's better off without me. Those are facts I can't change.

"Now that's where you're wrong, my friend." He takes a hit from the blunt. "You always have choices. Your choice is to give up."

I stare out into the ocean, wondering when my friend became so philosophical. As much as I want to push back, he makes a good point. Maybe I am choosing to give up. Maybe I'm not much better than my dad, choosing the easiest path. *No regrets, no remorse.* Were they just words I said and only applied them to playing ball? Was I not applying them to actual life?

I'm about to answer, but my phone rings. My heart practically stops when Coach Callahan's name flashes across the screen.

"Hello?" I answer, standing taller.

"I heard you're having a hell of summer." Coach Callahan's dry tone doesn't ease my nerves.

"You can say that."

"Give me one good reason why I shouldn't kick you off the team and pull the scholarship for the stunt you pulled."

"Sir, I have no excuse. Cassie and I have a history." I'm not delving into what our history entails. It's not his business. It's not anyone's business but ours.

Silence eats up the phone, and I want to run into the ocean and let the waves carry me away with my chances of staying on the team.

"Consider this your second chance. We've decided to suspend you for the first game."

"You're allowing me back on the team?"

Marty gives me a side glance. Blood rushes in my ears. I don't know if I heard him right.

"As far as I'm concerned, you never left. You're one hell of a player, but attitude is everything. We're used to dealing with over-inflated egos, but we don't like bad sportsmanship. We're a unit. Family. We play together. That's the lesson you were supposed to learn while staying at Greenburg's house."

I wince. I was a team player, all right, but that was for team Cassie and me.

"And that's what Coach Greenburg said you learned when he told me I'd be a fool not to take you back."

"He said that?"

"Don't get me wrong. Nolan's not your number one fan, but he said you're one heck of a baseball player, and any team would be lucky to have you. That I already knew."

My heart expands at the compliment. "Thanks, Coach."

"I expect you to report for weight training in August."

"Yes, sir. I'll be there."

A weight lifts from my shoulders as we hang up, but the relief that should follow it isn't there. I don't feel any better. I'm getting everything I want. Why don't I feel better?

"You're still on the team?" Marty's voice cuts through my thoughts.

"Yes."

"Thank fuck for that." He studies me for a beat, no doubt wondering why I'm not elated. But considering our previous discussion, I'm sure he already knows. I miss Cassie. I love her, and I won't be happy unless we're together. Jesus, I've messed this up.

I take off walking toward the truck.

"Where are we going?"

I spin the ring around my finger, each step with determination.

"The pawnshop."

"Wait, what? You need money?"

"Yep.'

"What the hell for?"

"A plane ticket."

"To get to school?"

"No. I'm going to see Cassie."

"You just found out you're still on the team. Why the hell would you risk losing your chance?"

"I told you before. I won't live a life of *what ifs*."

CHAPTER FORTY-ONE

CASSIE

I CLUTCH THE BOUQUET OF WHITE LILIES TIGHTER AS MY GAZE roams across the expanse of the cemetery. The morning fog lays thick and heavy, giving an eerier vibe than usual. I sigh deeply. Fighting the urge to retreat to my car, I trek across the drought-conditioned grass. Each crunching sound of my footsteps is a stark reminder that everything, including the flowers in my hand, dies. The visit is long overdue, but I couldn't make myself come sooner. Being here makes Mom's death real. Finalized. And that's what I hate most—the finality of it all.

Pushing forward, I think about my grandma. Of how she'd wake at the crack of dawn, pull her too-long hair into a bun, and truck to Grandpa's gravesite every day with his favorite donut. She'd place it on the headstone when she left. I always wondered who or what ate the snack because, according to Grandma, it never survived the night. Dalton said visiting loved ones can be therapeutic, but I have a hard time believing him. How can visiting a final resting place be reassuring? It's too heart-wrenching for that.

So, despite my reservations, I took a page out of my grandma's handbook, got ready, and drove my little fanny here.

I approach the black granite slab. It's a slanted stone. Dad passed on the upright one, stating it was too flashy. "We don't need anything elaborate," he had said. Then, he quoted 1 Timothy 6:6-7: Godliness with contentment is great gain, for we brought nothing into the world, and we cannot take anything out of the world. After he finished, I wanted to roll my eyes. I was so sick and tired of him continually being *on* instead of just being. He was always a preacher first but what I needed was a dad.

I stare at our namesake etched across the top center. A sprig of roses is engraved above each upper corner. Dad had wanted gaudy angles, but I talked him into the roses. I had argued that the large cross with supersized prayer hands in the center bottom should be the focal point. After all, the cross symbolized their religion—a statement he wanted to be passed on even in death. He agreed. But truthfully, my reasoning was selfish. I couldn't stomach a headstone littered with religious symbols. Where were the angels when I asked for a miracle? Where was God?

I crouch down beside the stone and replace the dead flowers with fresh ones. A humorless laugh escapes. It's just another reminder of how all things die. I sit there and absorb the peaceful surroundings. The dawn's chorus chirps in the distance, bringing a sad smile to my lips. I immediately think of Dalton. If he were a bird, his chirp would be the loudest and strongest, protecting his territory.

"I miss you, Mom." I look to the heavens, tears stinging my eyes. "I'm so mad at God for taking you away. Why do we pray for healing when it doesn't work? I feel so lost." I draw in my legs and wrap my arms around them, adding, "About everything."

A single tear slides down my cheek. What I wouldn't do to have this conversation in real-time. To have her with me again.

"I could really use your advice. I messed up. Remember the boy I met that summer when I stayed at Aunt Jan's? The one I got in trouble over?" I pause as if letting her recollect who I'm talking about. "You had told me I had a different path to follow. That if we were truly part of God's plan, we'd be together again." *Kismet.* "I know that was your gentle way of telling me to get over him, but guess what? He did come back, and we did get back together. Until I ruined everything."

Dalton hasn't called. Can't say that I blame him. I took his dream and smashed it like a cheap flower vase no one cared about. But I never expected to be shut out. Maybe it's his way of making sure I stay on the right path according to my dad, but Dad doesn't have all the answers—only God.

The realization hits. Was it God's will that brought Dalton back into my life? Had he not abandoned me after all? A few days ago, Dad questioned if I had lost my faith. I still see the hurt in his eyes when I told him the truth. Instead of repeating another Bible verse as I expected, he nodded and reached out to pull me into a hug. "Oh, Cassie," was all he said. I guess that was his way of being a dad for once.

But what if God did send Dalton my way. That would mean I'm not a lost cause. I feel as if it's my duty to help people. But maybe that person that needs help right now is me. I need to get over my pity party and fight for what I want. It's way past time.

I push off the ground, eying the headstone. "Thanks, Mom. I know what I need to do now."

Hope swells in my belly for the first time since forever. I guess Dalton was right. Visiting a loved one who's passed can be therapeutic.

I head back to my car, my thoughts consumed with Dalton. He makes me a better person. He challenges me. I would have never had the courage to confront Dad. Heck, I'd probably be engaged to the wolf in sheep's clothing if it wasn't for Dalton.

I'm so engrossed in everything Dalton I don't notice the person standing by the car until I'm upon them.

"Bobby?"

CHAPTER FORTY-TWO

CASSIE

BOBBY STANDS BESIDE MY CAR WITH HIS ARMS CROSSED OVER HIS chest. He watches every movement of mine, but there's a distance to his stare. It's as if he's dejected. A pang hits my chest, but I don't want to feel sorry for him. He brought this on himself. By his actions of late, how would I know if he's genuine or vying for my sympathy? Nope, I won't fall for it, nor will I cower to him.

"What are you doing here?" I ask when I approach him.

"Your dad told me where you were."

"It's a bit intrusive to show up, don't you think?"

He frowns. "I waited by the car."

You could've waited at home. I tamp down my anger. It's best to remember Bobby started as a friend.

"What do you want, Bobby?"

"I want to know why you suddenly dumped me for a . . ." His lip curls in disgust, but he doesn't finish that sentence. And in true Dr. Jekyll and Mr. Hyde fashion, his mood shifts from sad to angry.

I scan the surroundings. No one is close or nearby. An uneasiness creeps up my spine, but I don't understand why. It's not as if he'd do anything nefarious. Bobby was a friend who got me through some of my darkest days. He wouldn't hurt me. I shake off the feeling and move toward my car door. "If you can't be civil, we have nothing to discuss."

He shoves his fingers through his hair and keeps them there. "Tell me why you threw us away? I deserve to know that much."

Deserves to know.

My bullcrap meter just filled up and spilled over. I snap, no longer holding back. "I *tried* talking to you. You wouldn't listen. You cut me off. When I did talk, you minimized what I said. You told me how I felt. Gee, I wonder *why* I would want to end our relationship?"

"That's not true."

"But yet, it is. I told you I didn't want to work as a missionary, and you said it was just my nerves. I'm not nervous; I just *don't* want to go." I let out an exhausted sigh. "I'm not even going to touch the stunt you pulled at your welcoming party."

"I thought all you needed was an extra push to snap you out of this funk." He tugs at his hair that's still woven in his fingers. "Your dad is all for it."

"My dad doesn't decide who I marry. And a funk, really? I'm still missing Mom. Coming home this summer to her being gone is freaking hard. Have you ever considered that? So, no, I'm not in a funk. At least, I wasn't until . . ." I don't finish my thought because I'm certainly in one now.

"Until Dalton left?" he guesses.

I nod, looking at the ground. I hate hurting Bobby even though he deserves it. He's not completely innocent in this.

"You really like this punk?"

"He's not a punk. He's a sweet, caring guy."

"He's broody and standoffish."

I shrug. "Not with me."

And that's the truth. Dalton has been nothing but a gentleman to me. When he was mad, he still treated me with respect. I still wield power over him just as he does with me. We blend in a *Beauty and the Beast* kind of way—he, the brooding bad boy; me, all wide-eyed and innocent. Somehow, we work past the differences and click.

"That's real cute, Cassie."

"It's the truth, but even if he had never come into the picture, I still wouldn't marry you."

"But what about everything we talked about? You're just going to throw it all away?"

I feel like a broken record, constantly replaying my words. I don't know how to phrase it any differently. "This right here is why. You don't listen. You have this image of what a perfect housewife is supposed to be. It's not the same image as me. It never was. I told you that last year before you left for Peru."

"No, you didn't."

"Yes, I did. When we sat outside looking at the sky before you left, you mentioned it would be us going next time."

"Yeah, and you didn't say a word about not wanting to go."

"Do you even remember what I said?" When he stares at me blank-faced, I fill him in. "I told you that wasn't my dream. Do you remember what you said after that?"

His lips flatten. "You could've been more assertive."

"You told me you knew what my dreams were. You then went on to reassure me how great it'll be once we get there."

"Still. You could've—"

"No, I wasn't going to get into a huge fight right before you left. But when I tried breaking up, you still wouldn't listen. I tried multiple times the night you came back. You kept interrupting. I made it clear when we went out for dinner. You turned around and told everyone I accepted your proposal. Look, I'm not going to rehash it again." It seems like we're starting round three of the same song and dance. "I'm sorry if you feel like I led you on, but I did try telling you."

He studies the ground for a beat before turning his sorrowful gaze toward mine. "I thought we had something here."

You thought you found a good submissive.

"People in love listen to each other, Bobby. They don't try to

233

control the narrative, and they certainly don't try to control the other person. What we had wasn't love."

He tips his chin up and looks toward the heavens, not so much in a *Lord give me strength way* but more like *I messed up how can I correct this* way. When his gaze returns to mine, his voice is full of regret. "I should apologize."

"Can we just move forward? You'll always be my friend., but friendship is all I can offer."

Hurt or maybe shame coats his eyes, but then his chin juts as his body straightens. "The guy used you. He got what he wanted and took off."

I hate that he knows we got caught. Dad must've told him. My personal life isn't his concern. I may have offered an olive branch, but I didn't offer the entire tree. Why can't he accept the fact we're over and move on?

"Dalton took off because he was forced to."

"I can't believe you gave in to his will."

I gave in to his will a long time before now, but I'm not going to get into that. That's not Bobby's business. I don't justify that remark with an answer and glare instead.

"Has he even called?"

My bravado breaks into tiny shards that stab my heart—reality stings.

"I didn't think so," he scoffs. "I hope you know what you're doing." Bobby shoulders past me, leaving me alone.

"No, but I'm going to try," I say to no one in particular. A plan formulates, one I've thought about for a while but never dared to follow through until now. I hop in my car and take off toward Nicole's house. I need the internet to implement my plan. I let the conversation with Bobby go. There isn't anything else to say to him, but I'm glad we talked. It was long overdue, just like taking control of my life.

And that starts now.

CHAPTER FORTY-THREE

DALTON

"North Magnolia Avenue," the Uber driver announces my destination.

My gaze wanders to the stone and stucco ranch-style home. I mumble, "Thanks," but I'm not quite sure the driver heard it over the butterflies scraping and clawing like wild beasts in my stomach. I climb out of the woman's Mini Cooper, half tempted to beg her to wait for the sole purpose of being a witness to my slaying. I have no idea what kind of reception I'll receive from Mr. Greenburg.

I hitch my duffle bag higher on my shoulder and press forward. My sixth-grade teacher always used to say, "There's no better time than the present." He was referring to our homework, but it works in this case too. I take a calming breath and ring the doorbell, my mind racing with various scenarios: Cassie angry at the sight of me, Cassie happy to see me—this was my favorite one, Cassie reluctant to see me, and then the worst one—

"You have some nerve showing up here."

Of course, it would be the worst scenario—Mr. Greenburg peering down his nose at me. He looks about as impressed as a scout watching a supposed upcoming pitcher hurl mediocre sixty-five mile-per-hour fastballs. Bellow barks excitedly at my feet, wagging his tail. At least someone is happy to see me.

My mouth suddenly feels dry, but I stand my ground. "Sir, I owe you an apology."

Mr. Greenburg eyes me for a moment as Bellow weaves between my legs, continuing his happy barks. Coach shifts his gaze to the dog and sighs. When he steps back to let me in, I resist the urge to punch the air and yell halle-fucking-lujah. But this invite into his home is a significant step. I wasn't sure he'd let me through the door.

Coach motions toward the kitchen. "You want anything to drink?"

"No, I'm good," I say, even though my mouth feels like sandpaper. With the way my hands are shaking, I shouldn't have liquids. I honestly can't remember when I've ever been this nervous. I follow him into the kitchen, dropping my bag near the couch along the way. Bellow's bark subsides, but he remains by my feet when we reach the island. I pick him up and place him on my lap as I settle into the cushioned bar stool. Coach fills a glass with water from the faucet. When he turns back toward me, I clear my throat. "I need to start by being honest with you."

His right eyebrow lifts, and I regret not taking that drink. I need something to keep my hands busy. I settle on petting Bellow.

"I originally met Cassie three years ago when she visited Bellow Bay. I regret not being upfront about that when I first arrived, but I honestly didn't know how to handle it. I, uh, went about it all wrong." *As I do most things in life.*

His eyes narrow as he studies me. It's his constant assessment that drives me crazy. I never can read what he's thinking.

"I figured as much."

That grabs my attention. "How?"

"Cassie told me after you left, but I had suspected before that. Jan never put a name to the boy Cassie was sneaking around with. She only said he came from a dishonest family. The only family she ever trashed was the one who *ruined* her car."

"We didn't ruin—"

He puts his palm up to stop me. "Believe me, I was in the

middle of fixing it. *Eh*, more like over my head with it, but I could tell by how the engine was blown it was my sister's fault. After I saw your determination to fix the car, I put it all together."

I slump back in my chair as my chest lightens. It feels good to have someone finally believe us about that damn car. I'd be more relieved, but I still have another barrier to overcome. I somehow need to convince him to let me see the girl I love. "I still should've been upfront. And for that, I'm sorry."

"So you came here to apologize?" His hand curls around the glass he has yet to take a drink from.

"Yes, and to ask permission to date your daughter."

"You're willing to risk everything—your college admittance and your baseball career—over my daughter?"

"Sir, you once said, 'Do not love the world or the things in the world. If anyone loves the world, the love of the Father is not in him. For all that is in the world—the desires of the flesh and the desires of the eyes and pride of life—is not from the Father but is from the world.' I get it now. I'm not saying I'm reformed. Hell, I'm not even saying I'm a total believer, but Cassie is. I respect that about her and want to help her find her way again. She means more to me than anything I could possibly do or obtain on this planet."

He rubs a hand over his jaw. His voice resigned. "You really do love her, huh?"

"More than I thought possible."

"She isn't home. She went to the cemetery." He exhales heavily. "Make yourself comfortable. She's been gone for a few hours. I suspect she'll be back any moment."

"Thank you, sir."

He snatches his water glass and exits through the patio door. I place Bellow back on the floor and stand. Learning Cassie went to visit the cemetery surprises and elates me. Visiting her mom was overdue. Perhaps she's finally coming to terms with her loss. It's the first step in restoring her faith.

I step toward the couch, prepared to settle in for however long it takes, when the front door swings open. My gaze sweeps up to meet Cassie's. Her usually sculpted hair is disheveled as if she ran her fingers through it too many times. Her eyes are red rimmed as if being at the cemetery was too much. As unkempt as she looks, she's never been more beautiful. Bellow lets out a bark but doesn't leave my side.

"Hi," I say tentatively. If I was expecting a warm smile and welcoming reception, I didn't get it. She just stands there, frozen.

"You're here," she finally manages to say.

"I am."

"Why?"

"For you."

Confusion frames those beautiful blue eyes before they glance nervously around the room. This causes me to smile. My girl, the ever-loving rule follower.

"Your dad's in the backyard."

"Dad let you stay inside. By yourself?"

"We talked." I shrug and take a step toward her.

"About the team?"

"No. About you." Her mouth opens, but she's too perplexed to speak. I think I shocked her into submission. "I'm so sorry, Cassie. I should've never left without saying goodbye. I thought it would be better that way."

"I'm sorry too."

I step closer. Bellow wags his too-long tail. "You're my world. My life. Baseball, college, they mean nothing if the cost is losing you. I love you so goddamn much it hurts."

She lets out a whimper. "I love you too."

And then she springs in my arms. Her scent hits my nostrils, and I feel like I'm home for the first time in my life. Family doesn't always mean your biological relatives. Family means who you hold close to your heart.

"*What if* you agree to be my long-distance girlfriend?" This may be a spin on our *"what if"* game, but what I'm proposing isn't a scheme. It's real.

"Then I should be happy for the rest of my life."

"I'll never leave you again." My words come out in a whispered rush—a desperate attempt to drill my point home. I may physically be gone, but I'll be with her emotionally and mentally.

"I don't want you ever to leave."

My hands frame her face. I swipe my thumb under her eyes to wipe away what I hope are happy tears. "How was your visit to the cemetery?"

Her lips form a soft smile. "Therapeutic."

I pull her into a hug, amazed by her strength.

"I guess I'll have to get used to this." The deep baritone voice that sends shivers down my spine rings from behind us.

Cassie lifts off my chest. "I have something to tell the both of you."

The seriousness in her tone alarms me. My gaze meets Coach's. There's no doubt the panic displayed in his eyes mirrors mine. I brace myself for her following words, wondering how our minutes-long truce will hold. I'm not sure it would survive a surprise pregnancy. We had sex once without a condom, but everyone knows it only takes one time.

"I've decided to transfer to Cessna U this year."

My heart skips a beat. I steal a look at Coach. His jaw tics, and the vein in the side of his head pulses. I'm pretty sure he's less than thrilled but yet relieved not to be called grandpa.

"How do you propose paying for it?" he asks.

Cassie lifts her chin and straightens her spine. "Last I checked, the loans were in my name. If I need more, I will secure another loan. I'm an adult. It's time I act like one."

"You really want to switch schools for your last year?" I ask, a little taken aback by this development. Cassie at school with me? Hell to the yeah. This is like a dream I never knew could come true. "Won't that set you back?"

She focuses her sole attention on me. "I'm not sure yet, but it doesn't matter. Every chance you took had been for me. You sacrificed everything for me. It's time I do the same."

"This is what you want?" Coach asks with less bite in his tone.

"Yes. The process is already in motion."

"I don't know when I lost control." He sighs but smiles at his girl.

She squeals and hops over to him, tossing her arms around his waist. "Thanks, Daddy."

"Take care of my little girl." He peers at me over Cassie's head, his words more warning than sentimental. But the message is well received.

"I will, sir. With all of my heart."

I meet Cassie's gaze and all I see is pure love. I relax for the first time since being reunited with my girl because now, the only time I'll be left stranded on deck is during a real baseball game. I got caught looking at Cassie, but I certainly didn't strike out.

CHAPTER FORTY-FOUR

CASSIE

"ARE YOU READY?" I MEET DALTON OUTSIDE MY BEDROOM DOOR. He's dressed in his ripped jeans I love so much and signature white T-shirt. A sense of gratification settles over me, dueling with the hunger my body seeks. I can't believe this man is truly mine.

"Where are we going?" His eyes take in my casual appearance.

"I'm showing you the town in proper fashion." I give a curt nod. Between the baseball schedule and Dad's strict regime, Dalton didn't get a chance to see much of Baytown. "Believe it or not, there's more to the town than the baseball field and pizza joint."

He wraps an arm around my waist and pulls me close. Coming within inches from my mouth, he smirks. "Wanting to show me off, huh?"

"Maybe." I draw out the word. There is some truth to his question. It will be nice to parade my new boyfriend around town without the threat of being caught. If we catch any questionable glances from the church naysayers, then so be it. I'm excited to show off pieces of my past he hasn't seen.

"What do you have planned, Choir Girl?" His lips land on my neck, and I have to force myself to keep from moaning. But goodness, he feels good. I want to cherish every second we have together, especially since his lips on me are an added treat I thought was impossible.

"Once I show you the downtown area, we're going to walk to the park I used to play in. Then I want to take you to my favorite ice cream shop. Show you the best parts of town." Dalton's only here for one more day, so I want to make the most of it.

"The best part of the town is right here with you." His mouth dips farther along my neck as his fingers brush against my collar-bone. He rears his head back.

"You're wearing your cross." Surprised accusation edges his tone. I blush.

"While I was visiting Mom's gravesite, I realized I was wrong. God hasn't abandoned me."

"Yeah?"

"Yeah. He brought you to me."

Dalton leans his forehead against mine. "I love you so much."

His declaration holds so much meaning and feeling behind how he spoke it that I want to cherish this moment forever. We remain that way—one hand on my waist, the other framing the side of my face. That is until a throat clearing breaks our moment. Jolting apart, we turn to find Dad standing at the end of the hallway, his hands on his hips and scowl in place. Dalton casually slips his hands into his pockets. Dad's face screams anything but happiness, but he doesn't yell. Only grumbles. He's a work in progress.

"You kids getting ready to leave?"

I grab Dalton's hand. "We are. I want to show Dalton parts of the town he hasn't seen."

Dad adjusts his ball cap that sports the team's logo. Just our luck, they're leaving today for an overnight road trip. The timing couldn't be any more perfect.

"Have fun today." He mumbles something under his breath and takes off. I watch him leave and then turn back to Dalton.

"I'm sorry you're not going with him." It has to be hard on Dalton to see Dad in his coaching uniform and not be part of the team.

"Yeah." He runs his free hand through his dark locks. "It feels . . . different. It's definitely hard to get used to."

"At least it's only temporary."

"Thank God." But then he shoots me a devilish grin and pulls me up against him. "But I have you all to myself. Whatever shall we do?"

"What I have planned. That's what we're going to do." I laugh, but the sound fades when he places his lips on mine.

Thirty minutes later, we park the car and find ourselves walking along the various storefronts on the way to the city park. We stop in front of a sports collectibles store. The longing in Dalton's eyes as he peers through the window prompts me to ask, "Do you want to go inside?"

"Nah. I've seen enough in my lifetime."

"If I remember correctly, there was a cool sports store along the main drag in Bellow Bay."

"Bricks and Ivy." A smile lifts his lips, but it doesn't quite reach his eyes. "I used to go there a lot when I was little. Never had a chance to buy anything, though, but the decorations were cool. They had a bat on display that belonged to Mickey Mantle. I'm sure it prompted my love for baseball."

"Not that I don't think you will, but have you thought about what to do if you don't get drafted?"

"No. I never had a backup plan." He grimaces. "I never thought I needed one until this year. But working on your dad's car reminded me how much I enjoy working with my hands. I can work in a garage until I own my shop. But that's only if I don't make it. Nothing replaces the need for playing ball."

"It's a good plan. You're good at working on cars. Dad was impressed."

We remain silent as we enter the park. Walking past the swing sets, I point to the silver slide. "That's where I fell in love for the first time."

He quirks an eyebrow. "Should I be jealous?"

"Hmm, maybe. Jimmy was pretty dreamy to a six-year-old me."

"What does this Jimmy have over me?"

I laugh. "Nothing now, but he did climb to the top of the slide and declare he was going to marry me."

"Now that's a grand gesture."

"Second to the best."

"What's the first?"

"You coming back."

He smiles as if he likes what I said. "It took me some time to get my head out of my ass, but I wasn't going to let you go."

"I hate that you have to leave again."

"Me too, but we'll be together soon."

His leaving tomorrow will be rough, and long-distance will suck, but knowing we'll be seeing each other in a few weeks makes it all better.

"Is it going to be okay when you go home?"

"Honestly, I don't know. Let's just say Dad and I had a come-to-Jesus moment before I left."

"What do you mean?" I ask, worry settling in my stomach.

"I visited my brother before I came here."

I snap my head toward him. The last thing I expected him to do was to visit Steve. Dalton was more reluctant to visit his living brother than I was going to the cemetery. "How did seeing him go?"

"Surprisingly, the visit went well. Steve told me about his reasons for stealing. It turns out his reasoning had nothing to do with me."

"That had to be a relief." That night in Bellow Bay, when his dad blamed Dalton, I wanted to confront the awful man myself.

"Yeah, but I asked him why Dad treated me like shit."

I remain quiet as he unfolds the story. My heart breaks a little more for him. Everyone has a dysfunctional family, but some are worse than others. "Is that what brought on the argument with your dad?"

He nods. "I confronted him. Much to my surprise, Mom had an affair nine months before I was born."

"Oh, Dalton." I halt, tears pricking my eyes. How much more can this man take before he reaches his breaking point? "Is he for sure your dad?"

He takes a stuttering breath. "I don't know, but the results are in."

"You took a paternity test?"

He nods. "Dad was passed out when I got back from visiting Steve. It was easy to obtain the swabs. I got the email notification this morning."

"You haven't looked?" I watch the glide of his Adam's apple as he shakes his head. I seek out the closest bench and drag him to it. "Sit down. If you want to look, fine. If not, we'll rest here for a few minutes."

He pulls out his phone and opens the email app. His finger hovers over the email that determines his identity. I can't begin to imagine what's going through his mind. I don't even know what scenario to wish for. Either choice is unfortunate.

"Fuck it," he says and opens the email. He doesn't hesitate and hits the link. When I read the words 99.99% match, I breathe and take a peek at Dalton. He looks bewildered.

"Huh, I kind of thought it wouldn't be a match."

"Is this good or bad?"

"Honestly, I don't know. At least I don't have to worry about finding some random guy." He puts his phone away and waves my concern away. He stands, and I follow suit. He starts talking when we resume walking. "It's okay. I took your advice and sought professional help. There's a call-a-shrink service at the school open to athletes. I contacted them to set an appointment. I have my first session scheduled for when I get there."

"I'm glad you're seeking help."

"When I return home tomorrow, that'll be the last time I set foot in Bellow Bay. After this summer, I'm never going back."

"What about seeing your brother?"

"Once he's freed from jail, he can visit me. I'll do whatever it takes to buy his ticket, but I'm never going back there. If I ever get called up to the Majors, maybe I'll send some cash to Dad. But as far as I'm concerned, we're done."

I nod. I hope that someday they can resolve their issues, but it's best to cut the toxicity for now. His sanity is worth more than trying to please a bitter old man.

"What about your mom? Has she ever reached out?"

"No one has heard from her in years."

"I'm sorry you got dealt a bad hand when it comes to family."

He grabs my hand and tugs me into him. Stopping along the sidewalk about ten feet from the car, he kisses the tip of my nose. "We'll just have to make our own family."

"Yeah? Just how big of a family are we talking about here?" I'm half-joking, knowing full well he's only talking about us.

"Five," he soundly states as if he's given this some thought. "Well, seven if you include us."

"Five!" My eyes widen, not expecting him to put an actual number on kids. I hadn't even expected him to want kids. I step back and wave a hand over my petite frame. "Have you seen the size of me? I'll be lucky to pop one out of this body."

"I'll take whatever you give me." He erases the gap between us and plants his lips on mine. This kiss feels like a promise of spending a lifetime together. Hope bubbles inside me.

"Ah, I knew you two would get together."

Dalton backs away. Face red. I stifle a chuckle.

"Hello, Ms. Willow. You out for a walk?"

"Enjoying the beautiful weather. I knew this handsome boy had his eye on you." She winks. "Don't let me stop you. Although, you may want to tone it down some." She nudges her head toward the trio of church naysayers. "You'll make them go into cardiac arrest."

"You've got it."

The spirited woman turns to Dalton. "I'm glad you got your head out of your ass. Your girl was nothing but mopey after you left."

Now it's my turn to grow red.

Dalton laughs. "I think the same can be said for me. I'll take care of her. I promise."

"I know you will, boy. Where are you heading?"

"I'm taking him to get ice cream."

"Aw, showing him the finer things of Baytown." She lowers her voice and directs her following comment to me. "Good plan." Turning her attention back to Dalton, she says, "I better get moving. You take care of this girl."

"I plan to."

"Oh, I know you will." She winks again. Holy cow, I didn't know Ms. Willow was such a flirt.

Dalton grabs my hand, and we step toward the car. That's when it hits me. Something is missing from his finger.

"Where's your ring?"

He looks away. "I, uh, sold it."

"Sold it?" My steps come to a complete stop. I shoot him an incredulous look. "Dalton, that was important to you. What could've been so important to sell it?"

He shoves his hands in his pockets, clearly not wanting to answer. "My ticket to come here."

"Dalton!" I can't believe he sold something so sentimental for me. I have to find a way to get that back for him.

"I had to see you. We couldn't have this discussion over a text. And yeah, I loved Gramp's ring, but I love you more. No regrets, no remorse, remember?"

My throat tightens. This guy will stop at nothing for me. I can hardly talk I'm so overwhelmed by emotion. After a beat, I finally say, "You once told me that you would never judge me. I hadn't believed you at the time, but you stayed true to your word."

"You're my world, Cassie. I wasn't about to let you go." A shy smile crosses his lips. "It just took me a few days to realize I needed to act." His voice drops, almost as if he's afraid to ask. "You're actually transferring to Cessna U?"

"Yes. It may delay my graduation date, but I put in the transfer request along with Nicole."

"She's going to transfer too?"

"I'm not sure if she'll be accepted into the nursing program right away, but yes, she wants to transfer. I think she took a liking to Carter."

"Aw, following her heart. I know a guy who did that once." His mouth twitches.

"Yeah? How'd it turn out for him?"

"Not so well at first but pretty spectacular in the end. I think he's a little gun shy. He's worried that his true love's transfer will be denied."

"Ah, I see. Perhaps you can tell your guy that his love had been accepted into the program once, but she didn't go when her mom got sick because she didn't want to be that far away when things got worse." I erase the distance between us and tip my head. His arms wrap around my waist and tug me closer. "I'm done being apart."

"I can't believe we'll be together."

"Are you sure you're ready for me? I won't crimp the big jock's style?"

"Choir Girl, I can't wait to show you off. But most of all, we can get started on that happily ever after."

I can't stop the grin capturing my face. Who knew a big ole softie lay underneath that broody, bad boy? I peer into those warm chocolate eyes and melt a little more.

"I love you, Dalton Boyd."

"I love you, Cassie Greenberg."

He draws me into a kiss, and I don't hold back. I show him just how much I love him through every searing sweep of my tongue and nip of his bottom lip. The world fades to the background as I stake my claim on this man.

"You're going to make the old ladies talk," he murmurs. I can feel his grin against my mouth.

"Ah, screw them."

"I'd rather screw you," he says through a laugh.

I break away and tug his arm. He laughs some more as I practically drag him to the car—metaphorically speaking, of course. There is no way my small frame can overpower that beast of a man.

"Are we getting ice cream?"

"No, we're going home. I like your plan better."

And that's what we do. Dalton isn't leaving town without a proper goodbye.

CHAPTER FORTY-FIVE

DALTON

"ARE YOU SURE YOU'RE READY FOR THIS?"

I nod at my friend Marty and pat the piece of paper in my back pocket. The one I can't wait to show Dad. We grab the empty boxes out of his car and make our way into the house. This is the last time I plan on stepping foot in this house. Marty's parents agreed to let me stay at their home and they'll store what little belongings I have until after graduation.

"Let's just get this over with." I puff out a breath and make my way up the path. The sooner we get this over with, the sooner I can kiss this part of my life goodbye.

Marty says nothing as we pass through the dirty kitchen to get to my room. Once we reach my bedroom, I point to the desk. "Take whatever is in the drawers. The stuff on the shelves can stay."

I start in the closet and grab whatever clothes I hadn't already packed.

We're about done when Dad barges inside my room.

"What the hell are you doing?" He slurs his words as his gaze ping-pongs between Marty and me.

"Packing."

"You think you're leaving?"

I turn to face him. "Why would I stay?" It's a fair question, but one that makes his face deepen in color.

"Listen, you ungrateful—"

"Don't finish that thought," I warn before taking the piece of paper out of my back pocket and tossing it to him."

"What the hell is this?" His question comes out more like a growl. It's a tone I've heard most of my life. I'll be so happy not to listen to it ever again.

"In case your paternal instincts were ever in question, we're a match."

His eyes scan the document and then flick up to meet mine. A shocked expression squishes his face. He must have actually thought I wasn't his.

"That's right. I'm yours. But since you never wanted me as a son, you're getting your wish. We're through. I'm no longer your responsibility." As if he ever did anything to claim responsibility other than claiming me on his tax form. I look at Marty and nudge my chin to the door. He picks up my cue, stacks his box on top of a full one, and picks them up.

"Now wait one goddamn minute."

"No, I'm done waiting. Me and you"—I wave my hand between us—"are officially done. Hopefully, Steve makes parole and can help you out, but the results never mattered as far as I'm concerned. It makes zero difference going forward. Coming back was never the plan."

I pick up my box and shoulder past him with Marty on my tail. We make it to his car and shove my pathetic life belongings in his vehicle. How can an entire twenty-one years of existence fit into three boxes?

"You good?"

"I'm good." Or else I will be. Maybe someday, my old man and I can mend what he broke. Maybe not. Right now, I don't care because I refuse to let his actions define who I am. Those days are over. I found my family back in California. *No regrets, no remorse.*

CHAPTER FORTY-SIX

DALTON

TEN MONTHS LATER

I'M NOT SURE WHO'S MORE NERVOUS, COACH OR ME. CASSIE AND I sit on her couch and watch in awe as her dad directs his buddies where to place the television. Yes, I said television. I guess Coach bends the rules when there's a baseball draft to watch.

Okay, so I lied. I know who is more nervous. It's me by a long shot, but it has nothing to do with baseball and everything to do with this woman sitting beside me. I pat my pocket for reassurance and try not to dwell on circumstances I can't control. The draft is a three-day process, with round one televised. I don't want to get my hopes up, but it's about impossible when Coach goes out of his way, not to mention his beliefs, to host a televised party. Even Coach Callahan flew in earlier to join us.

"Dude, you're like ranked number ten on MLB.com's prospect ranking, according to Wikipedia," Nicole says.

Oh, yeah. There's that too. It's pretty hard not to get my hopes up. I had another phenomenal year at Cessna University. Unfortunately, our year came to a close at the regional rounds. It was a rebuilding year, and the loss of power from Braxton and Noah stung. Carter filled Garret's shoes nicely.

I look forward to seeing where the team goes next year.

Cassie graduated on time. She is currently employed at a nearby hospital, working as a registered nurse license pending. She constantly studies for her national exam, which takes place in July. She had gone to the library a few days ago, creating a perfect opportunity to talk to her dad.

"Sir, I don't know what the future holds for me, but I want to ask your daughter to live with me. But I don't want her living in sin." It took everything in my power to make that statement, but I knew that was what Coach believed. I could respect his opinion. "That's why I'm asking permission for her hand in marriage."

He did his thing where he analyzed the situation—face stoic, mind assessing. "You know you're not the person I envisioned for my daughter."

"I realize that, sir. I—"

He held his hand up to stop me. "I had pictured my girl attending my church, raising a family, working at church functions."

"I understand. Cassie can still do all that apart from attending your church elsewhere. Since I don't know where we'll live yet."

He smiled politely and nodded. "You may not be the ideal person I had in mind. You turned out to be better."

I thought my heart had stopped. It definitely skipped a beat. Was twenty-two too young to have a heart attack? He couldn't be saying what I think he was saying. "Sir?"

"I can't think of anyone better for my little girl. Of course, you have my permission."

"Thank you, sir." Emotion clogs my throat. "I, uh, plan to get her a ring soon. I just need to save up first."

"Hold on." He darts into his bedroom. When he returns, he holds a red velvet box. He opens it and reveals a vintage-style round diamond filigree ring. It's perfect for her delicate fingers. "This was her mother's. It's not big and flashy, but I have a feeling Cassie isn't looking for anything too flashy."

"Thank you, sir. It's beautiful."

"I think you can call me Nolan or Dad."

Tears pricked my eyes. And I was not a crier. "Thank you, Dad."

He's supported me during my last baseball season with Cessna

U. He's been to more games than my biological father. The transition wasn't smooth. It took him a while to get used to having me around. But Cassie insisted that I spend every break at their house.

I still don't talk to my father, but Steve made parole last summer, which helped alleviate the guilt. I speak to him periodically. He understands my reasoning and position. Maybe someday in the future, Dad will seek help and redemption. Until that day, there is nothing I can do. Dad has to help himself. That's the primary thing I learned in therapy. If he ever does, then I'll be open to communication. Until then, I'll stick with the family that accepts me.

The baseball commissioner steps to the podium. I grab Cassie's hand when he gets closer to my speculated round. She's been my rock this past school year and I can't think of anyone better to be with me. The room quiets as the commissioner says, "With the tenth pick of the MLB draft, the Boston Bears select Dalton Boyd, the first baseman from Cessna University."

Cheers erupt around the room as I sit in shock. *I made it. I actually made it.* The work ahead will be long and hard. I still have to get called to the majors, but I jumped the first hurdle without landing on my ass.

"You did it." Cassie leans over to kiss me. It's a chaste kiss, but one that holds promise for later.

"We did it."

Pats on the back pursued with both coaches beaming at me. My phone rings, the first call of many. The representative from the Boston Bears, my new agent, and my brother.

I grab Cassie's hand once the phone calls are through and the house empties. I need to get her alone. She seems to pick up on my disposition.

"You want to go to the park?"

"Yeah, I'm cagey. I need to get out of here."

Ten minutes later, we're walking hand in hand around the playground equipment. Once we reach the slide, I drop her hand.

"Wait right there. I'll be right back."

"What? Where are you going?"

"Just wait," I holler behind me as I run toward the slide. Once I step to the steps, I talk some kid into letting me cut in front of him, and then I climb to the top. Standing tall, I shout to the crowd, "I'm going to marry Cassie Greenburg."

Her hands go up to her mouth, and she stares at me with saucer-sized eyes. I slide down the shoot and jog over to her. Applause breaks across the park along with a few grosses and ew's from the kids.

"How was that? Did it beat Jimmy's declaration?" I pull her against me and kiss her nose.

"I don't know. Jimmy left quite the impression."

"Hmm, how about now?" I pull the ring out of my pocket and hold it up. "What do you say? Will you make me the happiest guy on the planet and marry me?"

She rolls her eyes in dramatic fashion, but that smile on her lips tells me she's anything but annoyed. "Some people will do anything to win."

I laugh. "I'm very competitive."

"Yes, you are. And, yes, I will marry you."

"So, what you're saying is I beat Jimmy?"

"Yes, you definitely won."

I won a lot more than, sweetheart. And I have a whole lot more wins to give you.

"And you don't mind living on the East Coast? That's where the Boston Bears affiliate teams are located."

"I don't care where we'll live as long as we're together."

I fully relax as I grab her hand. "Then come on. We have a wedding to plan. Because I want our happily ever after to start now."

EPILOGUE

DALTON

SIX MONTHS LATER

"You doing okay?" Marty asks.

I turn to my best man and smirk while pinning the boutonnière in place. "Why wouldn't I be?"

He shakes his head. "Glad to see your cockiness is still intact."

But I know he's kidding. And I know I'm not fooling him. I'm fucking terrified. But it's not about getting married—that's the easy part. I'm more worried about Cassie waking up and running away. How this sweet innocent girl wants to marry me still blows my mind.

"His cockiness is the one thing you can count on never changing," Garret speaks up.

"Fuck off," I say, straightening my jacket. Garret laughs. My phone pings a text before he can retort.

Steve: *Congratulations. Wish I could celebrate with you.*

A pang of remorse pinches my gut. Steve's the only family member I would want here, but his probation officer denied his request even though he's been out for a year and four months. It sucks, but I get it. Cassie offered to change the venue to North Carolina, but I shot that idea down. I don't need my brother around to get married. I just need her. This wedding is more for her benefit than mine. I won't deny her the dream of getting married in her father's church. I'm good as long as we're together.

Me: *I'll ship you some cake.*

Or, in our case, chocolate cupcakes. Cassie may have wanted a small, traditional wedding, but that's where the tradition stops.

"The crew is here." Garret pops up and heads to the door.

Noah, Braxton, and their girlfriends file into the room a moment later.

Marty stands with his hands in his tux pants. He's trying to act casual, but I know he's in awe at my friends. Garret didn't get called up this year, but Noah and Braxton did.

Shannon wears a huge smile as she makes her way to me. When she reaches me, she throws her arms around me and hugs tightly. "It's your big day!"

"How'd your interview go?" I ask.

"This is your big day, not mine." Shannon had a job interview with *Valvemor*, an upcoming trendy fashion company. They reached out to her this summer when she was interning abroad.

"That doesn't matter. I still want to know."

"I got it," she squeals.

"I'm so happy for you. I bet Noah's relieved."

"I am." Noah approaches and shoots Shannon an appreciative glance. "But we would've been good either way. It's just a lot easier when you're in the same country."

I laugh and give Noah a man-hug. "True that. Hey, man. Good seeing you. Glad you could make it."

"You know I wouldn't have missed it."

Braxton and Cara step behind Noah, holding hands.

"There's the groom," Braxton says and gives me a one-arm hug, with Cara following suit.

"Thanks for showing up, man. It means a lot."

"We wouldn't miss this for anything," Cara says. She scans the room. "Where's Lexie?"

"She's with Cassie and Olivia," Garret says. Olivia is Garret's daughter. I'm surprised he hasn't proposed to Lexie yet. Out of everyone, I thought they would've been the first to tie the knot.

"Oh my gosh, I bet your little girl is such a cute flower girl," Shannon gushes.

"She's so excited, even though we had to bribe her to wear the dress." Garret laughs as Shannon heads to the door.

"Where are you going?" Noah asks.

"To go find the girls."

"Wait for me." Cara rushes up to her. They exit, and the guys shake their heads. Braxton punches my arm playfully.

"I can't believe you're the first one to get married."

"Yeah, you're making us look bad," Garret says.

I give them a wicked grin. "I can't help that you're all wusses."

"Hey, I bought the ring. The opportunity hasn't risen yet." This comes from Braxton. "It won't be long. I can't wait too much longer. We won't be able to make it official until she graduates though." Cara has two and half years left of veterinary school.

"Yeah, I plan on asking soon as well." Noah shrugs. "I was waiting for Christmas."

"Not to sound like a parrot, but I was going to pop the question during the down season too."

Marty shifts, and I feel like an asshole forgetting that he doesn't know these people. I make the proper introductions and try including him in our conversations.

"We need to make a pact. We get together every winter break," Noah says.

"We should drink to that." Garret looks around the room. "Where do they hide the sacramental wine?"

I shoot him an are-you-kidding-me look. "Does this look like that kind of church? I was lucky to get the man to marry us."

He shrugs. "Should've brought some, I guess. Why didn't I think to do that?"

"Because it would've gotten confiscated," a deep voice that still sends shivers down my spine says. The glare Coach shoots Garret's way causes him to retreat. I hold in a laugh. Out of all of us, Noah drank the least, but Garret, who wasn't around most weekends, came in a close second. Coach turns to me. "Can I have a word?"

I have never seen a room clear out so fast. *Wusses.* But who am I kidding? Coach and I may have come to an understanding, but that doesn't stop the spike of adrenaline shooting in my veins. I figured this talk was coming, but I also figured it would've come before now, not ten minutes before Cassie's due to walk down the aisle. My thumb grazes the bottom of my right ring finger. Even though the ring has been missing for months, I still haven't shaken the habit. I swallow hard and ask, "What's on your mind?"

"I wanted to properly welcome you to the family. I know you'll be a good husband to Cassie. All I can ask is you always treat her with as much respect as you did the night you defended her honor."

My gaze flicks to his. Did he find out what that prick said that made me lose my mind?

As if reading my thoughts, he nods. "Yes, I know what prompted the fight."

"How?"

"Son, there isn't anything that happens around these parts that I don't know about."

My throat clogs with emotion I'd never felt with anyone besides Cassie. *He called me son.* And even though his admission comes across as a warning, I extend my hand. "I won't let you down. Taking care of Cassie is my top priority." And to drive home my point, I add, "I appreciate your understanding my need to take my shot, but she will always come first."

And I mean that. We have a plan. She'll work as a nurse while I take my shot. If I don't get called up within the next few years, then I'll work on becoming a mechanic. I'm fairly certain I'll be called up shortly.

"You'd be a fool not to take that shot. You're one heck of a player. But you'll make an even better husband." With our hands still clasped, he pulls me into a hug and then pats my back. "Now, let's prove me right, shall we?"

I smile and nod. "I'm ready."

A few minutes later, I stand near the altar as Cassie's father walks her down the aisle. I have to catch my breath. My hand goes to my chest. My girl stands there dressed in an all-white boho gown. Beaded spaghetti straps and lace motifs over tulle overlay complete the look. Her hair is pulled into an updo, exposing her tanned neck that calls to me. *Damn.*

I'm totally captivated during the entire ceremony. And when we get to the rings, I'm floored.

Nicole hands Cassie the ring. When she holds it up, my breath is knocked away for the second time. Gramps's ring, the one I sold to come back to California, lays in her palm.

"Is that—"

"Your grandfather's ring." She beams up at me.

"How?"

"I called Marty after you told me what you had done and wired him the money. I had him go back to the pawnshop and buy it back. I'm so glad he went with you that day."

"I can't believe you did this." My voice is barely above a whisper. I'm blown away. This is the nicest gift anyone has given me. That includes the '57 Chevy Cassie's dad gave us for our wedding present.

"This ring meant a lot to you. I couldn't bear to see you give it up."

"I'd give up anything for the chance to be with you but thank you." I pull her in for a hug, paying particular attention to her hair and makeup. Her cucumber-melon scent wafts in the air between us. Before we get too far into the hug, a stern throat clearing breaks us apart. A rumble of laughter follows suit.

Biting back smiles, we get into position as her dad continues. When he finally announces us husband and wife and I kiss my bride, relief like I've never known settles through me. Our world is just beginning and there are a lot of unknowns, but I'm right where I belong. We break apart, hands still clasped together.

Resting my forehead on hers, my throat clogs with emotion as I say, "I love you so much."

"I'm so happy to be called Mrs. Boyd. I can't wait for our life to begin."

I smile. There was a time when I wanted to escape my last name, but that was before a new chapter started. I lean further down and whisper in her ear, "I can't wait until after when we're alone."

She practically moans, but I don't miss the slight blush creeping across her cheeks. My grin widens at my not-so-innocent girl. The music starts playing.

"Let's get to it then," she says.

"Yes, ma'am." I squeeze her hand as we turn to face the audience. With my best friend by my side and the friends that have been more like family to me seated nearby, I stand in awe. Then I escort my wife down the aisle.

When we make it to the end, Cassie's gaze lands on mine. I know at that moment, I'm the luckiest man in the room.

No regrets, no remorse.

To RECEIVE NEWS ON UPCOMING RELEASES, SPECIAL SNIPPETS, ARC opportunities, bonus content, and more, join my reader group on Facebook here:

Author Kimberly Readnour's Book Gang!

What's next? Don't want to miss any new releases including Cessna U Football and Hockey? Go to website www.kimberlyread-nour.com and join my newsletter to receive updates. As a bonus, you will receive two free novellas for your enjoyment. Enjoy!

ALSO BY KIMBERLY READNOUR

Cessna Wildcats Series:

Swinging Strike

Behind the Count

Full Count

On Deck (Prequel)

Caught Looking

Heartbreak Hitter (Cocky Hero Club)

Bad Boys Redemption Series

Second Chance Hero

Swing for the Fences

Bottom of the Ninth

Bad Ball Hitter

All American Boy Series

Celebrity Playboy

KB Everyday Heroes World

Sworn to Duty

An *Unforeseen Destiny* Series:

Impossible Love

Unexpected Love

The *Mystical Encounter* Series:

Visions

Deceptions

Vanished

ACKNOWLEDGMENTS

Thank you so much for reading *Caught Looking*! I can't tell you how grateful I am for your patience in completing this series. Although I have many more ideas for the Cessna U world, including hockey and football, I appreciate you hanging in there until the end!

There are many people to thank that helped me bring this book to life!

To my trusty beta reader, Nikki. Thanks so much for you awesome input. Once again, your thoughts and suggestions were on spot. I can't express how much I value your insights!

To every single book blogger, bookstagrammer, and ARC team member. I keep saying this but it keeps holding true. Your shares, posts, reviews, and overall hype from the cover reveal to release day is greatly appreciated. I wouldn't be anywhere in the publishing world without your help. Thank you so much!

To my editor, Missy. I can't express how much I love your insights and experience. You make my manuscript shine! Your help is invaluable!

Katie, I don't know what I would do without you! Thanks so much for always being there for me. I'm so glad you're part of my team!

Linda and Alissa, thanks so much for once again being there

for me and promoting the heck out of my books. Foreword PR & Marketing makes it possible for me to keep doing what I love. Thanks for everything.

Kelly, I appreciate everything you've done to promote this series. Inkslingers and you have added that extra reach I needed!

Angela, you are my rock in all of this! You help in so many ways. There can't be a better PA than you!! Thanks for everything!

And lastly, to my family for putting up with me. I tuck away into my office and emerge once and awhile to give you all love. Thanks for being supportive so I can live in this imaginary world. Ha-ha.

ABOUT THE AUTHOR

Kimberly Readnour lives in the Midwest with her husband and a very snuggly cat.

Having a true passion for romance and HEA's, she took the leap from the young adult genre to romance and never looked back.

Kimberly worked as a Registered Nurse for fifteen years before hanging up her stethoscope. When she isn't running her own business, you can find her tucked away writing.

Contact me at:
kimberlyreadnour.com
kimberly@kimberlyreadnour.com